Bert and Norah

INTO THE LIGHT

Bernard H. Burgess

Cover designed by Kristy Kennedy-Black, Idea Creative Services
Kristy@IdeaCreativeServices.com

This book is a work of fiction. Names, characters, places, and incidents either are products of the author's imagination or are used fictitiously. Any resemblance to actual persons, living or dead, events, or locales is entirely coincidental.

Bernard H. Burgess
Visit my website at www.facebook.com/Coywolf.publishing

Email:bb2975@hotmail.com

Printed in the United States of America

First Printing: July 2019
Coywolf Publishing

ISBN-13 978-0-9600069-1-5

DEDICATION

I dedicate this book and story to my grandchildren and great grand-daughter. This story touches upon the mystery of this thing called love and how it transcends time and distance and even death. I hope that my writing, and this book especially, can connect my life to theirs as the years pass. Hopefully, long after my own journey into the light.

TABLE OF CONTENTS

CHAPTER ONE: THE NEW HIRE

Bert Lynnes knew that Wyoming Governor Sam Patterson had called it correctly. After the last two high profile and highly publicized cases, the requests for help from his company, B & N Investigations, were increasing. By the end of November 2017, Bert felt the pressures of having a successful business. He'd known that he might not be able to keep up with the growing demand and might have to expand his company one day. It was just coming sooner than expected. Bert did the math and was compelled to hire another private investigator. In addition to Norah's continued presence and assistance, they were going to need more help if they were to maintain their reputation for excellence.

Albert, Bert as he was known, leaned back in the chair at the kitchen table of his Cody, Wyoming, log cabin. He rubbed his chin as he stared out the kitchen window into the mountains to the north of his house. Bert loved those grey and brown mountains of this part of Wyoming, just to the west of Cody in the North Fork Valley leading to Yellowstone Park. They were beautiful, rugged, dangerous, and spiritually uplifting, all at the same time. He considered this mountain valley the major steppingstone which led to the designation of Yellowstone as the nation's first national park.

He wondered if his former career as a military officer had really prepared him for the demands and challenges of having his own private investigation business. He could lay down a deadly trail of bullets on an enemy, and lead soldiers into danger, but could he build a successful small business? When those doubts surfaced, he would remember what his paternal grandfather used to say: "It doesn't cost any more to dream big."

A glance at his small library shelf bolstered his confidence. One of his favorite books, also one of the smallest books he owned, always seemed to provide that mental boost when he needed it. James Allen wrote one of the most amazing little self-help books ever published, as far as Bert was concerned. He opened "As A Man Thinketh" to page 17. He read part of a paragraph: "Men do not attract that which they want, but that which they are." He read on and focused on the last two sentences. "Not what he wishes and prays for does a man get, but what he justly earns. His wishes and prayers are only gratified and answered when they harmonize with his thoughts and actions."

He closed the book and placed it back in its place of honor at the head of his self-help group. It was time to get his actions in harmony with his thoughts. It was time to call upon the wisdom of his spirit wife, Norah, and get the ball rolling.

Bert was blessed with the gift which allowed him to both see and communicate with this beautiful spirit of his lovely wife and companion. He had always adored her from the first time they met. Fate had brought them together at the same moment in time on a hiking trail in a state park in Minnesota. The beauty of the changing leaves that October morning was matched by the beauty of the shapely, red-haired, young woman with the bubbly personality and lovable sense of humor. From the first word she said to her last, he fell head over heels in love with her. To this day, that memory and her spirit held his undying love. He would love her beyond his own grave.

They had many years together, good years. She followed him through most of his twenty years in the Army, and during their transition into civilian life. However, those years passed far too quickly. When the unexpected medical condition hit like a bolt out of the blue in 2016, it was guaranteed to negatively impact their fledgling investigation business. The full impact hit a few months later, though, when that beautiful life was snuffed out in an instant. Bert was left stunned, numb, and unsure about anything, including his own life.

Just when the darkest time seemed too dark to go on, something miraculous began to happen. A previously unknown and undeveloped gift began to bring Norah back into his life. He began to not only see her spirit frequently as a full bodily manifestation, but he could also communicate telepathically with her. Her spirit became the new version of his wife and his business partner. She still possessed her own gift of psychic insight and was able to continue adding this dimension to their investigations. Not even death could break the bonds of love and devotion which they shared. She chose to remain attached to his world instead of moving on to the next dimension. She chose an indirect path toward the light. Love bound their two worlds together into a present reality shared by both.

Their world was also shared by Missy, their coywolf companion and tracking animal. At three years of age, her reddish-grey coat was thick, full, and beautiful. She weighed about 45 pounds, just a little larger than most of her wild cousins. However, as a well-trained sidekick to Bert, Norah, and the business, she ate a little better than they did. Since her rescue as a tiny pup from a Wisconsin hillside, she had become an integral part of both their family and the business.

Bert turned to his spirit wife and they discussed how best to find another investigator. An ad in the paper might get responses, but it wasn't going to be easy to find someone with the temperament and aptitude for this type of work. Investigation work could be tedious;

demanding mentally, emotionally, and physically; and was at times potentially dangerous. It wasn't for everyone.

Norah suggested that they put an invitation on their Facebook and website pages and attempt to pull from the realm of people who followed or were already familiar with their business. These people crossed all walks of life and were from all over the country. They soon began to get a few inquiries from a spattering of people familiar with their business.

Bert began to line up a few interviews from several promising inquiries. The first was a 25-year-old man from St. Joseph, Missouri. This lad was the cousin of one of Myrtle Kennedy's friends. He didn't get beyond a telephone interview. The young man just didn't sound very mature nor did he seem to have the temperament that Bert wanted. He was a "thanks, but no thanks."

An older man, in his forties and from Sioux Falls, South Dakota, seemed over the phone to be mature and well grounded. They even arranged to meet roughly halfway between their locations, in Chadron, Nebraska. After that personal interview, though,

Bert was left with the impression that this fellow, although probably capable, wanted to do it only for money. Not the right reason for this work, Bert knew. Another no.

He and Norah again reviewed the inquiries. One caught his eye, a female who was working for a PI company already. The name, Rebecca Abigail Thompson, had not caught his attention during the first screening. He wasn't seriously considering a woman for this job, anyway, believing there were too many potential issues with a female investigator. He wanted someone he could eventually just let go and not have to worry about. As he looked over Thompson's resume, though, he was impressed with her writing skill and apparent intelligence. It didn't hurt that she already worked in the field so would know by now what she was getting into. She listed her residence as being in Wellington, Wyoming. He wasn't sure where that was. It didn't matter, right now. Norah thought it might be good to have a female on the team, because a woman could bring a fresh perspective to their cases. So, Bert sent an email to Thompson inviting her to give a call.

That evening, Bert received a call from Thompson. "Good evening," he answered her initial greeting, "this is Bert Lynnes of B & N Investigations. How are you doing tonight, Miss Thompson?"

"Doing well, Mr. Lynnes, thanks for asking and thanks for giving me a chance to compete for your position there."

"I see that you already work as an investigator for another

company. Why are you wanting to change?" Bert was a little suspicious when someone wanted to change companies.

She replied matter-of-factly, "I like the work, but not relating well with the people I'm working with and for. I'm getting the impression that it will be a long time before I'm trusted to take on cases. I got into this line of work because I want to work, not just be a pretty fixture in an office. I like to explore and investigate challenges, and I want to solve them, Mr. Lynnes. I expect to learn but I don't want to sit on the sidelines. I've looked into your company since you helped the Governor get his daughter back. I would like to first learn from you and then be an asset to your company."

Bert liked what she was saying, but he was wrestling with a feeling that he somehow knew this woman. How could that be, though? "Where are you now working, and how long have you been there?" He asked.

Thompson answered. "I work for Cowboy Investigations out of Cheyenne, and I've only been with them about three months now. I know I probably don't have all the experience you'd like to see."

He reassured her, "Experience isn't the major criteria for us, Miss Thompson. We can train you. Your attitude and temperament and aptitude for this kind of work are what we consider important. How old are you and are you married?"

She laughed, "Well, Mr. Lynnes, I'll forgive you for asking a woman for her age, this time." She laughed again. "I'm 43 as of last month, and I recently finalized a divorce from a ten-year marriage that was a mild disaster. I hope we can just leave it at that. Not my favorite subject."

"No problem," he answered, "I don't need to know that. Do you have any recommendations?""

"Does Governor Patterson count?" she asked. "I also have several from people who worked with me in prior jobs."

Bert sat in stunned silence for a few seconds, digesting her words. "Governor Sam Patterson gave you a letter of recommendation?"

She laughed again, "Yes, he really did. I talk with him sometimes several times a week and we've become good friends."

He sat quietly for a few seconds, as Norah nodded in agreement. "Well, Miss Thompson, the Governor is also a friend of mine. If he recommends you, then you're a serious candidate. How about we meet in a few days in Caspar. That's about halfway between Cheyenne and Cody, where I'm headquartered. Today is the 5th of December. How does Friday, the 8th, work for you; maybe around 2:00 that afternoon?"

She seemed to be checking her schedule before replying. "Yes, that should work okay with me. Just call me when you're getting close and tell me where to meet you. I'm looking forward to working with you."

Bert was somewhat confused by this candidate. He felt a little bit of familiarity yet couldn't figure out how he could possibly know her. He didn't know anyone named Thompson. "That sounds good, Miss Thompson. I'll see you on the 8th then, about 2:00 that afternoon. Take care and thank you for your interest in our position."

They hung up. Bert turned to Norah, who had been listening to the discussion. Well, what do ya think?" He asked.

"She seems intelligent, witty, and wants to do this type of work. I think you should definitely interview her and see how it goes," Norah replied.

"Yeah, might be a diamond in the rough," Bert suggested. "I'll see how she handles herself in person on Friday." He turned his attention back to the several requests for help that they'd received today. "We can sure use some qualified help, I'm beginning to realize," he told Norah.

They studied one request in particular. It was intriguing in that it didn't seem to involve someone missing or a white-collar crime of some kind. A mother in Red Lodge, Montana, was experiencing strange things with her seven-year-old daughter. Her husband didn't want to make a big deal of it. The mother, however, felt that the girl needed help. She didn't know what was needed but was asking if B & N Investigations might investigate it. Bert looked at Norah and they both shook their heads. It wasn't the kind of case they would typically take. They put it on the back burner for now. Bert emailed the woman back and said they might be able to get to it in January.

There was another case involving a child custody dispute which they could do the following week. While not their preferred type of investigation, it was one of those they had to take now and then to pay the bills. It probably wouldn't take more than two to four days to document the involved child's living conditions. It just required video surveillance. Norah and Missy could probably stay home. Bert messaged that new client and began to make arrangements.

* * *

Friday, December 8th, arrived with grey sky and a bitter wind. Snow flurries were possible but otherwise the weather should be reasonably good for Bert's drive to Caspar. It would just be a cold 18 degrees with a wind chill around zero. At his home outside of Cody, Bert rechecked his winter travel bag. He always double checked this emergency and survival gear before any significant drive in the winter. Caspar was nearly a four-hour drive from Cody, and anything could happen on Wyoming roads in the winter. Better safe than sorry.

Bert scurried around the cabin, getting coffee and a light breakfast, tending to Missy's needs, and chatting with his spirit wife. Despite the obvious barrier, they still had many good talks about a multitude of things. This morning, as Bert was getting ready to leave, they started talking about the small town of Meeteetse. Its name came from an amalgamation of Crow and Shoshone phrases, one of which meant "meeting place."

Situated at the bend in the road which marked the departure from the long agricultural valley and entry into the hills, Meeteetse was about thirty minutes from Cody on Bert's route. He lamented about the closing of the old Cowboy Bar and its Outlaw Café. However, he also enjoyed stops at the Elkhorn Bar and the Chocolatier. A host of characters were associated with the rich history of this rugged cow town. Butch Cassidy, Marty Robbins, and Amelia Earhart are among the well known to have connections with the town. Amelia even lived south of there for a while. Whenever he had the time, Bert loved to take a pause and learn a little more about the history of that place. The drive this morning would not provide him the luxury of time.

At the same time, Rebecca was also leaving Cheyenne for her travel to the interview in Caspar. Like Bert, she also carried an emergency bag with the basics for survival. She brushed back her shoulder-length blonde hair, adjusted her light green pants suit, and tossed her black, lined leather coat over the seat. She would exchange her winter boots for the more business-like dress shoes once she arrived in Caspar. This interview made her more nervous than she cared to admit. It could be that dream job she was hoping to land at some point in her career as a PI. Anyone could see that she was a "looker," mesmerizingly beautiful. They had to know her, though, to discover that she was also intelligent and very driven to succeed. She focused her blue eyes on the road as she proceeded north on Interstate 25.

Rebecca always enjoyed the beauty of this winding and hilly interstate highway. It traversed the transition between the

Great Plains and the Rocky Mountain foothills region. The mostly open hills and valleys were dotted with small stands of cottonwoods along the various creeks. The occasional antelope, also known as pronghorn, could be seen grazing not far from the road. Shortly after leaving Cheyenne, she passed through the small town of Chugwater.

She'd been doing her homework on her new residential state, and she was surprised to learn that Chugwater was known for the nearby vertical sandstone cliffs, once used as buffalo jumps by the first Americans. Legend has it that the name came from the sound made by the buffalo hitting the water below the cliffs. The cattle and ranching history of Wyoming had a link to Chugwater, where the railroad became a conduit for cattle heading to the Omaha stockyards. A rodeo bucking horse, Steamboat, was raised on a Chugwater ranch. Ridden by Chugwater ranch hand, Clayton Danks, at the Cheyenne Frontier Days rodeo in 1909, the picture of this horse and rider became the logo for the state of Wyoming. To this day, the legendary ride is depicted on the state license plates, one of which was on the back of Rebecca's black Dodge Hemi, extended cab, pickup. This logo also represents the University of Wyoming.

Steamboat was eventually inducted into the Pro Rodeo Hall of Fame and the National Cowboy Hall of Fame. He's the only horse to be buried on the grounds of the Cheyenne Frontier Days rodeo, near bucking chute nine.

Chugwater was also known for its chili. Various recipes

celebrate the town's spicy dishes. A well-known landmark is the Chugwater Soda Fountain, carrying on the small-town tradition.

Another hour or two farther north, Rebecca passed by the town of Glendo, and the large reservoir bearing the same name. She glanced into the Glendo State Park just east of the interstate, a popular regional recreational area. The Park surrounded the large reservoir which was formed by a half-mile long earth-fill dam across the North Platte River. This area was a common crossing point for the Oregon, Mormon, and California Trails. It was also the end of the trail for one of the nation's last known train robbers, William Carlisle, captured there in 1919.

Two more hours of driving brought Rebecca into the city of Caspar. The backdrop of snow-covered mountains to the south and west, as they faded into the ghostly white of light snow flurries, gave the feel of a ski town rather than a rodeo town. She answered her ringing cell phone.

"Good afternoon, Miss Thompson. Bert here from B & N Investigations. I'm just twenty miles west of Caspar. How about we meet at the Branding Iron restaurant. It's not too far away from I-25 and just south of the Yellowstone Highway, which I'll be following into town." Bert was being very professional.

She replied cheerfully, "That sounds good, Mr. Lynnes. I'll be there. If I get there before you, I'll just go inside and get a table, if that's okay with you. I'm craving a coffee."

Bert readily agreed and resumed his drive toward Caspar from the west of the city on State Highway 20, also known as the Yellowstone Highway. He was ready to get out of the car and have a coffee, himself.

About thirty minutes later, Bert walked into the Branding Iron Restaurant. He removed his tan winter coat as he scanned the dining room. To his surprise, he saw a familiar face. He looked closely and rechecked his memory. Yes, that was Becky Moreland at a table near the far window, by herself. He wondered what she was doing up here; maybe working a case? He knew he had to say hello before he looked for his prospect.

"Well, what a surprise. Hi Becky, how are you doing? How are things going in your job down there in Cheyenne?"

"A surprise indeed," Becky replied. "I'm doing well. How are you doing? I didn't know you lived around here. Can you sit and join me for a minute?"

Bert looked at his phone. It was 1:40; twenty minutes before he was to meet Miss Thompson. "Sure, I can sit and talk for a few. I'm meeting someone in about fifteen minutes. Enough time to bring me up to speed on what you've been doing. We haven't talked since Cheyenne a couple months ago."

She made a frown. "Yeah, I know. I hoped to keep in touch with you but when you finished the job you were on you just vanished. What've you been doing, Cody?"

Bert sat back in his chair and looked out the window. She called him Cody, his alias when he worked for the Governor in Cheyenne. He suddenly realized that she didn't know his real name or occupation. Maybe he didn't really know who she was, either.

"I'm curious, Becky," he said, "this might sound strange, but what's your full name now?"

She was a little puzzled by his question but answered him. "Well, when we met at the restaurant, I was Becky Moreland. Last month, though, my divorce was finalized, and I reverted back to my maiden name, Thompson."

"Let me guess," he replied, "I'm betting that your full name is Rebecca Abigail Thompson. Right?"

A hint of realization was coming over her. "Yes, that's right, Cody. So how do you know that?"

"Hang onto your seat, Rebecca Thompson, because I'm not Cody. Cody was an alias I used when I was working for the Governor. My real name is Bert Lynnes, owner of B & N Investigations."

"Oh my God," she exclaimed. "So, you're here to interview me." She adjusted her posture to sit fully upright from previously leaning toward him.

Bert laughed, a little nervously. "Yup, I guess so, Miss Thompson. So, I only have three questions for you."

"Well, don't keep me in suspense, Mr. Lynnes. Shoot."

He leaned forward, resting his arms on the table. "Why do you want to work for us?"

She was getting over the shock. "Well, sir, aside from the fact that I know the owner and think he's a pretty good guy that I would enjoy working with, I like the nature of your company. You employ an unusual tracking animal, and I love animals and would really love to know how you use her. Thirdly, you enlist the aid of a psychic. I believe I have some ability of 'clairsentience', clear thinking, otherwise known as an empath. I'd like to work for a company that understands and accepts that as an asset. Lastly, I want to be successful, and it helps to work for a successful company."

Bert could tell that she'd done her homework. She'd obviously studied their business website, because she knew Missy was a female. He realized that the absence of personal pictures, typical for many PI companies, had kept her from knowing that "Cody" was the owner. "One more question, then, Miss Thompson."

"What's that, sir?"

"How do you feel about working with a psychic? Especially one who stays in the background, out of sight. I'm the only one who communicates directly with her? Any questions you have for her would have to be channeled through me."

She replied, "Mr. Lynnes, I suspected that there might be such a relationship when I studied your website and looked into a few of your cases. I'm actually kind of excited by the opportunity to learn how you make that work and to try to become a part of it in some way. I've had a lifelong interest in, not just investigation, but in the paranormal."

"Last question, then," he said with a smile. "When can you start?"

"Does that mean I've got the job?" Becky asked.

Bert answered with a chuckle, "Yes, you've got the job if you want it, Becky. And from now on, I'm Bert. I'm not a formal guy, as you know."

She became serious. "I should give my present company a two-week notice. So, with the holidays coming on, I think I should probably aim to start working for you about the second or third of January. I'm renting a place in a small town a few miles south of Cheyenne, so need to move, I guess. I assume I should try to find a place to live up here around Cody, right?"

"Yes, it would be better if you lived near us. That will likely take some time, so until then we can work with you by phone. I know a bed and breakfast in downtown Cody which would make you a pretty good deal on a few months of temporary off-season lodging until you find something permanent. For now, how about we have lunch?"

He reached across the table and shook her hand. "Welcome to B & N Investigations, Becky Thompson."

CHAPTER TWO: RED LODGE

Tuesday, January 2nd, 2018, was clear and cold. Bert and Norah looked out their picture window onto the three inches of fresh snow. It had turned the early morning landscape into a brilliant mix of glistening white, broken by the scattered trees and rock facings of the surrounding mountains. The sun was just rising over Cedar Mountain, which rose sharply to the southwest of Cody.

Wyoming's second national monument, designated so by President Taft, now sat nearly abandoned on Cedar Mountain, nearly three-quarters of the way up Spirit Mountain Road. This road left the vicinity of the world-famous Cody Night Rodeo grounds and wound steeply up the mountain until a visitor could arrive at the steep ledge which led to Spirit Mountain Cave. What could have been another national treasure, this 2,000-foot-deep cave with its sparkling crystals was largely sacrificed to the development of Yellowstone Park. This morning, no visitors were there to witness the spectacular sunrise as it crept over the mountain to light up the North Fork Highway to the west. It wrested the valley from the night and brought its majesty to Bert's and Norah's view.

Bert shifted his gaze from the morning spectacle to Norah. They were once again discussing the ongoing emails with Elizabeth Hayden, in Red Lodge, Montana. She was the mother of the seven-year-old girl having some kind of emotional issue. Elizabeth, or Lizzie as she liked to be called, had taken her daughter, Summer Irene, to three different psychiatrists. They each offered different diagnoses, ranging from post-traumatic stress disorder to schizophrenia. Lizzie just didn't buy any of that. She said she couldn't help but believe there was something else behind her daughter's strange behavior. She had studied the B & N website and felt strongly that they might be able to help her child.

Norah agreed with Lizzie. "I'm sensing that Lizzie is right about the psychiatric evaluations. That profession wants a label and a psychosis for every human feeling and action. They're not happy unless they can put you into one of their boxes. The PTSD evaluation might come the closest. It could be that some traumatic event happened to this child that her parents don't know about."

Bert nodded. "Yeah, babe, I'm changing my mind about this one. I'm thinking we should take this case. The parents are well off, so money is no object for them. Perhaps we're the only team with the tools to answer their questions."

"I'm thinking this might be a good case for Becky to cut her teeth on, Honey," Norah suggested. "She wants to work and she's a self-starter. As an empath personality, she might be able to connect with this child in a way that few others can."

Bert added, "You're right, I think, Sweetheart. She got out of her lease down by Cheyenne and is moving into the Robin's Nest B & B on Alger Avenue this week. This is one of those unusual cases that might be tailor-made for her limited investigative experience."

"Have her come out soon as she's able so I can see her, Bert,"

Norah requested. "I've heard you talk about her, but I want to meet her. Well, you know what I mean. I'm sensing that she's ugly as a mud fence, right?" She smiled.

He grinned a little sheepishly. "Well, dear, not quite like a mud fence, but close. I'll see if she has any time this afternoon."

A phone call to Becky caught her in a reception zone as she traveled just west of Caspar. She'd gotten an early start this morning with her pickup loaded down with her last possessions. She said she should be able to come out to their place later this afternoon.

While Norah spent some time with Missy, Bert went back to checking email. A new inquiry popped up. A guy in Nebraska asked if B & N Investigations would consider a very cold missing person's case.

Bert thought about that for a minute before replying that they would consider such a case. However, he needed to know more details in order to decide.

Missy was wandering around the living room, acting restlessly. Bert knew she needed to go out and get some exercise, so he donned his winter boots and coat and they headed out the back door and into the snow-covered mountains. She sprinted ahead of him, stopping periodically to look back and keep him in sight. She excitedly searched under rocks and fallen trees for any sign of a furry snack.

Can't take the country out of the coyote, thought Bert.

"Damn, that's gonna be a bruise!" He rolled over slowly, checking his right hip to see if everything still worked.

He carefully picked himself up from where he'd fallen. Snow covered rocky trails were not a place to get in a hurry. He could enjoy the scenery more at a slower pace, anyway. The rest of their nearly three-hour hike went well, and man and coyote thoroughly enjoyed themselves. Alone in nature, Bert could not only relax and enjoy the serenity, but it was where he did his best thinking.

Back at home, Bert fed Missy and left her to her bed in the garage. From there she had access to their large fenced yard. He went inside to check email again and communicate with Norah.

The guy from Nebraska had emailed again. The name of this 23-year-old man was Robert Sturdevant. He lived on the outskirts of Nebraska City, Nebraska. He said that his mother, Vicki, disappeared in 2010. Both the volunteer search and the investigation came up empty. After a couple of years, the case went cold. His mother had been a very successful real estate investor, leaving him well off as her only heir. Emotionally, he was having a difficult time living without knowing what had happened to her.

Bert discussed this latest email with Norah, as he sipped a coffee. "I have some reservations about taking a case this old and cold," he said. "We've never tried to reach so far back in time before. This guy sounds so distraught, though."

Norah had moved to the opposite side of the cozy sitting area in front of the large picture window. They both paused to drink in the early afternoon view of the North Fork Valley, spreading before them to the south and west. "I'm also apprehensive about this one, Honey. But there's something about this man and his obvious pain that pulls me. I think we should try to help him."

Bert nodded as he watched the light January traffic on the Yellowstone highway. It was mostly locals who either lived in the valley or were heading for the east entrance to Yellowstone for some snowmobiling or cross-country skiing. "Yeah, Sweetheart, I agree. This one is tugging at me, also. I'll tell him we'll take it. And ask when he might be able to have a telephone call to get into more details."

Shortly after his call to Robert, his cell phone rang. It was Becky. Bert greeted her warmly and asked how the move was going.

"OMG, don't ask!" She exclaimed. "I'm sure you've done enough moves to know the drill and the frustrations. But hey, I'm ready for a break after moving my last bags into the room and my other stuff into a storage unit. Ready for a chat with you guys."

She always sounds so upbeat, Bert thought to himself as he noted Norah's nod of approval. "Fantastic, if now is a good time, come on out." He proceeded to give her directions.

"Guess we're going to find out how this will work with our first new investigator. Ought to be interesting." Norah laughed. "Get to see just how much she resembles a mud fence."

Bert wondered if his face was red. "Well, she isn't exactly ugly, Honey, but she's a good person and I think she's going to be great working with us."

"I'm just teasing you, my Love," Norah said with a laugh in her voice. "I've already perceived that she's a very beautiful woman. Remember, hun, I'm a bit psychic. I know you chose her, though, because of her abilities. I trust your judgment."

"Thanks, baby, you're right about all that," Bert said as he began to tidy up the kitchen and living room.

The knock at the door followed the black Dodge pickup's arrival on their driveway. Bert glanced at Norah as he walked to the front door. She stood near the chair to the left of the picture window, a big smile shimmered on her face.

Bert opened the door. "Hello Becky, welcome to the headquarters of B & N Investigations." He shook her hand and waved her inside with a sweep of his hand.

As Becky stepped inside and looked around the warm and cozy log cabin, Bert glanced at Norah. She looked at him and mouthed an approving "Wow!" Although Becky was wearing denim jeans, a short sleeve camo tee shirt, and her ankle high lace work shoes, he knew Norah was thinking, "Not a mud fence."

Bert smiled and gave Becky a tour of the downstairs, then directed her to the sitting area by the picture window. She marveled at the view for a minute, then turned to Bert, ready for his guidance. He'd been marveling at the view, also.

They engaged in small talk for a few minutes. After that, Bert transitioned to discussing their business. Becky had numerous questions about their past cases and how the team worked together. She was especially fascinated with the psychic inputs.

"So, your psychic wife, Norah, always works in the background?" She asked. "Will she stay in the background, even with me?"

Bert knew this question would come up. "Yes, for now she wants to stay in the background with everyone but me. I know that may seem a little strange, but in time you'll understand."

Becky nodded. "You'll tell me then what she thinks of me? And what she wants me to know?"

"Yes, for now we'll work it that way. I can tell you already that she likes you and thinks you'll be a real asset to our team."

"Really?" Becky wanted to know. "She hasn't met me; how

can she know she likes me?"

Bert was struggling more than he expected with this. "Well, don't forget, Becky, Norah is a psychic. She senses you already." He wasn't happy with the way that answer felt.

Becky seemed satisfied for now. "Yeah, I forget about that. I'm sure it will take some getting used to in order to have a relationship with a psychic that I don't directly interact with. However, if you're okay with my steep learning curve, then we'll figure it out as time goes on." She smiled that killer smile and her blue eyes sparkled.

Bert knew it was time to get down to business before he continued to stumble over this situation. He glanced at Norah, who was smiling at his awkwardness. "Let's discuss a possible case for you, Becky."

"Are you serious?" Becky was caught by surprise. "I haven't even gotten my feet on the ground with you guys and you already want me to work a case?"

Bert laughed. "You said you wanted to work, so we're going to work you."

"Well, I thought I'd have an air-conditioned office, a staff car, and a couple of assistants for a year or two before I started working cases," she said laughingly.

"Nope; not with us," he replied. "I recognize your abilities and Norah agrees with me. In fact, this one is her suggestion. It's a rather unusual case a couple of hours from here, in Red Lodge. You could either drive back and forth or stay in a motel there, depending upon the need."

Becky leaned forward from the easy chair. "Then give me the rundown, boss, and I'll get back to the B & B and finish moving in today. After that, when would you like me to get started with it? Tomorrow?" She took out a notepad and pen from her purse, ready to get the details.

Bert retrieved the email traffic from Guy and Elizabeth Hayden. He read the several exchanges out loud, pausing to allow Becky to ask questions and make notes. "I'll give you copies of these messages, so you don't need to make notes on them. I think this case will probably require a bit of interaction with the parties up there, especially the child."

"I'll call Elizabeth and Guy tonight and arrange a time to visit and get started, then. When they're ready, I'll be ready." Becky was thrilled about being entrusted with a case the day she walked in. "Got to tell you, Bert," she added, "I'm really excited to be working with you and to get to work on this case. I'll do my best to not let either of you down."

"No worries, Becky," Bert said, "We want you to do the Red Lodge case because we think you're best suited for it. You have an empath personality, and that may be exactly what's needed to find closure for this little girl. Just call and discuss it with us any time you feel the need. Otherwise, run with it."

Becky was bubbling with enthusiasm as she walked to the door. When she reached the door, without thinking, she gave Bert a hug. "Oh sorry," she exclaimed, "My family and I are huggers and it's just second nature to me. I hope you don't mind?"

He quickly relieved her concern. "That's okay, both our families are huggers, too. You'll fit right in. Good luck with the rest of your move. If you need help, give a shout. Just let me know how the case is proceeding."

She left. Bert turned toward Norah, where she was watching Becky drive away. Norah turned back toward Bert.

"I like her," she said. "I love her bubbly and enthusiastic personality. I think she'll be a great member of our team. I just wish she was a bit ugly, though." She chuckled at that. Her husband was dazzled by Becky's beauty, and she knew it.

"Well, look at the bright side." Bert said a little apologetically. "Her beauty and smile can probably get her into worthwhile conversations when I wouldn't stand a chance."

"You're right about that, Honey," Norah agreed. "Most men would likely bare their souls to her." She laughed as she looked Bert in the eyes.

* * *

Rebecca Thompson felt strangely eerie as she drove back to her room. Norah wasn't there when she met with Bert, so why did she feel that Norah was there. Though she was only talking with Bert, she couldn't help but feel a three-way conversation. There was obviously a lot she had to learn about this psychic relationship.

Becky arrived back at her room and continued the chore of unpacking her things and putting them away. Fortunately, she was traveling light for the time being. Just the very basics to tide her over in this room until she found something more permanent. Of course, that depended upon how permanent her job was. That was going to depend upon how well she handled this first job. She needed to contact the Red Lodge family and get that ball rolling.

Becky listened to her phone ring about five times. Just as she was about to hang up, Elizabeth Hayden answered. "Hi Mrs. Hayden, I'm Becky Thompson with B & N Investigations." Boy, she liked the sound of that! "I've been assigned to your case. I'd like to arrange a time when I can come up there and begin the process of trying to help you with your daughter."

Elizabeth quickly asked to just be called Lizzie. She said her husband, Guy, knew she wanted this investigation, but he wasn't convinced that it would do any good. So, Elizabeth, Lizzie, would be the primary point of contact with Becky. They arranged to meet the day after tomorrow, Thursday. The snow which was forecasted for tonight and tomorrow should be passed by then.

Becky thanked Lizzie for putting her trust in her and the company and said good-bye. She was glad they weren't meeting until Thursday. It gave her another day to get her room setup to her liking and get mentally prepared for the unknowns this case was certain to bring her way.

She went back to work on her room. Outside, a light snow was beginning to fall in the darkness of 6:30 PM in Wyoming. The thermometer outside her window said it was fifteen degrees. If she wasn't sweating from arranging her room and putting her things away, she knew she'd be suppressing a shiver and putting on a sweater.

West of the Buffalo Bill Dam, Bert and Norah were on the speaker phone with Robert Sturdevant. He was describing the horrible day in July of 2010 when his mother was last seen. Several times, the child in this man surfaced as he broke down crying. The third time, he wept for well over a minute before regaining enough composure to continue.

Bert inquired gently, "Do you have any idea what she was doing and who she was associating with during the months leading up to her disappearance?"

"I'm very sorry, Mr. Lynnes, but I just can't remember much of that. I've had a lot of mental problems, and one is that I can't remember a lot about my early years. A couple of the doctors I've been to think it may be amnesia brought on by mom's disappearance. Kinda like PTDS, they say."

Bert thought about that for a few seconds. "Robert, if I may call you Robert, just call me Bert. I'm not a formal guy. Do you mean PTSD? Post-Traumatic Stress Disorder?"

"Oh yeah, I'm sorry, sir. Yes, that's what they called it. Do you think it could be that?"

Bert replied carefully. "I don't know that, Robert, and I'm not a doctor. I couldn't diagnose that. It does seem like a plausible explanation, though."

"Yeah, it makes sense to me," Robert admitted. "So, can you help me find out what happened to mommy?"

"Robert, all I can promise you is that we'll do our best. This is a very cold case and will probably be difficult to resurrect and solve. I think we should get together soon and go over as many details as you can recall. Today is January 2nd, Tuesday. Would you be able to meet me about a week from now? I'll have to look at the weather forecasts, but right now I think I can drive over there around Tuesday or Wednesday of next week."

"Oh, yes sir," Robert responded quickly. "I'm not really working; just trying to manage mom's investments from home. I'll meet with you anytime you can get here." He sobbed again.

Bert wanted to channel this man's obvious grief in a positive direction. "Robert, I need for you to meet with the police and get a copy of their report about your mother's case. Also, make notes about anything or anyone that you believe might help us. Friends, acquaintances, coworkers, and so forth. Anything you can remember or dig up. If you find people who're familiar with the case, get their phone numbers and addresses so we can contact them."

Robert seemed anxious to help. "Oh yeah, Mr. Lynnes, I'll get those for you if I can. I mean, Bert. Sorry. I'm just used to being formal with my superiors."

"No problem, Robert. I'm just Bert. And I'm not your superior, I'm just the man you've hired to try to find out what happened to your mother. I'll call you in a few days to see how you're doing with those things, and we can finalize a day and time to meet. Take care of yourself. Okay?"

"Oh yes sir, I mean okay, Bert. I'm very anxious for you to get started. I really want to find out what happened to mommy. Goodbye, sir."

After ending the call, Bert looked at Norah with a look of confusion. "Honey, this case just got a bit stranger, I think."

Norah was nodding vigorously. "Yes, dear, you're right. I'm picking up on an unusual degree of hurt in this young man. He's not even begun to heal from the loss of his mother. To him, it's as if it happened yesterday. You must handle him with kid gloves, Bert. He seems very fragile."

"Well, 2018 is starting off with a bang, my Love," Bert concluded. "I think we're going to have our hands full in Nebraska City. I wonder if it will be any easier for Becky in Red Lodge?"

Outside, the wind was picking up, now about 25 miles per hour. It was swirling the new snow, now coming down at a much faster pace. By morning, it was forecasted to be a winter storm, with up to 12 inches of snow by late afternoon, when it was predicted to subside. At the ski lodge and its runs at Red Lodge Mountain, owners and skiers would be excited. This best kept secret of the downhill community would reap the benefits of fresh snow, even as the roads would initially prevent Becky from making the trip.

From her room at Robin's Nest B & B, Becky peered out her window into the lighted back yard. The snow, dancing in circles around the trees and lawn ornaments, reminded her of the rush of anxiety dancing in her head about the case she would go to on Thursday. The 10-degree temperature exacerbated the chill she felt as she tried to imagine what was going on with the little girl. Now, though, she kicked off her fuzzy slippers, adjusted her pajamas, and climbed under the covers. Red Lodge would come soon enough.

CHAPTER THREE: SUMMER

Becky took one last look at the cherrywood bar given to Bill Cody by Queen Victoria. This ornate bar spanned a major portion of the west wall of the Buffalo Bill Restaurant. She had decided that her first meal out in Cody just had to be at the internationally known Irma Hotel on Main Street, named for Bill Cody's daughter. When she walked the roughly five blocks to the hotel and its restaurant, the storm had subsided to just light wind and flurries. Even this light snow gave a surreal appeal to the senses as it passed through the streetlights, which had come on at dusk on this Wednesday evening, January 3rd.

Walking through the bar area to the east of the restaurant dining room, Becky slowed to look at the pictures scattered around the walls of this rustic cowboy bar. She paused at the signed picture of her friend, Governor Sam Patterson. Her heart warmed as she thought of the enjoyable chats she had with him and Cody, now Bert, back in Cheyenne. She remembered fondly how much she had looked forward to them coming into the restaurant for their working lunches.

She exited through the side door onto the sidewalk. The ten-degree temperature was more than enough incentive to hike up the collar of her heavy wool coat, tug her knit cap over her ears, and pull on her lined leather gloves. She took a deep breath, enjoying the cold air that seemed to invigorate her lungs. The snow was as beautiful as before, drifting and swirling now more softly from the dark sky. She had to admit that she was a northern girl, addicted to the four distinct and often harsh seasons.

The streets were plowed and her walk back to Robin's Nest

was easy and enjoyable. Once inside and settled on the living room couch with a hot chocolate, self-served from the kitchen, she called Bert.

When he answered, she greeted him warmly. "Hi there, this is Becky. Getting psyched up to begin the case tomorrow and thought I'd see if you or Norah have any words of wisdom for me before I head out around dawn."

Bert sounded pleased that she'd called. "Hey there. I don't have anything to offer that you don't already know, but Norah may have some insight."

She replied enthusiastically. "Fantastic, Bert. Hey, do you realize that I haven't called you Cody even one time since I got here. I'm amazing myself with that, because I totally knew you as Cody down in Cheyenne."

He laughed at that. "Yeah, I have noticed that, Becky. Funny, the twists and turns of PI work."

"Yup," she laughed. "Anyway, boss Bert, what insights does Norah have for me?"

"She says she's getting two feelings about your case right now," Bert relayed. "One concerns the mother. Norah feels that the mother is genuinely concerned and will be honest with you. That can be significant because our clients often have ulterior motives or hidden agendas."

"Oh my, that is great," Becky responded. "What's the other thing?"

Bert was more somber now. "She senses that the key is the child. Something has happened to this kid, and if you can find out what that was, you'll help this family cope with it."

Becky sat with the phone to her ear, not saying anything. After what seemed like minutes, she finally answered. "Wow, that's heavy. It was weighing on me before, but now . . ."

"You'll do fine, Becky," he said. "Just follow your instincts and use common sense. They rarely lead us too far astray. You always have us to bounce ideas around."

"Thanks, and please thank Norah for me. I can see I'm going to appreciate and rely on her insights."

"I'll pass that on," he promised. "Be careful traveling tomorrow. It sounds like the roads should be mostly clear, maybe just a few patches of snow or ice to watch for. Give a call if you have any questions or need assistance. Good luck, Becky."

Becky wished them a good night and put her phone down. She sat quietly sipping her remaining hot chocolate, now a lukewarm chocolate. She re-read the messages again between the company and Lizzie. "What secrets are you hiding, Summer Irene?" she said aloud to herself. She was alone in the living room since there were no other guests this time of year.

It was nearly 10:00 and time to get to bed. The anxiety about her case was suddenly sublimated by a sense of loneliness. As she ascended the stairs leading toward her second-floor room, not even the owners were in sight. She felt all alone in this big, quiet house. It was so quiet that she found herself tiptoeing to quiet the squeaks in the wooden steps and floor. Quietly, she opened and closed her bedroom door, and stood for a couple of minutes, surveying the room with its mix of cute accoutrements, some theirs, some hers. It looked warm and friendly. Yet, the very warmth of the room made her more aware that she wasn't sharing it with anyone. A trickle of tears dampened her cheeks and spotted her T-shirt as she felt loneliness closing over her like a dense fog.

She'd been so intent upon her jobs and new career that she hadn't really mourned the end of her marriage. As bad as it had become, she still missed the companionship, especially at night. Her husband could be the nicest guy when he wanted to be. Out in public when things were good, they made a stunning couple. Both men and women would send glances their way. She shook her head and suppressed a sob though, as she recalled the times that weren't so good.

When she moved to Cheyenne back in the fall, her double black eyes and swollen lips had just gotten healed back to normal. The rages and beatings had progressed to the point that she knew she had to get out or she'd eventually be killed. She knew that some things you just can't change, and you must think about your survival. Her best girlfriend said the one thing that made her decide to go. "A leopard doesn't change its spots, Becky." Becky knew in her heart that was true. Her ex was not going to change from his fits of jealous rage every time another man looked at her. She knew that her only option was to leave Ron Moreland while she could. She had to leave the area, because she knew he would not want to let go of her.

Once she had made the decision to get out and get away, Becky had known that she wanted to help others in similar situations. She'd considered numerous options and occupations, but none really related to her. When she looked into private investigator, though, something had connected with her. If there was anything she could do to help someone else who felt alone, abandoned, and hurting, then she wanted to be able to do something. She needed a paying job fast, and she wanted to help people who were in trouble. She liked mysteries and she liked to solve them. She had decided that she, Becky Moreland, now Thompson, was going to become a P.I., a good one.

All of that mattered, and yet it didn't seem to make much difference right now. Through the windows, the snow was still swirling lightly against the panes and outside around the pine needles. The thermometer added to her chill, as she read five above zero.

She pulled back the covers and stood in her flowery pajamas looking down at the bed. Even in the darkened room, there was something about an empty, cold bed that brought the reality of a failed relationship back into the light.

* * *

Carrying her usual emergency gear as well as her PI bags,

Becky headed north from Cody at 7:00 Thursday morning. With the fresh snow everywhere she looked, Highway 120, locally known as the Belfry Highway, would be more scenic than usual, despite the high overcast clouds. At first, she glanced frequently at Heart Mountain, the east side of which was a common hiking challenge just a few miles northeast of Cody. After it began to fade in the rearview mirror, the beauty of the Absaroka Mountains to the west was awe-inspiring. The Belfry Highway paralleled the seam between the eastern front of the mountain range and the high plains foothills to the east.

Roughly halfway to the Montana border, Becky passed the exit for Crandall Road, Wyoming Highway 296, also known as the Chief Joseph Scenic Byway. This winding mountain road followed the trail taken by Chief Joseph as he led his Nez Perce tribe toward Montana from what is now Yellowstone Park, in 1877. The 46-mile drive from Cody connected to the Beartooth Highway at Cooke City, and brought the traveler to the northeast entrance of Yellowstone Park. She had been on this road several times when she lived in Billings but reminded herself that she needed to drink in the beauty of this drive at the first opportunity in the spring.

As she entered Montana, her road became Montana Highway 72. A short time later, she turned west on Highway 308 at the town of Belfry. It wasn't long before the road passed through the town of Bearcreek, Montana, site of the worst coal mining disaster in Montana history. She stopped briefly to read the marker left in tribute to the 74 men who died in a methane gas explosion on February 27th, 1943. This event decimated the town of Bearcreek, turning it into the ghost town that remained today. Mine 43 never reopened and the rusting buildings and entrance still stood guard over the spirits of those lost. Becky wiped tears from her eyes as she resumed her drive to Red Lodge. She could feel the pain all around her.

The remaining drive to Red Lodge was peaceful. As Becky pulled into town, she had to admit that she didn't feel ready to take on the responsibility of this case. "You can't think that way," she said aloud to herself. "Got to be positive and just do what needs to be done. You've got this, Becky, so suck it up."

She called Lizzie, who answered immediately.

Lizzie suggested that she meet Becky alone for coffee and breakfast at the Café Regis. Summer was staying with a friend this morning. Lizzie said the café was a little off the beaten path. However, she said the food is great and hopefully the place wouldn't be overwhelmed by skiers. They could talk about Summer while eating.

Becky located the restaurant on her phone's map program. She wanted to get there quickly to satisfy her craving for a coffee. When she walked into the restaurant, she immediately felt the stares from several of the ski bums. Even though she was dressed very casually in her denim jeans and checkered flannel shirt, she always seemed to attract attention. She paid them no mind. She was after coffee right now.

Ten minutes later, Lizzie Hayden joined her. She was a cute brunette with wavy hair, nicely built, and seemed very friendly and outgoing. Lizzie also wore denim jeans but with a beige pullover sweater. Her winter walking shoes were very practical for the weather and time of year. She said she was originally from Idaho but moved here after college for the ski scene. That didn't last as long as she intended because she met her future husband and married a year later.

After introductions and ordering breakfast, they began to discuss the daughter, Summer. Becky asked what major problems the child was experiencing.

"Mainly, Summer has outbursts at unexplained times, and she gets obsessed with certain activities, such as drawing. In most respects, most of the time, she's a perfectly normal seven-year-old," Lizzie said.

Becky listened intently. "As far as you know, Summer has never been abused or attacked in any way by someone?"

Lizzie answered, "No, absolutely not. She's rarely been out of our sight. Just a few times when we hire babysitters, usually teenagers we know. When she was pre-school, we had her in a daycare facility for one year when I was working. Other than that, she stays with Guy's parents for the most part when we're doing something."

"How about at school? I assume she's about a second-grader?" Becky asked. "Could anyone be bullying her?"

Lizzie was slower to answer. "No, we've asked around among

the teachers and have no indication of that. Summer is one of those kids that's normally very bubbly and liked by everyone. She likes school and is always anxious to go. Not the demeanor of a child being bullied."

Becky considered that for a minute. "When did her strange behavior first start, Lizzie?"

Lizzie responded, "Well, I don't know if it's part of what we're experiencing now, but around the age of two, she began having night terrors. This was pure hell for us. The episodes were almost nightly and often lasted over half an hour. Summer finally outgrew them when she was nearly five."

"I've heard of those, what are they like?" Becky inquired.

Lizzie took a few seconds to wipe a tear from her cheek. "Heart wrenching! Your child seems to wake up screaming bloody murder. Some think they aren't awake, but in an altered state of sleep. You learn not to wake them. Just let her scream until it finally subsides, and she goes back to real sleep."

"Oh, wow. That had to be awful for all of you." Becky sympathized. "Was it just crying and screaming. No words?"

"All screaming at the top of her lungs. Piercing!" Lizzie seemed to shudder as she recalled those memories. "No words. Well, I don't know that for sure. When she was older and nearing the end of the terrors, she sometimes seemed to be screaming for a baby."

"Really?" Becky said. "Do you remember exactly what she'd say?"

"She was very young, so it sounded like she was saying 'be-be', but it had to be her attempt at 'baby'."

Becky considered that, then asked, "why do you think that, Lizzie?"

"It became apparent shortly after that. We bought her a little boy doll. She almost immediately began to call it 'be-be'. She still does to this day. It goes everywhere with her, even in her bag to school. It's her 'be-be'. Her security blanket."

Becky leaned back and sipped her last bit of coffee. "Anything else that you find unusual?"

Lizzie reached in her bag and pulled out several sheets of paper. "These. About the time she finally came out of the terrors, she wanted to draw. She's like a fledgling artist. Many are different and what you'd expect from a girl her age. However, these show a consistent theme for the last three years. She'll draw something like this sometimes three or four times a week." She passed the sheets to Becky.

Becky studied all the sheets without a word. Most of them appeared to be a stick figure, seeming to be a girl, judging by the hair. The figure was standing between two posts. That was it. A plain white sheet with three stick figures. The other pictures seemed to show two circles; a smaller one with a large circle around it. It looked as if the little girl would trace around both over and over, dozens of times.

Becky couldn't make any sense of either. "Do you have any explanation for these?"

"No. I was hoping you might." Lizzie almost pleaded.

Becky shook her head slowly. "Sorry. No, I sure don't. Does Summer say anything about her drawings?"

"No. When I ask her about them, she doesn't seem to know why she draws them." Lizzie looked worried. "She gets upset if you press her on it. I need your help to make sense of all this."

"Thank you," Becky told Lizzie who picked up the tab for breakfast. "You don't need to pick up my bill, but I do appreciate it. I'll get the tip. When do you think I might be able to meet with your daughter and get to know her personally?"

"She'll be back home after lunch. Would you be able to come to our place about 1:00 and I'll introduce you?" Lizzie was excited. "You can stay as long as you want."

Becky was equally enthusiastic. "That's wonderful! Just let me put your address in my phone and I'll find your place with my map app."

Lizzie gave her their address. They lived in the rural part of town just to the north. "Say, if you need a place to stay sometimes and don't want a hotel, we have a guest cottage off to the side of our house. Has its own driveway, kitchen, etcetera. You're welcome to use it any time you're up here. Just sitting empty."

"Well thank you for that offer. For tonight, I think I'll get a motel room so I can get acquainted with your town. After tonight, though, I might take you up on that." Becky wanted to see more of Red Lodge.

They said adieu. Becky looked at her phone. It was almost 11:00, so she had some time to find a motel and settle in before going to Lizzie's.

After driving South Broadway Avenue, the length of the town, looking over the selection of quaint motels, hotels, and eating places, Becky decided to stay at the Beartooth Hideaway Inn for this first night. A bit more than she was comfortable spending, but it would do for now. It'd give her the opportunity to get more familiar with this small, country, ski town, and its 2000 plus residents. It was a gateway mountain town, having an elevation just over a mile high.

Time passed quickly. It seemed to Becky that she had barely gotten checked into her room when she was surprised to see that it was nearly a quarter until 1:00. It was time to head for

Lizzie's house and her meeting with Summer.

She pulled up to the Hayden's house a couple of minutes before 1:00. It was important to her to be prompt and on time with her clients. Lizzie and Summer met her at the front door of the two-story log and rock house. It was situated in the middle of a well-cared-for, mostly level, five-acre property, dotted with numerous trees and shrubs. Obviously an affluent family, Becky surmised.

Lizzie greeted Becky warmly, shaking her hand profusely and welcoming her to their home. Daughter, Summer, was a little shy and hugged her mother's leg while eyeing this visitor and saying nothing. She was very tuned in to Becky, though. Becky could sense that this child was more complex than usual. She knelt to Summer's level. "Hi Summer, my name is Becky. I'm hoping we can spend some time together and get to know each other. Would that be okay?"

The little girl nodded her head in agreement. She still didn't say anything, though. Her eyes did not leave Becky. It felt to Becky like she was making a connection with this new woman.

Summer Irene Hayden was a cute, slender, and small statured little girl with dark hair. At seven years old, her height barely reached Becky's waist. She was very alert and gave the impression of being inquisitive and intelligent, even if a bit shy with this new stranger. Her eyes sparkled with a mix of friendliness tempered with caution.

Becky stood up and turned her attention back to Lizzie, sensing that she needed to begin slowly with this child. She said she was excited to see their beautiful home and asked if Lizzie and Summer would show her around?"

With Summer in close proximity, they led Becky on a tour of the house. When they approached the bedrooms upstairs, Becky looked to Summer and asked if she could see her room?

This time, Summer responded. "Sure, ma'am, I have a great room." She began to show her new friend around the room, pausing at favorite toys, drawings, and books. A small boy doll was on her bed, lying against a pillow.

Becky pointed to the doll. "And who is this, Summer? Is this your baby?"

Summer pulled the doll off her bed and hugged it to her chest. "My be-be," she said.

"That's nice, Summer. What do you call your baby?"

"Be-be," she replied.

Becky could feel Summer's strong connection to this doll. "So, his name is Be-be. Does he stay with you all the time?"

She nodded affirmatively. "Yes, ma'am. He's with me everywhere."

"I see that you like to draw. Is this your only picture?" Becky had paused to study a crayon drawing of a nature scene. It was obviously drawn by a child of her age.

"I love to draw," said the little girl. "I have lots of drawings. I'm an artist."

"Wow, that's fantastic, Summer," Becky praised her. "May I see some of your other drawings?"

Summer opened a drawer of her dresser and pulled out a small presentation folder filled with pages of her drawings and artwork. Becky and Lizzie sat on the bed with her as she proceeded to show page after page to Becky. The first couple dozen were all bright drawings in crayons and colored pencils. Most depicted some kind of natural scenes with animals and birds. However, there was one like those shown earlier by Lizzie. It was a pencil drawing of the double circle. There was no color, and nothing was in crayon. The stark contrast between this picture and those done in crayon was almost startling.

Becky focused on the picture without really seeing it. She was feeling confusion and fear in this child. This was not just scribbling. It was an expression of something dark, maybe even sinister. It represented a feeling more than a fact or a figure. As much as she wanted to ask Summer what this picture represented, she sensed that would not be productive. Not now, anyway. Maybe some other time when the girl trusted her more. She asked to see the other pictures.

47

Before long, the other picture which Lizzie had told her about, surfaced. Like the ones shown by Lizzie, the stick figures looked as if they were drawn by someone else. Especially those done more recently. Although slightly more sophisticated, they continued to be eerily similar to those of earlier ages. Again, Becky sensed fear in the child as she looked at these couple of pictures. She decided to chance asking a question.

"These are all very good, Summer. Would you tell me what you are thinking or feeling when you drew these two?"

It was a wrong move. Summer didn't answer but instead turned away, hunched her shoulders, and crossed her arms.

Becky had to regroup. "Oh, I am so sorry, Summer. I didn't mean to make you sad by asking. I'm very sorry. Would you forgive me?"

The child slowly relaxed and regained her posture. There were tears slowly running down her cheeks, though she didn't make a sound. She looked at her mother.

Lizzie took the cue. "Summer often takes a nap after school and before supper, so she's probably getting tired. I think we should let her take a nap now if she wants." She looked at her daughter, who nodded her head.

The women left the room and Lizzie closed the bedroom door without latching it. She looked at Becky, knowing that Becky was mortified that she had seemed to blow it with her daughter. "Don't worry, I just let you go without giving you any suggestions or precautions. She's reacted that way before with me. I hoped it might be different with you."

"Your child exudes fear when those two pictures come up. Even as she draws them, she's feeling fear. I just wish I knew of what."

"That is the question, isn't it? Or at least part of the question." Lizzie sighed as she exhaled deeply. "So, you think she feels fear with both of those? I haven't been sure what she thinks or feels."

"Yes, I'm sure that fear is the dominant force behind both those drawings, Lizzie. I sense what she's feeling. I'm getting a feeling of fear from them, myself. Summer can't begin to heal until we can identify and help her deal with that fear."

Lizzie walked over to a kitchen cabinet and opened the door. "How about a glass of wine and just some girl talk for a while? I need a break, a drink, and a woman to talk with."

Becky was up for a glass of wine. There are times when it is not only okay to drink on duty, she rationalized, but might even be necessary. She picked up her glass of a semi-sweet, red, Montana wine, and toasted her client. They proceeded into the living room for that girl talk.

As they sat into the two rustic log chairs, Lizzie confessed. "Hey, listen Becky. I know this isn't the best decorum to have a drink the first afternoon. I won't suggest this but rarely if ever again. Today, though, you don't know how good it feels to share this burden with someone who understands. I've kept this to myself for so long. My Guy just doesn't grasp the gravity of Summer's conflicted mind. So, I really have nobody to talk with. I hope you don't mind?"

Becky leaned toward Lizzie, who was rapidly becoming a friend as much as a client. "No, I don't mind, and I do understand. Just don't tell my boss that I'm drinking on the job." She laughed.

Lizzie almost scoffed at that thought. "Oh, don't you worry. You're on the job right now and this is what your client needs. I think we should give Summer a break the rest of the day, and you can try to get into her trust tomorrow. I want you to just spend time with her and see for yourself the other things."

"The other things?" Becky asked.

Lizzie gave her a serious look. "Yes, there are other things, and I think it's best if you just find them out as you get to know her. Summer is a very normal seven-year-old girl; except when she's not. Would you stay and have supper with us when Guy gets home?"

Becky thought it unwise to get too close any faster. "I really appreciate the offer, but I want to just unwind over a burger downtown and get back to the room. I need to check in with my boss, too. Can we do supper another time?"

"Sure," said Lizzie, "My husband will be home in just a couple of minutes. How about meeting him before you go?"

They talked about Summer for a few more minutes before she came down from her room. Shortly after that, Lizzie's husband, Guy, arrived from his work at the airport. He and Becky talked for about twenty minutes, before she left.

As she drove back toward her motel, Becky couldn't help but debate her thoughts about Guy. On the surface he seemed nice enough and was friendly toward her. However, something about him didn't sit right with her. It was just a feeling; nothing concrete. Maybe it was partially fueled by his seeming disinterest in helping Lizzie find out what was going on with their daughter. She wondered if he was hiding something.

She decided to detour into the Snag Bar on Broadway Avenue before reaching the motel. She'd heard about the beautiful but rustic wooden bar and the reputation for having good burgers, beer, and atmosphere. It seemed like a good spot to have an evening bite before calling Bert.

It wasn't long after she sat at the bar before a younger man, apparently one of the skiers in town, hit on her. He was a handsome guy, probably in his late twenties or early thirties, with dark hair and blue eyes. She didn't mind having some company while she ate so accepted his request to sit with her. Alex, as he introduced himself, was from out of town, someplace in eastern Iowa. They chatted while she ate her burger and finished a lager beer. He picked up her tab before she could pay it.

51

Becky wasn't naïve, she knew where this could go. It was tempting. She'd been divorced for about five months now and hadn't been with a man that entire time. She didn't know if she was ready now. What was clear was the loneliness that she increasingly felt. Was this the answer to that feeling, though? She debated that question for another ten minutes as they talked.

Alex finally got to the question she knew was coming. He invited her to his motel for a "night cap." She knew it was for more than a drink.

She took a silent and long inhale. "Alex, I just got divorced not long ago. I'm flattered by your interest, but I'm just not ready for that. You're a great looking guy and very nice, but I just can't. Not now. I hope you understand."

Alex's look of disappointment said everything. However, he was gracious as he said good-bye and rejoined his table of friends. Becky quickly left the bar and drove back to the Beartooth Hideaway Inn. She hadn't noticed the lone man who was sitting in a dark corner of the bar and who left while Alex was hitting on her. In her distracted state, she didn't pick up on him as he followed her to her motel, staying a block behind with his dark, two-door pickup.

Safely settled in her room, she struggled to understand the buyer's remorse she felt at not accepting Alex's offer. She needed companionship, and she wanted a man's touch again, but she wanted more than that. Certainly not just a one-night stand thing. Something kept her from taking that plunge. What was it?

She called Bert's number. It was time to check in and tell them about the day with Summer's family. As the phone rang, she knew she'd made the right decision.

Becky told Bert and presumably Norah about her time with Lizzie, Summer, and Guy. When she had recounted the major events, she asked if he had any suggestions or if Norah could offer any inputs.

Bert apparently put down his phone to talk with Norah. Becky could hear him in the background but didn't hear Norah. Soon, he returned to the phone. "I think you're on the right track, Becky. You must understand what's in that child's head if you're going to help her. Norah said the same thing, and she is sensing that the two pictures are very significant. Something is hidden in those drawings. If you find out what that is, you'll probably find the answers to the child's dilemma."

Becky told them about her plan to spend the next few days, as long as it took, really, to get to know this family and Summer. Especially, she wanted to spend time with Summer. She would immerse herself into the family and see if Summer would open up more with her. Bert told her that he and Norah both agreed with that approach.

They talked for a few more minutes about non-business stuff. Nothing in particular but Becky enjoyed just having a regular conversation for a while. She liked Bert. She felt she'd like Norah, too, as she got to know her. If she got to know her. That relationship was a little perplexing. The first night when visiting their house, she felt like Norah was there, even though Bert said she wasn't. It was an eerie feeling.

  After saying good-bye and good-night, Becky changed into her pajamas and leaned back in bed with a glass of beer. It was a good time to recap her time with the child and let the beer relax her into sleep. This case was more than a job to her. Today, it became a passion to understand and eliminate the fear, the demon, which seemed to haunt this small child. After readying for bed, she turned the light off and pulled the covers to her chin. Tomorrow was a new beginning. She closed her eyes and asked the darkness one last question. "What's going on with you, Summer?"

CHAPTER FOUR: DIGGING UP BONES

Friday morning, January 5th, 2018, greeted Bert and Missy with clear skies, light breeze, and five below zero temperature. They were both animated and full of energy as they took their morning walk into the mountains north of the house. This would be a short walk of about a half hour. Just too cold to stay out a lot longer, even for Missy. Walks were as much for Bert as for his animal. He always welcomed the time in nature, and it helped him clear his mind and think.

Norah chose to stay with the house this morning. Her inputs and ideas had been key in first finding and then updating the little two-bedroom log cabin years earlier. It was the fulfillment of a dream and became her sanctuary when they weren't out of town on a casc. She was attached to their home nearly as much as to Bert. Both held her to them.

When Bert returned, he fed Missy and let her into the living room. She loved to lie on a rug a few yards away from the fireplace. After her usual couple of spins, knocking down the invisible grasses ingrained in her genetic code, she yawned, laid on her side, stretched, and went to sleep. Bert chuckled as he watched her ritual and then told Norah he thought it might be wise to go see Robert in Nebraska soon. They'd check the weather channel again in a minute, but last night's report seemed to favor the trip sooner rather than next week. Norah was also watching Missy and smiling. She nodded.

Bert paused to drink in the beauty of his spirit wife for a moment. Her shoulder-length, auburn hair seemed to literally shimmer as she stood near the front picture window. Her round face, wonderful smile, and laughing eyes betrayed the often-warped sense of humor that always lurked just below the surface. She always had a nice, trim figure and great legs. Even as a spirit, Bert could see the beautiful woman who won his heart many years earlier and still held it today. He sighed a deep, longing sigh. He hoped she wouldn't see the lone tear that slowly slid down his right cheek. The TV gave him the reason he needed to turn away.

The morning's weather report called for several more days of clear and cold weather, but the talk was now focused on what appeared to be a significant winter storm expected to move across the region by the middle of next week. Bert just nodded to Norah, and then called Robert in Nebraska City.

He talked briefly with Robert, asking if it was okay for them to come there the next day, Saturday. Robert was enthusiastic about that and said he'd been able to get as much of the information as possible. Bert told him they could be there probably around mid-afternoon Saturday, January 6th. They'd have to scramble around and leave by noon today. It'd require an overnight stay somewhere, probably in west Nebraska.

"Robert seems relieved that we're coming there soon," he told Norah. "He's anxious for us to get started. We'd better start getting ready and try to leave before noon, if possible. Also need to do a quick call to Becky and let her know. See how she's doing. Looks like we're all going to be digging up bones in these two cases."

"Yes, she's probably at the Hayden's by now. I hope she can begin to understand what's going on with Summer. I'm starting to get a strange vision, Bert. It's a scary one, because it feels like I'm being drawn into a portal. Then it vanishes. One second it rushes at me, and then it's gone. I hope it doesn't mean this child is going to be taken in some way or disappear. You'd better warn Becky to watch for something like that."

"Oh wow, that's scary, Sweetheart. I'm going to call her in just a minute, soon as I get a coffee." Bert fixed another coffee, sat down in front of the picture window, and called Becky.

Becky answered on the fourth ring. "Hello, boss, how're things down there in the tropics? Kinda mild up this way; a balmy 12 below zero this morning still. Might need to wear socks today." She laughed.

Bert laughed back. "I guess we're having a heat wave compared to that. Only five below here now. How's everything going there?"

Becky was upbeat. "I'm having coffee with Lizzie right now and she's treating me to eggs and toast at her house. We're waiting for Summer to get dressed. Then we're going to take her out window shopping around town. The kids don't go back to school until Monday. A chance to spend some time with her."

"Fabulous!" Bert said. "Sounds like you're on a plan. I wanted to pass along a couple things."

"Okay, shoot." Becky responded immediately.

"For one thing," he said, "Norah's having a vision you should know about. Are you on the phone speaker?"

"No. Just you and me."

"Good. I think the client doesn't need to hear this; at least not yet. Norah sees something like a portal and she's disappearing into it. Very quickly. She's concerned that Summer might somehow be taken or vanish. We don't know what to make of it beyond that. Just be aware and keep a sharp watch. Norah's visions may take a while to understand, but they're usually significant."

Becky took a moment to collect her thoughts before she replied. She didn't want Lizzie to hear the sudden concern in her voice. "Okay, Bert, I'll do that. What else do you have for me?"

"We've talked with the Nebraska client, looked at the coming weather, and decided to drive over to Nebraska City now to meet with him. We'll leave just as soon as we can get packed up. We'll have to stay overnight somewhere, probably in west Nebraska."

"I understand," she said, "drive carefully, boss. Don't want to lose you two. I mean you three; I'm sure Missy is going with you."

He smiled at that. "Yup, she's a part of the team. You'll get to know her in time. She'll love you. You'll love her, too. Well, good luck up there. Tell Lizzie that we say hello and can't wait to meet her someday. Bye for now. Call anytime if you feel the need."

Bert disconnected the call and turned back to Norah. "She's aware of it and has a plan going, Sweetheart. I'd better get ready. It's over thirteen hours to Nebraska City."

He gathered up their bags and gear, placed Missy's favorite blanket in the back area of the SUV. The doghouse, as he often referred to it. An hour before noon, they pulled out of the driveway and began the drive toward the Nebraska Panhandle and Interstate 80.

* * *

In Red Lodge, Becky and Lizzie gathered up Summer and went to Lizzie's van. It was time to do some serious shopping. At Summer's insistence they drove first to a sweet shop for some hot chocolate and a donut. Becky felt her waistline and looked at Lizzie. Lizzie just smiled and nodded in understanding. More temptations to try to ignore, thought Becky. Last night wasn't enough, apparently.

A half hour later, they left the store, feeling only a little guilty. The ladies had split a bag of glazed donut holes with a cup of tea, while envying the child as she snarfed down a whole cinnamon roll.

"Oh, to be young again," Becky said wishfully. "Would you mind if I get something for Summer, maybe clothing of some kind?"

"That's fine," said Lizzie, "there's not much that she needs, though. There's a neat western store on the main drag. Lots of temptations. We'll go there. It's one of my favorite places to browse."

"Oh God, more temptations." Becky silently braced herself against her shopping DNA. She'd been noticing that Summer seemed to be cold, despite the heavy coat and hat. She thought about something like a balaclava with an animal face and ears; or maybe a scarf. Hopefully the western store would have something like that.

They hurried inside the store to get out of the bone-chilling cold. A young man ambled over to assist them. While Lizzie followed Summer to the youth section, Becky asked this lad if he had any balaclavas or scarves. He led her to that section of the store. Only the scarves seemed to have some potential. Becky picked out a brightly colored scarf with animal patterns. The young clerk asked if she'd like to try it with the little girl first, just to be sure she liked it. That seemed like a good idea, so they strode over to where Lizzie and Summer were looking at vests.

"Hi little lady," the clerk said to Summer, "let's see how you look in this." He leaned forward and gave a quick wrap of the scarf around Summer's neck.

Summer let out a scream that caught the attention of the entire store. She ripped frantically at the scarf and threw it on the floor as she ran to her mother and threw up her arms. Her screams were turning into tears and sobs. She grabbed her mother's neck tightly as soon as she was picked up and buried her face against Lizzie's neck. Three shocked looks were on the faces of the adults.

The clerk and Becky simultaneously began to apologize to the child and mother. Becky was shocked as she realized she was witness to one of the "other things" which Lizzie had referred to. What just happened, she wondered.

"Oh my God," Becky cried out. "I'm so sorry, Lizzie, what did we do?"

Lizzie was also confused. "I don't know. I've never seen her react so strongly to a scarf before. This is a first."

Becky instinctively stroked the child's hair as she clung to her mother. In doing so, she felt an intense sense of fear. It was clear that this young girl was petrified of the scarf. Or was it having it placed around her neck?

She needed to know. Becky picked up the scarf and held it normally in front of herself. She moved casually around behind Lizzie so that Summer could see her. As she did this, she watched Summer's reaction. The child clutched her mother tighter but didn't seem to get any more intensely afraid. Becky moved the scarf in her hands. "See, Summer, this is just a scarf. It keeps you warm. It won't hurt you."

Standing about three feet away, Becky slowly wrapped the scarf around her own neck. She snuggled into it and tugged it up to her chin, keeping out the imaginary cold. The child continued to watch her intently, but her demeanor didn't change. It's not the scarf, Becky thought to herself.

Becky removed the scarf and slowly moved it toward Summer. The child instantly reacted, nearly cutting off the circulation to her mother's neck. She began to whimper. Becky knew if she moved it any closer, Summer would begin to scream again. She brought the scarf back down and handed it to the young clerk. He'd been watching everything with almost bug-eyes. He didn't know what to think or say. He took the scarf and returned it to the rack.

"She's afraid, deeply afraid, of having something around her neck," Becky said to Lizzie. "Has she ever had an incident with something around her neck, perhaps making her gasp for breath for a second or two?"

"No, not to my knowledge," Lizzie replied. "I guess we've tried to get her to wear a scarf a time or two several years ago, and she refused. I don't remember this much reaction, though."

It was obvious to Becky that this mother was going through her memories, trying to find any such incident. "Then maybe the individual is a part of this, not just the scarf, not just the wrapping it, but a stranger doing it?"

Lizzie nodded. "That could be it, Becky. When we tried to get her to wear a scarf, she kinda pitched a little fit about it and we quit pushing it. Nothing like with the clerk, though."

"So, the question becomes, what happened to her to give her such fear?" Becky reflected on her own question. They left the store without buying anything and moved on to another.

There were no other incidents with Summer and the child acted completely normal again. They browsed through three other interesting shops, and then decided on pizza and a shake at the Red Lodge Pizza Company. Becky discovered that Summer loves meat and veggie pizza and chocolate shakes. While they were eating, a young woman entered carrying an infant.

Summer pointed to her and told her mother, "look mommy, that lady has a baby just like mine."

Becky noticed that the child had no problem saying the word, "baby." She didn't know what that meant, except that it was distinct and separate from "be-be," the name she gave to her doll.

Following a nice lunch and leisurely chat together, the three left the Pizza Company and Lizzie gave Becky a tour of the town and immediate surrounding area. She pointed out the ski runs on Red Lodge Mountain, to the west of their home. "Best kept secret," she told Becky.

Becky agreed. She'd skied there a couple of times when she lived in Billings; only a couple hours or so drive to the northeast. She wasn't a great skier, maybe intermediate skill level, but she sure loved the exhilaration of sliding down the mountain. It had great runs; nice and wide with plenty of room for a novice skier.

Her ex, Ron, was an excellent skier, and had taken her there during the first two years of their marriage. They stopped going after a drunk ski bum started hitting on her at the lodge. Ron had decked the guy and hurt him pretty good before the lodge cops pulled him away. That night at the motel was the first time that Ron verbally abused her and slapped her around, making it out to be her fault. It would not be the last time.

Back at Lizzie's home, Summer was sleepy, so she went upstairs to take a nap. The ladies sat at the table and began to discuss her. In most respects, Lizzie described a perfectly normal child.

"She just has these outbursts occasionally. Usually when you don't expect them, something will just set her off," Lizzie told Becky.

"You said that you put Summer in a daycare facility for about a year when you were working. How did that go? Did she ever have problems there?" Becky asked.

Lizzie told her, "It was not a problem more than you'd normally expect with a four-year-old. The staff said she had a couple of fits, but they didn't make any big deal out of them."

Becky picked up on this. "Lizzie, would you mind if I go there and talk with some of the teachers and staff? I just want them to go into more details for me. Maybe there's something there to know."

Lizzie was all for that. "Anything that might help my daughter is okay with me. Tell them to call me if they need my permission to talk with you."

With that, Becky left and drove to Honeybee Daycare on the edge of town. They did have to call Lizzie for permission to discuss Summer. After that, Becky first spoke with the facility director, Shonda. The director said that Summer had been a little sweetheart while with them and she wasn't aware of any issues at all with her. She suggested that Becky discuss her with one of the regular teachers, though. They would have more firsthand experience with the child.

Teacher, Gayle Strum, said that she taught during the year Summer was with them. She described Summer as a very dear little girl who was a pleasure to work with. There were just a couple of minor disputes with the other children.

"Would you describe those disputes for me, please, Gayle?" Becky asked.

"Oh, you know how children can be with one another," she

answered. "One time another little girl tried to take her drawing and Summer became very irate about it; she started yelling for me to get it back for her."

"Did you know why they both behaved like they did?" asked Becky.

"Suzanne, the other child, wanted to tear up Summer's drawing because she said it wasn't the Smokey Bear they were supposed to be drawing. Summer became very possessive of her work and pulled Suzanne's hair trying to get it back."

Becky pondered this, then asked, "did you see Summer's drawing?"

Gayle nodded with a smile. "Oh yes, Suzanne was right about it not being the assigned task. It was just a couple of circles, one inside the other one. Nothing more. However, I got the drawing returned to Summer so she could work on it more, but she never tried to do more with it."

"Okay, thanks. What about the other incident?"

Gayle said that one of the little boys had grabbed Summer from behind one class period. He had grabbed her around the neck but didn't mean anything by that. The little guy was just trying to get Summer's attention. "However," Gayle added, "Summer came unglued and began to scream. I had to rush over and calm her down, even though the boy let go of her the minute she yelled. It took me about a minute to quiet her down. Lizzie quit her job just a week or so after that and pulled Summer from the class."

Becky was making mental notes of this for later. "Were there any other unusual or notable events involving Summer?"

"Well," Gayle said, "I don't know that this is anything noteworthy, but Summer seemed to have a phobia against one of the male teachers who was working here at that time. He only filled in for me a few times, but Summer seemed to dislike him and be afraid of him every time. She wouldn't go near him and if he got too close, she'd start crying and whimpering."

"Was there any reason that you know of for Summer to dislike him?" Becky asked.

"No reason at all that we could tell," Gayle responded. "This lad was a local kid, in his mid-twenties. He'd only been out of college a couple of months. Another staff member knew his parents really well."

Becky continued to inquire into this young man, Jeremy Hinderman. She found out that he had graduated three years ago from the University of Wyoming in Laramie with a degree in Early Childhood Education. From his application, there were no warning flags that would make his employment questionable. Gayle said he was a tall and slender guy, about 6 foot 2 inches. He had sandy blonde hair. Becky took her notes, said her thanks and good-byes, and drove back to Lizzie's home. She'd decided to take Lizzie up on her offer of their guest cottage.

Lizzie convinced her to have supper with them. Once Guy got home, they all shared a bottle of wine, visited with Summer about her artistic interests, and then sat down to the meal. Becky found out more about Guy as they ate.

At six feet tall and 185 pounds, dark-haired Guy was imposing and intimidating, although a somewhat good-looking man in his early forties. He was from Eugene, Oregon, and graduated from Oregon State University with a degree in Airport Management. Shortly after landing a job at the Red Lodge Regional Airport as a deputy manager, he met and eventually married Lizzie. She had moved there a year earlier from Bozeman to work as an assistant manager at the ski lodge. On the one hand, Guy was impressive, and yet Becky still felt something was amiss with this man.

With head spinning from three glasses of wine, and feeling a slight unsteadiness in her feet, Becky said her thanks and good night. She wasn't used to ever having more than a drink or maybe two, and rarely drank more than once or twice a week. She was known among her friends as a cheap date, a title she wasn't exactly sure was complimentary.

She was almost back to the little cabin, a couple hundred feet from Lizzie's house, when a slick spot in the path sent her right leg forward in far too much haste. Nothing else could catch up to it, and she fell on her right side into the snow piled at the side of the walk. She wasn't hurt and rolled onto her back and quietly laughed as she looked up at the star-filled night sky. She found it almost enjoyable, and lay there for several minutes, trying to identify some of the constellations.

Other than Orion, the big and little dippers, and the North Star, all other orbs were spinning a bit too much for identification. The rising moon was starting to wash out the dimmer stars. She rolled over, got up, and cautiously made her way on to the cottage. Can't drink that much wine again, she thought to herself. Did they mean to get her drunk? Guy had made sure that her wine glass was never less than half full. Or was "cheap date" just at it again?

Inside the cozy and warm little one-bedroom cabin, Becky kicked off her boots and laid down on the bed. Flipping the blanket over her, she vowed to get up soon and get ready for bed. She felt that she should call Bert and see how their travels were going. Tomorrow she felt the need to try to talk with Guy's parents. They did a lot of babysitting of Summer. Perhaps they could shed some more light on their granddaughter's strange behavior. Maybe on their son as well, she thought. She really did intend to call Bert, but sleep came before her good intentions.

CHAPTER FIVE: NEBRASKA CITY

Down in southwestern Nebraska, at a small town of Oshkosh, Bert stood in the cow pasture just across the road to the south of their little Shady Rest Motel. While Missy rummaged around nearby, relieving herself in several different places to mark her new territory, Bert surveyed the dark sky. He had always loved to identify the stars and constellations every chance he had. As an Army officer, he had to be skilled at using the stars for night navigation. After about ten minutes of this, he was sure that Missy was set for the night. He scanned the sky one more time for aircraft, since they were not far from the county airport. Not seeing any airplanes or vehicles moving, they crossed highway 26 back to the motel. Back to where Norah waited patiently for them.

While he fed Missy and watched her bed down for the night, Bert discussed the continued drive the next day with Norah. They would stay on US Highway 26, also known as the Western Trails Scenic and Historic Byway, through the town of Lewellen. A short drive after Lewellen, he wanted to pause to let Missy out at Ash Hollow State Historical Park, a historically significant rest stop. This place was near the Platte River and Clear Creek and was a favorite watering spot for both Native American Indians and pioneers traveling the Overland and Oregon Trails. It was also the site of an early battle in the Indian Wars. Considered a victory in September 1855 by the soldiers of the US Army under the command of General William Harney, it also carried the black eye of a massacre.

With a numerically superior force, more than twice that of the Lakota Sioux, led by Chief Little Thunder, 86 Indians and 27 soldiers were killed. Half of the Sioux killed and captured were women and children. This engagement was called the Battle of Ash Hollow or the Battle of Blue Water Creek. However, it was also referred to as the Harney Massacre. Bert loved history and he also admired the Native American culture. He knew before he got there that the natural beauty of this popular state park would be tempered by the knowledge and the pain in his heart of this tragedy.

After the brief and emotional stop at Ash Hollow, they would continue past Lake McConaughy, a massive man-made lake formed by one of the largest earthen dams in the nation across the Platte River. At the cow town of Ogallala, they would begin their speedier crossing of Nebraska on Interstate 80. With luck and a 6:00 AM start, they should be in Nebraska City around mid-afternoon. Now, however, they needed to bed down for the night.

Norah had been listening to Bert's discussion of Ash Hollow. When he started to say good night to her, he realized the intense sadness in her eyes. He knew that he had passed his emotional connection to Native Americans on to her and she was sensing and feeling his saddened heart. Her sense of humanity and her loving spirit were among the many things he adored about Norah. She was not only a beautiful woman and spirit, but she retained the heart and soul of a saint. It was one of the major reasons why he could not bring himself to let go of her. In life as well as in death, her genuine goodness made him a better person and he knew it.

"Good night, my dear Norah," he said. "I'm sorry I upset you with my sense of tragic history."

"It's okay, Honey," she answered. "I've always known your heart, and this is only a reminder of what I love about you. You're a good and caring man, Bert. Don't ever change, my Captain Kirk."

As he turned off the light, the lump in his throat and the tears in his eyes made it impossible for him to say anything more right then. This was one of those times when he ached to wrap his arms around her and just hold her tightly. Until sleep came, it would be one of those nights when he would dread the day, somewhere in the future, when she would go into the light.

* * *

Bert, Norah, and Missy had just gotten onto Interstate 80 at Ogallala, when Becky called. It had warmed up to a balmy 20 degrees this Saturday morning in southern Nebraska, but she said it was still only about five above zero in Red Lodge. For January 6th in Montana, they all knew that was typical. After a discussion of the weather and their travels toward Nebraska City, Bert talked briefly about their earlier stop at Ash Hollow and the mix of emotions that elicited. He knew from Becky's tone that she was in tune with his feelings. He asked how her case was developing.

She brought him up to date on the recent scarf episode and her questions about the daycare worker and the girl's father. Bert agreed with her assessment about the scarf. He relayed a feeling that Norah was getting. She had the sensation of difficulty breathing and feeling overpowered and panicking. She felt this was coming from the little girl and transmitted through Becky. As Becky talked with Bert, she wondered why she wasn't hearing Norah in the background. A poor connection, apparently.

"So, this daycare worker is suspect, you think. How are you planning on checking him out? Bert asked.

"He's related to one of the daycare staffers. I thought I'd talk with her first and see what she can offer," replied Becky.

Bert listened to Norah's advice before answering Becky. "Good idea. Norah also suggested that you see what you can find out from his school, UW I think you said. His college days might be more revealing than his time at home. If there's a discreet way you can get Summer around him, her reaction could be telling, too."

Becky's voice came back over the phone, "Oh yeah, good ole college days. The things that go on in college can be both revealing and damning. Glad nobody was following me around taking notes during my years at Montana State." She laughed.

"Hmm, guess we'll have to check out your storied past at MSU." Bert laughed back.

She was chuckling as she answered, "Well, it would probably be a bit boring. The biggest story of my college years was discovering that I can't hold liquor. I somehow got the reputation of being a cheap date. Still haunts me. Can't even handle three glasses of wine."

Bert looked at Norah and saw that she was laughing at that. Then he got back to business. "And you're going to get with Guy's parents and see what they can bring to light about Summer?"

Becky replied, "Yeah, they babysit her a lot so could have some insight into her other behaviors. I'll have to be low key when it comes to their son. They may not want to tell me too much about him, especially if it's negative."

"Like the daycare kid, the father's college days at Oregon State could be telling," Bert said.

"Oh yeah, that's a great idea, Bert. I'll see what I can find out from those days." Becky was excited by that suggestion.

Bert checked his phone. "Hey, Becky, I think we're about to outrun the cellular reception at this point on I-80. Better be signing off. Keep up the good work up there. We think you're doing great."

Oh, one more thing if we can get it in. "Norah's asking if they go to church. Summer's family. She's getting a feeling of being inside a church," Bert said. "She says it's like she's near the altar and looking out at the congregation. Says it's a strange feeling."

"I'll have to find that out," Becky responded. "Hasn't come up in conversation yet. If they do, I'll see about going with them tomorrow."

With that, they ended the call. Bert, Norah, and Missy continued east on Interstate 80. They passed North Platte, which was another place laying claim to Buffalo Bill Cody's life and times. Besides the museum, there was the interesting tour of the Buffalo Bill Ranch State Historical Park, when one had the time to go there. This morning, they didn't have time even to stop at the Fort Cody Trading Post. Bert wanted to stay on track for meeting Robert by 3:00 PM.

He decided to stop at Kearney for a quick lunch and to give Missy a run. He pulled into the parking area of the Great Platte River Road Archway Monument, a magnificent structure which spanned the entire interstate. He'd been inside the museum before and wished that they had time to do it this morning. Sadly, they didn't have time, and he didn't want to rush the trip. The museum was a historical celebration of Kearney's connection to the westward expansion in the nation's early days.

Kearney was at the confluence of the Oregon, Mormon, and California trails, and was a key stop along the Pony Express mail route. The Lincoln Highway was built to join Kearney to the state capitol. As the railroads pushed their way westward, the growing city became a major hub for connecting east to west. Among the many attractions is the Museum of Nebraska Art, which houses the state's official collections and spans nearly two centuries of history.

Bert walked Missy around the outdoor display area for about fifteen minutes, while drinking one of his smoothie fruit drinks. This one had a heavy dose of lemon, peel and all, and really made him pucker at times. He hoped it made him healthier, because it could be a little hard to get down sometimes.

Missy didn't seem to particularly care about Bert's smoothie issues, as she was hot on the trail of some vermin near one of the small frozen ponds. She bounced around from spot to spot, alternately burying her nose in the snow and then standing perfectly still to listen for the tiny sounds from under the crusty stuff. Bert smiled as he watched her very slowly cocking her head from side to side, changing the angle of her ears ever so slightly to get a better listen. It didn't surprise him when she jumped straight up and came down with her head driven into the foot-deep drift. It did surprise him a little when she came up with a mouse and ate it in one gulp. It made him wonder just how sublimated all those wild genes really were.

After Missy's hunting expedition, they resumed their trek toward the east. Around 1:30 they bypassed the south edge of Lincoln. To the east and north stood two familiar landmarks. The first was the Nebraska State Capitol building, considered to be one of the most beautiful in the nation. The acoustics inside the rotunda were reported to be stunning for the occasional musical performances held there. The second was Memorial Stadium, the home of Nebraska Cornhusker football. On a football Saturday at home, the typical sell-out crowd qualified as the third largest city in the state. Bert wasn't stopping to enjoy the attractions, though, and the city was soon in the rearview mirror as he guided the doghouse east on Nebraska Highway 2.

Bert cast more glances toward his spirit wife and marveled again at her beauty and grace. He wondered if her shoulder length red hair was getting longer. It wasn't but gave that impression right then. Even with her spirit, the love he always felt for her was hard to describe.

"Sweetheart," he said, "I'm very anxious to know what kind of signs or visions you pick up once we meet up with this young man."

"I know, Honey, I'm curious about that also. The one overriding feeling I get from this case so far is that of intense sadness. I feel that this lad has suffered emotionally more than we know." Her face was devoid of happiness.

He knew she was feeling a pain that she didn't understand; feeling it deeply. During some of these cases, he felt sorry for his wife. She experienced on some level what the victim's lived through, but without the understanding which they may have had. It was tough on her.

Bert called Robert to update their arrival time, which looked to be just a few minutes before 3:00. Robert asked if they could meet downtown at the Buck Snort café, a place well known locally for its American cuisine, especially hamburgers. Bert couldn't help but chuckle at some of the other connotations for the name, one of which involved flatulence. His chuckle turned into an outright laugh, which Norah was soon repeating. They alternately laughed and tried to get serious for several miles before getting past the humor. Bert couldn't help but wonder why their client chose this place to meet. They nevertheless drove into downtown Nebraska City and parked near the front of the restaurant.

After meeting Robert Sturdevant outside the café, however, it quickly became apparent why he chose that place to meet. On Thursday, July 8th, 2010, Robert had lunch there with his mother, Vicki. When they left about 1:00 PM, it would prove to be the last time he saw her. He hadn't been back to the place since then, until meeting Bert there.

Bert suggested that they go inside and see if the setting could trigger latent memories which might be helpful. Norah would sit unseen near them and quietly listen and read the hidden messages which Robert might divulge. Missy hunkered down in the back of the doghouse, dividing her time between watching the street and napping.

The former Army officer studied this 23-year-old young man as he removed his dark brown, hooded parka. Wearing tan slacks and a light blue dress shirt, he looked to be about 5 feet 8 inches tall, with slender build, thick and somewhat unruly dark hair, brown eyes and a slightly narrow face which seemed incapable of smiling. He spoke quietly, almost timidly, in a halting and seemingly unsure manner. He immediately gave Bert the impression of someone who lacked self-confidence. He felt a sense of sadness come over him for this lad. Robert was the first client for whom he felt pity.

Robert described how he had taken a lunch break that hot day in July from his fast food job to meet his mother for lunch. He was sixteen at the time, in high school and very devoted to his mother. She was equally devoted to him, her only child. His father had died years earlier in a vehicle accident. Robert was five at the time he lost his Dad, so Vicki essentially raised him by herself. She was a bookkeeper and did office work at several local places in order to provide for herself and her son. Because of the long hours she worked, usually six days a week, he didn't get to spend much time with her. Not nearly as much time as he wanted.

"What did you talk about with your mother that day, Robert?" Bert asked.

Robert thought for what seemed like several minutes. "I think she mostly kept telling me how much she loved me and wished she had more time with me," he replied. "She seemed to be sad that day. And was upset about something, I think."

"Did she say why she was upset?" Bert inquired.

Robert said, "No sir. She told me she had to do something after lunch, though. It seemed to be hard for her. She seemed kinda mad."

"It must not have been a very good lunch meeting, then, if your mom was angry," Bert suggested.

"You're right about that, sir, Bert. She seemed to be distracted.

She went to the bathroom once. I think she also made a phone call."

"Was she working that day?" Bert asked.

"No, sir," Robert responded. "It was her day off that week. I do remember that. But she said she had to go do something. She didn't say what."

"Do you have any idea who she called? Or who she was going to meet?"

"No, sir," Robert said.

Bert asked, "where was your mother working at that time, Robert?"

Robert wasn't sure but thought she might have been working for an insurance company that week.

The police report would provide most of the details that he wanted, so Bert continued to probe Robert's memories about that day and his mother's state of mind. He found out that Vicki did temporary bookkeeping and office work for the insurance company, two real estate firms and one church. With the four employers, she worked nearly sixty-hour weeks, often six days a week. On the side, she pursued her own business in real estate investment. Robert didn't realize until after his mother's disappearance that her net worth was almost a million dollars. She had become wealthy and almost nobody knew it. Yet, she had become very unhappy in the months leading up to her disappearance and nobody seemed to know why.

The police report about his mother's disappearance was in Robert's possession, and he handed his copy over to Bert. As Bert had requested earlier, he also brought along his mother's favorite silver hairbrush. The few intertwined hairs should provide enough scent for Missy, Bert hoped. His mother was a bit of a loner. However, Robert had located one of her old friends who was willing to talk with him. Patricia Domenica and Vicki had met in church and were friends for about ten years before Vicki vanished.

"Do you still go to the same church as before when your mother was here?" he asked Robert.

"Yes," Robert said, "I've been going to the same church with mom for a long time; at least the same one as when she was here."

"What church is that?" Bert asked.

"We were going to the Calvary Community Church at the south edge of town," answered Robert.

"Is that the church she did books for?" asked Bert.

"No," Robert said. "She did books for another church, a

Catholic church."

"Oh, okay. I guess that's a big church that needed her services."

"Yeah, I guess so," said Robert. "She worked there for many years; I think. I don't remember much about that period."

The next day was Sunday, and Robert invited Bert to go to the morning service with him. At first Bert was about to decline, but he decided to go and see what else might be learned.

The strain on the young man's face told Bert it was time to wrap up the interview. Now that he had the police report and the name of a friend to talk with, there were things he could do without his client being present. As he walked with Robert back to his car, he knew the fellow was fighting back tears. Bert knew he shouldn't let his own emotions get in the way of the investigation, but it could be difficult sometimes. This was probably going to be one of those times. He waved as Robert drove away and then he returned to his own vehicle. Norah was already there, along with Missy.

"Well, Sweetheart," he asked, "what do you think of the talk with Robert?"

She answered in a quiet voice. "Honey, I'm getting a dark vision; dark emotionally. As he talked, I began to see him standing looking through an open door into another room. That room was empty and totally dark, as if it's a void. I think it represents the pain of a very dark side of him or maybe the past."

Bert took that in. "Umm, that's interesting. So, is he hiding something from us; or is there a part of his past that has been shut out? A memory too painful to accept into his consciousness. Could it be both?"

"What if he did something to cause his mother's disappearance?" Norah asked. "He's suffered for a long time and he still suffers."

"Wow," Bert replied. "Could he have done something to his mother, and then be hiding behind the shame and guilt to the point that his mind denies the reality?"

They pondered these questions as they drove in silence to a motel on the edge of town. Missy needed some nearby open space in which to run for a while and maybe find another mouse. After that, it would be time to call Becky and the friend of the missing woman and then begin to read the police report. It was already a long day; they needed some down time.

After closing her phone following the morning call with Bert and Norah, Becky leaned back in the comfortable easy chair and enjoyed the small but cozy wood stove in the Hayden's cabin. She had decided to have a breakfast of fruit and cereal by herself on this Saturday morning and plan her pursuit of the truth regarding the principals in this case. The first person she wanted to look more closely at was daycare worker, Jeremy Hinderman.

A call to Jeremy's aunt, who worked at Honeybee Daycare for about fifteen years, didn't tell her much. According to this lady, Jeremy had always been a nice kid, never got into trouble and was generally liked by everyone. She didn't know much about his college years other than he graduated with a degree in a child-related discipline. The boy's parents had both died some years earlier, so this aunt was his family in Red Lodge.

Becky searched online to see what she could find out about Jeremy via his University of Wyoming public records and his social media use. She eventually found out that he had worked as an intern at a local Laramie elementary school and part-time at a daycare facility. It took a couple of hours of calls to finally get in touch with someone at both places with some knowledge of Jeremy.

A teacher named Karen told Becky that Jeremy did a lot of his assistant teaching in her second and third grade classes. She didn't see anything that she considered a problem, although she did finally admit that he seemed to show a little favoritism toward the girls in the classes. Karen didn't perceive any real issues with that, though, because everyone has their favorites.

The daycare was cautious about giving any information over the phone, so Becky arranged to drive to Laramie on Monday and meet with an assistant director who claimed to know about Jeremy's work there. They set aside two hours at a nearby coffee shop to meet and talk. By the end of the call, it was nearly 1:00 in the afternoon and she still hadn't talked with Lizzie. Becky called her.

Lizzie was starting her Saturday at a slow pace, cleaning the kitchen and doing laundry. She told Becky that Summer was going out with her grandparents soon for a couple of hours that afternoon and said they'd probably not mind if she went with them. It'd be another opportunity to be around Summer as well as pick their brains about her. Becky was excited about that, so Lizzie called them to arrange it. They'd be at Lizzie's house to get Summer in about fifteen minutes. Becky scurried around the cabin getting herself ready to go.

Becky greeted Summer with a warm hug and a brief talk, kneeling to the child's level. Then she stood up to introduce herself to John and Sandy Hayden, Guy's parents. Both were moderately tall and good looking, like their son, and their dark hair was greying. John was the talkative one, while Sandy was quiet but warm and friendly. An obvious gentleman, John opened the door of their Jeep wagon and held it for Becky.

"How about one of those great pizza's and a shake, sweetie, then we can check out that new rock-climbing place?" John said to Summer.

"Oh, yes, yes, Grandpa. I'd like that," replied his granddaughter.

"You up for some pizza, Miss Becky?" asked John.

"Well, I'm up for it, if my waistline will agree," Becky said with a chuckle. "That'd give me the chance to get to know you and your family better."

"That would be great," said Sandy. "We love to talk about our family. Right Summer?"

Summer nodded her agreement without saying anything.

They drove down to main street and back to their favorite pizza diner. Over pizza, Becky found out that the grandparents also knew about Summer's frequent and mysterious drawings. Sandy told Becky that Summer would draw one or the other, sometimes both, nearly every time she stayed with them. She admitted that this might be partly because they usually encouraged Summer to work on her artistic talents. Neither grandparent had an explanation for the two odd drawings. They both said that Summer couldn't explain why she drew them. It would upset her if they pressed her for an explanation.

Becky turned the conversation to their son, Guy, and asked about his background. Sandy described a son, normal by most standards, but did admit that he was a little wild as a teenager.

He fancied himself a lady's man, she said.

"I understand that Guy went to college at Oregon State University," Becky said, "was he a good boy in college?" She laughed.

"Oh my, how does a mother know the answer to that?" Sandy said. "All I can tell you is that he graduated with a B average and got a good job back home. And we now have a beautiful little granddaughter." She stroked Summer's dark brunette hair.

Becky then asked, "was Guy always interested in the airport business?"

"Yes," his mother answered, "he even got hired as an airline steward and did that for the first couple years after graduating."

"I bet a good looking' guy like him was a thrill to work with for the female flight attendants," Becky said with a smile.

Sandy laughed. "Oh yes, he loved the work. We were very surprised when he suddenly quit after two years and applied for the airport job here."

Becky answered, "Oh, yeah, that would have been a big surprise. Did he say why he left such a cushy job for so much responsibility?"

"I think he got tired of all those beautiful women hitting on him," laughed his dad. "Us guys in this family get tired of being sex symbols."

They all laughed at that. Sandy chimed back, "Well, I wouldn't get too tired of it, Honey, because you might lose the title if you don't behave."

John laughed. "Yes, babe, I'm very aware of that. You've tamed me, just like Lizzie tamed our son. We're now under control of our gals and glad to be."

Sandy looked at Becky and gave a wink. "Well, just keep the bridle on, Sweetheart, and you'll be fine. How about we go see how well Summer can climb. I'm very curious about that new wall climbing business."

Becky listened intently to the talk. She perceived more than was being said between John and Sandy. It felt like there was an undercurrent of friction hidden beneath the words. Was Guy more like his father than had been let on? The apple doesn't fall far from the tree, they say. Are there secrets inside the walls of these seemingly perfect families? If so, to what extent do they touch Summer?

When she looked at Summer, Becky felt a feeling of anxiety and uncertainty. Was this feeling emanating from Summer? Or was it really Becky's own insecurities about the case? Was she qualified to be working a case like this? She knew she could not allow such a thought to dominate her thinking. Like it or not, she was working this case and she just had to keep her head clear, think with logic and reasoning and press on.

Becky closed her eyes and cleared her mind for just a couple of seconds, focusing on the child. Yes, she thought, the anxiety is coming from Summer. The question is "why?"

"Hey, let's go see that new climbing wall, ladies," John said enthusiastically. "I want to see our granddaughter scale that thing like a pro." He stood up, took Summer's hand and headed for the car. Becky and Sandy followed in close pursuit.

A short drive later, they arrived at the tall metal buildings which now housed the rock-climbing wall that was the buzz of the town. The old building had formerly been a grain storage facility but had gone out of business several years earlier before a local partnership bought it and developed it into the climbing wall. Now, all the local climbers had a place to tune up their skills before tackling the real mountain walls just a few miles out of town. The kiddy wall was becoming popular with the young future climbers. With their safety harnesses on the kids had as much fun losing their grip as making it to the top. This would be Summer's first trip to try this new adventure.

Once they had paid for their time slot, Summer stood quietly while the teenaged attendant fitted and tightened her safety harness and gave her some basic instructions. The young man then led her to the kiddy wall and assisted her with the first couple of halting grips. He stepped back and left Summer clinging to the wall.

Becky watched the child with a growing uneasiness. She sensed that something wasn't right. Her empathic personality was meshing with the feelings of the little girl and a sudden burst of anxiety flooded her consciousness. Summer wasn't just nervous about the first-time climbing experience. Something else was happening. Becky felt a deep fear bordering on terror.

Suddenly, Summer began to cry as she began to frantically grab at the climbing grips with her hands while her feet flailed to find the footholds. She seemed to have no fear of the height as she struggled to scale the wall at a pace far faster than the other children. She reminded Becky of the time one of her cats had gotten onto a screened window. Spread-eagled, the animal had almost ripped the screen to shreds as it fought to get to the top of the window. It was obvious that this child was in a mental place removed from the wall itself. Becky jumped from her chair and raced to the little child.

She was just able to reach Summer and pulled the girl from the wall. Hugging her tightly and stroking her hair, Becky placed her cheek against the girl's face and spoke to her calmly, telling her she was safe now. Summer clutched Becky around the neck ferociously.

John and Sandy had watched in stunned silence, unsure what to make of the situation. Finally, John spoke. "What's going on, Becky? Why'd you do that? She was doing just fine, far better than the other kids."

Sandy turned angrily to her husband. "John, you ignoramus,

Summer was scared to death and Becky knew it. She literally rescued our granddaughter from a situation she didn't understand."

Becky tried to defuse the tension. "Sandy is right, John, and it isn't your fault that you didn't know. I'm able to connect with Summer's feelings and I knew she was terrified of something about that wall. She wasn't climbing the wall, guys, she was trying to escape from it."

John looked at Becky appreciatively. "Oh my gosh, I guess I didn't pick up on that. Guess the grandfather in me wanted to think she was overachieving. So why is she afraid of it?"

"I wish I knew, guys. That's the $24,000 question," Becky replied. "I don't think it's the wall, I think it's something that the wall represents."

Sandy tried to ask Summer what she was afraid of, but to no avail. Her granddaughter just sobbed as tears trickled down her cheeks. She seemed to have no idea why she was so afraid. It was obvious that her experience at the climbing wall was over. The adults left the business without understanding what had happened.

Back at the Hayden's home, Becky and Summer said good-bye to the grandparents. Becky then discussed the events at the climbing wall with Lizzie while Summer took a nap. Guy had gone into town to watch a college basketball game at Foster and Logan's Pub and Grill with a work friend. Lizzie poured them each a glass of red wine and invited Becky to sit in front of the fireplace with her. They chatted before the fire, basking in the warm glow of the flickering flames. Outside, the mountains to the west cast a shadow over their log home and the entire town. The temperature seemed to drop ten degrees almost instantly as the sun sank below the peaks. The state of dimming twilight would last another half hour.

Becky savored her first sip of the semi-sweet elixir and studied her female employer. Lizzie was a very cute, round-faced, woman. Her naturally wavy dark hair just touched her shoulders. She sat barefoot with her legs pulled up inside the big log chair, staring at the embers as she tugged at her sweater. Becky felt a connection to her that went beyond that of work. She felt like they could become best friends. It was easy to see why Summer was such a little cutie.

"Lizzie, I'm very puzzled by what happened today." Becky kicked off her own shoes and pulled her socked feet under her. "Do you have any idea what might have happened to set your daughter off about that wall?"

Lizzie turned her gaze from the fire back to Becky. "I've been trying to think of anything remotely like that. The only thing that comes to mind as even a slight possibility is a camping trip last year. We went with Guy's brother and his son to the Ovens. It's an area of limestone and dolomite cliffs not too far south of here. It's sort of a beginner's climbing area. The boy and Summer went hiking around there for an hour or two. They apparently got a little too close for Summer and she wanted to go back to camp. He said she was scared."

"Did they actually try to climb any of the formations?" Becky asked.

"Not according to the boy. He said they just walked along the base of the first major cliff and Summer kept saying she was afraid of them."

Becky asked, "nothing like the panic she had today then?"

"No, not at all. She just seemed to not like being that close to them," Lizzic said.

"What was happening today went beyond fear," Becky said. "She was feeling a combination of terror and outright panic."

"I haven't seen that before. But you see what I meant by other things. Every so often, without any warning, something like this will happen. It catches you by surprise and you have no idea why." Lizzie wiped away a tear.

"I'm so sorry," Becky said. "We'll keep after this until we figure it out."

"Thank you, Becky," Lizzie replied. "I know you probably need to check in with your company soon. Would you like to go to church with us tomorrow? We haven't been there for a couple months. Maybe it's about time."

Becky was thrilled to be asked. She agreed to meet them for breakfast in their house about 8:30 and go with them to the Red Lodge Community Church. It should be a clear and sunny morning, though very cold.

She felt her heart begin to ache for Lizzie. It had to be very frustrating and painful to see your child go through these unexplained episodes. She could also sense a degree of fear in Lizzie; fear of the unknown and what else it might bring. Somehow she had to get to the bottom of this and help the mother and her child. For now, though, the wine in her cup was nearly gone and a wave of sleepiness hit. It was time to go back to the cabin, take a short nap, grab something to eat somewhere, and then call Bert and Norah.

* * *

In the dusk of the sinking sun, the last rays peeked over the western horizon and then disappeared. Bert strolled slowly in the snow along the tree-lined gully bordering a fallow cornfield a short distance from the Nebraska City Holiday Inn Express. He decided to pull the earmuffs down on his cap to subdue the increasing cold of impending darkness. He was normally somewhat impervious to the chill of winter, but when he felt his ears begin to sting he knew it was time to cover them. His eyes strained to pick out Missy as she roamed at the edge of the gulley, in and out of the trees. If not for the snow-covered ground, her thick reddish-grey coat would have been very difficult to discern from the terrain in the fading light.

Missy was in her element. Most of the time, the snow would support her 45-pound weight, but every now and then she would break through and sink almost up to her belly. Bert got a kick out of watching her leap from the drifts until she found harder crust to walk on. The wild in this animal always had her senses on high alert. A furry snack was always on the menu. There just might be a mouse in the clumps of grass or a rabbit in the trees.

Bert turned to his spirit wife, who had accompanied them on this evening walk, and nodded toward their vehicle. She nodded back. It was time to get back to the motel and do some work before darkness overtook them. He whistled for Missy.

Back at the motel, Bert took care of Missy's needs as he talked with Norah. Besides being his wife, he valued her opinions and inputs into their business. Her spirit was as attractive to him as when she was alive.

"Well, Sweetheart, I'm thinking the first order of business is to call that friend of Robert's mother," Bert said. "Patricia Domenica I believe her name was. Do you have a better idea?"

She paused and then answered, "No, Honey, I think that's a good first move. I'm getting good vibes about her. I'm also seeing a telephone, Bert. I think we need to pay attention to the phone logs in the police report. I get the feeling that something is in those logs."

"Yeah, Sweetheart, I think you're right. There must be something the police missed about her calls. Her son thought she made a call from the café. Did they pick up on that? Surely it registered."

"If Becky calls later, please tell her about my church vision. I'm continuing to see the parishioners, as if from the altar. She might be going to church with the clients out there, just as you're going with Robert here. I'm not able to tell if my vision relates to Red Lodge or here. Right now, it could be either case."

Bert nodded affirmatively. "I'll tell her tonight, Norah. She said she'd call. For now, let's see what we can find out with Miss Domenica."

He took a longing look at his wife's spirit and blew her a kiss. She held up her hand and blew it back to him. He dialed the number for Patricia Domenica.

Patricia seemed to be expecting his call. Robert must have laid the groundwork well. She answered in a strong voice with good English, although there was an undercurrent of Spanish dialect. Bert introduced himself and explained why he was calling. He could tell that she was reluctant to talk much with him. This was often the case with phone work. People weren't comfortable talking over the phone about sensitive issues with someone they haven't met in person. He needed to meet her face to face.

It turned out that Miss Domenica attended the same Calvary Community Church as Robert; the same church they were going to tomorrow. Bert arranged to meet her an hour before the service started. She suggested getting a coffee at the Phillips 66 station near his motel at the intersection of highways 2 and 75. If they needed more time, she would meet him again after the service.

With that settled, they turned to the police report. They first began to scan and identify common elements within Vicki's cell phone logs. The detective had identified to whom the calls were made. Vicki called her places of employment several times weekly. These were Billingsley Insurance, Wilson and Wilson Realty, Century 21 Real Estate and the Holy Mother Catholic Church. She had apparently kept books for these organizations for several years with the Wilson Realty and the catholic church being the longest. During the week she disappeared, Vicki had called the church business office on Monday and Tuesday, once each day. On Wednesday and Thursday, she called the insurance company office, once Wednesday and twice the morning she vanished. Those two calls were made at 9:23 and 10:12 and lasted about ten minutes each. Very few of her calls exceeded fifteen minutes. There were no calls made during the lunch time frame.

Vicki had few friends it seemed. Most of her non-business calls were to Patricia, two or three times a week. She only talked once or twice monthly with her one sister who lived in Omaha. Vicki had no land line since early 2008.

Her most frequent calls were to her son, Robert. It appeared that she called him daily during school or work breaks. Few of those calls went over five minutes. The record gave the impression of a mother just keeping in touch with her son.

Bert leaned back and looked at Norah. He knew she thought the same thing he did. Robert must have been wrong about his mother making a call during their lunch. So, what made him believe she did? Did it matter?

The long day was beginning to catch up with Bert. Missy was already curled up in her favorite place near the window. He told Norah it was time to get hold of Becky and see how she was doing with the Red Lodge case. He dialed her number.

The phone rang four times before she answered in her usual upbeat way. "Hello boss Bert. How are things down east?"

"Hi Becky," he replied. "We're making some headway here I think, considering we just got here." He proceeded to give her a quick recap of their activities.

Becky brought him up to speed on her day's activities and the newest development with the climbing wall. She told him about the plan to go to church with their family the next day.

Bert looked at Norah and nodded his understanding. "Becky, Norah continues to have the same vision inside a church. We're going to meet our client here at his church tomorrow, also. So, we aren't sure which case she may be picking up on."

"Wow, how bizarre is that," she exclaimed. "Does Norah still have that portal vision?"

"Yes, she still sees that unsettling portal. And she just now told me that she's getting a strong feeling of fear and terror in your case."

"I felt that same thing from Summer," said Becky. "Whatever is going on with this child, she feels genuine terror from it."

"Just be careful, yourself, Becky," he said. "We don't know how much of the fear may apply to you or us. There can be an element of danger even in the most mundane cases."

There was greater concern in her voice. "Okay guys. Good advice since I'm digging into the background of that daycare worker as well as the father. I can only imagine what skeletons may be in those closets." She laughed somewhat nervously.

"Well, good luck tomorrow. Looks like we're all going to church. It may be interesting to compare notes tomorrow evening and see if we have more hope or confusion." Bert laughed.

"Good night, boss," Becky said. "I hope you, Norah, and Missy all have a good sleep and learn a lot tomorrow. Talk with you then."

Bert put down his phone, leaned back in the swivel chair, and placed his bare feet on the foot of the bed. Norah was at the head of the bed. "I love you, Norah," he said. "I don't know what I'd do without you here to give insight into these cases. Even on this first day, your gift has given us a direction to focus on. Vicki's phone records."

"I have loved you from the first day we met, Bert," she replied. "I'm happy that I'm still able to help you with our business and to share your life. Someday you'll join me on this side, Honey. Until then, I'm glad I can join you on your side."

Bert held back tears. "Yup, this is truly a blessing, Love. I'd be lost without you, but I don't have to be lost." He reached for the report. "There's another question that just came to me, Sweetheart."

"What's that, Honey?" she asked.

"Where did they find Vicki's car? That might provide some more questions, if not answers." He looked over the report's table of contents until finding the section on vehicles.

He scanned the vehicle area until finding the report on the victim's car. It was a small 4-door sedan, black in color. It would not have stood out. The location where it was found caught him completely off guard. The police found it in the back part of a parking lot at the Table Creek Golf Course.

Bert told Norah what he'd just read. He continued to scan that section of the report as he asked what she made of that.

"I think we need to find out if she had any connections to golf or to that location," she said. "It seems obvious that she either met someone there, took someone there, or someone put her car there. Maybe Patricia will know if she was dating a guy who golfed there."

Bert was listening as he scanned. "Good thoughts, Sweetheart. It sounds like the detective was thinking that also. He reports interviewing a Daniel Simmons several times. Apparently Vicki dated him off and on, and he was a golfer. He was a suspect early on, but they ruled him out because he had a solid alibi. He was in Kansas City at an amateur golf tournament all that week. Friends corroborated his story and said he stayed in KC all the time."

They both mulled over this bit of information as Bert continued to look over that section of the report. This was apparently one of the big stumbling blocks to this case. The church where she worked was about three-quarters of a mile from the golf course, but she reportedly always parked at the church when she was working. She normally worked when there were no church events, so parking should not have been an issue. On a Thursday, there were usually no events and often nobody at the church. Besides that, she was working at the insurance agency that day. The detective concluded that Vicki had met an unknown person at the golf course. He felt that that person knew something about her disappearance, but the police could never make an identification.

"Let's go by that golf course tomorrow, Honey," Norah said. "Maybe I'll be able to pick up on something that can help us."

Bert agreed with that. He reluctantly put the report aside. It would take many hours to digest it all, and it was after 11:00. He needed to get some sleep. Sunday was shaping up to be a big day.

"Good night, first officer Norah," he said as he turned off the light and crawled into bed.

"Good night, Captain Kirk. See you on the flight deck."

Though his eyes were closed, he could see her sweet face and smile enveloped by her radiant red hair. He focused on her image and her goodness, as he fought to not feel the longing to touch her. In the darkness, he felt the tears slowly trickle down his face.

* * *

In Red Lodge, Rebecca Abigail Thompson reflected on her phone call with Bert. How wonderful it was to be working with a company composed of good people, people who appreciated and trusted her. She hadn't been back outside since leaving Lizzie and taking a nap in the cabin. The cheese, sausage, and crackers had been filling and seemed a good compliment to the glass of wine she'd had earlier with Lizzie. She felt no need to go anyplace for food, but she did feel like getting out for some night air. She pulled on her boots and zipped up her winter parka. As she went outside, she tugged on a warm pair of mittens and stepped onto the sidewalk. This time, she looked for slick spots.

"Why, hello Becky, what brings you out on this chilly night?" It was Guy Hayden.

Becky wondered what Guy was doing outside on this chilly night. "Well, Guy, I guess I could ask you the same thing. I just decided that I'd like a little night air and a stroll under this big sky we all talk about."

"That's funny," he said. "That's exactly what brought me out. Sometimes it just feels stuffy inside and I must get out for a little while. Seemed like a good, clear night for a short walk. Care to walk with me?"

"Sure," Becky replied. "I'd love to have some company, especially since I don't really know where I'm going."

They strolled down the unlighted highway. Between the snow-covered ground and the moon and star light, they could easily see around them. Becky enjoyed the sheen of the snow and the dark star-drenched sky.

"So, Becky," Guy finally asked, "do you really think there's something going on with my daughter?"

She knew she had to answer carefully. "Yes, I do, Guy. I can't explain it yet, but the fear she feels seems to be palpable and comes on instantly from out of nowhere. I don't think she has any idea why this is happening to her. My job is to try to find that out."

He walked for a while, saying nothing. Finally, he responded, "Well, as you may or may not know, I've often been a bit of an ass throughout my life. I haven't always been the altar boy that mom sometimes thought I was. Having said that, I want my daughter to be free of whatever is tormenting her. I will help you in whatever ways I can."

Becky was surprised by his response. She'd felt like he was a bit of an ass. To have him admit it and want to help wasn't what she expected. She had to make herself relax, breathe deeply, and let her clairsentience seek the truth with this man. She walked calmly and just listened to him talk about Summer.

They talked about his family and his years at Oregon State. He asked her about how she got into being a private investigator. Becky didn't discuss the marital influence but told him about her deep desire to help people using her gifts of problem solving and relating to others. She didn't know if he'd understand her being an empath, so she avoided the topic. For now.

When they arrived back at Guy's house, he asked if she'd care to join them for a nightcap. She thanked him but said no. Then she had second thoughts and asked if Lizzie was still up. When he said she was, Becky accepted the offer. Maybe it was the best approach to continue getting comfortable with them.

Once inside and a glass of wine in hand, Becky began to realize why Guy was out for a walk. It became evident to her that he and Lizzie had been arguing or having a fight, probably over Summer. When she saw him go to Lizzie and hug her tightly and heard him say he was sorry, she began to realize the good she might do for others. It felt like her walk with Guy had opened his mind and heart to both his wife and to the reality that something was really happening to Summer. A warm feeling came over Becky. This is why she became a PI.

They talked about just stuff. Anything that came up was fair game. Becky enjoyed just having a normal conversation with two people she liked and was getting to know. After one glass of wine, which she sipped slowly, she knew it was time to get to bed. It was almost midnight and she was joining them for breakfast at 8:30 and then going to their church. She didn't want to stray too far from professional decorum.

She walked carefully back to the cabin, just in case the spot of clear ice was still there. Once inside, she got into her pajamas and sat on the edge of the bed. Like her room at the B & B in Cody, this rustic and cute little cabin reminded her of the undercurrent of loneliness she often felt at such times. She debated for a few minutes if she was ready to date and maybe have a relationship. Then the realization hit her that her job would probably make it difficult to have a real relationship. At the least, she'd probably be on the road a lot.

As she laid down and pulled the covers up to her chin, she concluded that it might not be possible to have it all. Her dream job could make it difficult to have a dream relationship. For now, she knew the job had to take priority over her personal life. Something about this job and this company pulled at her heart and tugged her down that path.

CHAPTER SEVEN: CHURCH

Becky blinked her eyes as a ray of sunshine hit them from a small split between the curtains on the east facing kitchen window of the cabin. It seemed like mother nature was shining a flashlight in her eyes to tick her off. She turned over in the cozy queen bed to avoid the bright light, looking again at the cute interior of the little log cabin and savoring the last glowing embers of the fire. The covers were so warm, and she knew the wood plank floor would be cold as ice. It was very tempting to pull the down comforter over her head and sleep longer, but she knew she had to get ready for the morning plans with Lizzie's family. She flipped back the covers, rolled onto the side of the bed, and slipped her feet into her fleece-lined slippers. The little kitchen and its coffee pot were calling.

"Ah, elixir of the gods," she said aloud as she took a sip of the freshly brewed coffee, pulled the curtain back, and drank in the mountain valley view. "Gonna be another day in paradise, with some actual sunshine on the menu. Might even warm up to freezing today." She settled back in the one easy chair and continued to enjoy her coffee. For a few minutes, she indulged that darn sense of loneliness again. It was times and settings, like now in this neat little cabin on a beautiful morning, when she felt so alone. She had always figured it would hit her worse during gloomy weather and in dumpy situations. Those were bad, but it was the inability to share the good times that was the hardest. That's when she most missed having a man in her life. She sighed deeply and reminded herself that if she avoided the wrong men then the right man would eventually find her. With that bit of self-analysis, it was time to get ready for her visit.

As she dressed, she wondered what Norah's vision of the inside of a church meant. They were going to church in Nebraska with the Nebraska client, Bert had said. Did Norah's vision pertain to the church there, or to the church in Red Lodge? For that matter, could it be about a different church altogether? So many questions, she thought, and so far so few answers. She pulled on her wool dress coat, grabbed her cap and gloves in case she needed them later, and left the cabin for the short walk to Lizzie's house.

Becky walked into the Hayden's kitchen just before 8:30 this Sunday morning and said her greetings. Because of the cold, she'd decided to wear a black pantsuit with a white cotton shirt. A pair of nice looking, black, cold weather, dress boots finished off her ensemble. She was comfortable yet felt like a million bucks. She'd been on the Hayden's case now for only three days, but it felt like a month. On this fourth day, she expected a routine breakfast but was apprehensive about what the Church had in store for them. She had an uneasy feeling about it. Maybe it was just a reaction to Norah's vision.

Their kitchen's green stained pine cabinets, all handmade, provided a stunning contrast to the honey colored pine logs of the house. The large cedar table and chairs also looked to be a one-of-a-kind creation. Becky especially loved the old-time, deep, twin sinks and the outdoor garden-type faucets for hot and cold water. They gave a real sense of rustic charm to the overall décor. This house was a pleasant blend of beauty and function, modern and rustic.

While Lizzie scurried about getting her servings of toast,

scrambled eggs, and deer sausage on the table, Becky enjoyed the view of mountains below a mostly blue sky with scattered high clouds. The thermometer hanging outside the multi-pane thermal windows above the sinks read a chilly 18 degrees. She turned to greet Summer as she arrived from her bedroom, neatly dressed for church.

"Well, good morning, Summer. Don't you look great this morning. Are you ready for some breakfast and then church?" Becky said.

"Yes, ma'am," Summer said. "I'm hungry."

Becky smiled as she recalled how this sweet little girl had such a big appetite. This was confirmed again when they all sat down to eat. Summer ate her generous helpings with gusto, while saying little. Becky also enjoyed the food, especially the sausage. It took all her will power to not take a second one. She hated that it could be such a chore trying to keep her nice figure. She took her mind off it by focusing on the conversation with Lizzie and Guy, mostly discussing the weather and their families. Summer seemed to have a quiet nature and didn't say much. She appeared to listen to the grownups talk and chimed in occasionally when something especially interested her. The small talk was interesting but didn't reveal much of substance, though she did find it interesting that there was a new Pastor at the church, and this would be their first time with him. The little bit of time passed quickly before they had to make the ten-minute drive to their church.

Guy had warmed up their car for a few minutes before the ladies got in, so the seats weren't quite like sitting on ice. Summer seemed to liven up as they made the drive down to South Broadway, and she became chattier. Becky got the tour of downtown from a seven-year-old's perspective. When they approached the church, Summer was first to point it out. The child was anxious to get there.

"We haven't met this new priest yet," Guy said, "I hear he's quite different from our previous one."

Becky asked, "How so?"

Lizzie answered, "Apparently, for one thing he's much taller and slimmer than Pastor Eldredge. That's the former priest. Eldredge was pretty short and chunky."

"I hope you guys don't have anything against us short, chunky people." Becky laughed.

"Oh my God," Lizzie said, "you're kidding, right? Most women would kill to have your figure. Right, Honey?" She looked at Guy.

Guy shook his head, "I ain't saying nothin' about Becky's figure. I may be stupid but I'm not crazy. Hadn't noticed, anyway."

Summer had to chime in with the innocence of a child. "You've seen her, daddy, I've seen you look at her when she walks away."

They all had a good laugh about that. Two people were a little red-faced as they opened the car doors. A blushed Becky stepped from the parked car and surveyed the church. It was very different from others she'd been in. Not only was it a tall, red brick, building, but it had two flat-topped towers. The left tower appeared to be the main entrance and was considerably larger than the shorter but otherwise identical tower to the right. A central cathedral separated the two. The towers almost gave the impression of guard towers for a fortress, ironic for a church. All in all, though, she thought it an attractive structure and looked forward to seeing the inside.

The ushers greeted them, and Becky followed Guy, Lizzie, and Summer to near the middle on the left side. The interior was beautiful, and the general layout reminded her of many other churches she'd been in. As they waited for the service to begin, Guy and Lizzie said hello and chatted with a few other people nearby. Summer squeezed Becky's hand and pointed out some of her friends. While this was going on, Becky found herself imagining the view from the altar, looking across the parish. She realized that the altar kids, musicians, and the priest all would have this perspective. What was Norah's vision trying to tell us, she wondered.

The service began in typical fashion. There were two singers who were quite good, accompanied by a guitarist and pianist. The priest, Father John Hightower, was a reasonably dynamic speaker and aptly named. He was indeed a high tower, must have been about six feet four Becky reasoned. Everything, though, went off in the usual manner, she thought. Nothing out of the ordinary. Maybe Norah was picking up on something at the church in Nebraska.

When the service ended, Becky meandered with the Haydens toward the front entrance. Summer was getting comfortable with Becky and wanted to hold her hand as they walked behind her parents. Guy and Lizzie chatted with a couple of friends as they worked their way to the church entrance, where Father Hightower was greeting everyone individually, many for the first time. The line was moving a bit slowly, though nobody seemed to mind.

Their turn came to meet the priest. As they approached him, Becky felt Summer's grip on her hand tighten and the child began to hug against Becky's leg. Becky could sense a sudden unease in the little girl. It was strange and out of character for Summer to be pulling away from this new man, even if she didn't know him. This was a time when an empath personality was helpful. Becky was feeling not just distrust from Summer but a sense of fear. Why?

Becky watched as Guy and Lizzie exchanged their introductions with Father Hightower. Guy then reached for Summer to lead her to meet the new Priest. Summer at first pulled away from Guy, but when he persisted, she literally jumped onto her dad and threw her arms around his neck. She turned her back on the Priest and pressed hard against her father. Becky could see that Guy was embarrassed and a little miffed with his daughter's actions. He tried to force Summer away and turn her toward Father Hightower, but she kept turning away from the man and her face betrayed the silent cry and tears about to come.

She didn't want to meet that man. She's afraid of him, thought Becky. This didn't seem like the typical reaction of a shy child. More was going on. Why?

Lizzie came to Summer's rescue and took the girl from Guy, holding her closely and telling her it's okay. While Summer didn't cry, she didn't want to meet the Father, either. Lizzie didn't push her to do so. Father Hightower was understanding and very nice about the episode, seeming to take it matter-of-factly. After apologizing and another minute of talk, Guy and Lizzie headed for their car. Becky walked just behind them, studying all of them, especially Summer. It was obvious that Guy was quite upset with his daughter while Lizzie was more understanding.

After entering the vehicle, Guy turned to Summer and said angrily, "What's wrong with you, Summer? I ought to spank you right here for behaving like that."

"Honey," Lizzie said, "she's not used to him. Let's just give her some time and space to get to know him. He's new to her."

"She didn't act like that with Father Eldredge, even when she first met him," Guy replied. "So why the big drama with Hightower?"

Becky now jumped into the conversation. "Guy's, I don't know why this reaction, either, but I can tell you that she's experiencing something like fear. She doesn't understand it, but she doesn't trust him. I'm able to sense her emotions and this is real apprehension. The question we need to ask is why?"

Guy settled down somewhat and his anger subsided into inquisitiveness. "Well, we know she's never met Hightower before, so it has nothing to do with the past. So, what else is different from Eldredge?"

Lizzie added, "We know she doesn't react to other strangers like this when meeting for the first time. Something is different here."

"Has she met other men at the church before?" asked Becky. "Could it be the church setting itself?"

"Oh yeah, she's met a number of our male friends and even visiting strangers at the church," Lizzie replied. "She never acted like that with any of them."

"Hightower was wearing his regalia, robe and all," said Guy. "Could it be the fact that he looks like a priest, I wonder?"

Summer was leaning tightly against her mother while this talk about her was going on. The few times they asked her about these things she just shook her head and silently turned her face against Lizzie. She didn't seem to know why she was feeling whatever she felt. Becky could sense that the little girl was confused and bewildered about it all.

Becky then said, "But Father Eldredge would have been

wearing his official clothing, too. She wasn't afraid of him, didn't you say? So, it must not be the robe."

"What's left then?" asked Guy. "Only other thing I can think of is body type. Eldredge is shorter and somewhat fat, Like Becky," he laughed, "while Hightower is tall and lanky."

Becky laughed back. "Oh, so the truth comes out now, huh. Back on my diet, I guess. Regarding that, doesn't she meet and know other men who are both short and tall, chunky and lean? Does she react like that with any of them?"

Guy and Lizzie pondered that. Finally, Guy answered, "Yes, and no. Yes, she's around all body types and no, she doesn't act like that with any of them that I can remember."

"That's right," Lizzie continued. "So, what's left?"

Becky finally broke the ensuing silence. "Only thing I can think of is a tall, lanky priest, dressed in his robe, and in a church. But how would you explain that?"

She sat with the other adults sat in the car, silently. Guy started the engine and turned toward the women. "I can't explain it. None of us can."

Lizzie added, "Since the priest theory is ridiculous, we still have to try to understand what's going on in her head. How about we go out to eat and not worry about it for now."

Becky agreed with them about that. Guy pulled out of parking and headed downtown for another of their favorite restaurants. Becky would be driving back to Cody for the night, right after they got back to the Hayden's house. She wanted to cut a couple of hours off her early morning drive to Laramie Monday morning to discuss Jeremy. It wasn't lost on her that Jeremy had been described as tall and lanky.

* * *

In Nebraska City, earlier that morning, Bert had taken Missy out for a sunrise stroll around the same field as the previous day. The patches of snow were crusted over from the night's cold and they shimmered like diamonds in the early light of the southeasterly rising sun. Missy's breath had been like puffs of smoke from a cannon in the still morning air. She had a ball running on each glistening patch and grabbing at the chunks which broke off under her feet. She even had a good chase of a cottontail which happened to be grazing on a clump of grass. It narrowly escaped her sharp teeth as it darted under a pile of limbs in the tree line. Since hunger was not her motivation, she had quickly lost interest in that new toy and looked for other things to chase. By the time they returned to the doghouse, Bert's cheeks and nose had started to tingle from the four degrees above zero temperature. The moisture from his breath was frozen to his face. He knew his cheeks were probably redder than those of a four-year-old child after outdoor recess.

Back at the motel, Bert had told Norah about the chase, fed Missy, and prepared his questions with Norah. They wanted the meeting with Patricia Domenica to be professional and productive. Norah had been in a chatty and typically bubbly mood. Her lively and energetic personality shone brightly when she became engaged in an issue. She had sat back against the headboard, watching Missy dine on a mix of dog food and deer, while sharing notes about the case with her husband. Bert's emotions ranged from enlightenment, to love and admiration, and to amusement, as he listened to his wife's often witty assessments. Whether a living or a spirit woman, Norah was always a pure joy to him. He always felt in love with her.

A few minutes before 9 a.m., Bert pulled up to the gas station and went inside for a coffee. Patricia was already there, just beginning to sip on her cup. She was a dark-haired little woman with a pleasant round face which seemed to have a permanent smile. She was short, barely five feet tall, and on the plump side. With her tan and brown dress and yellow shawl, she looked like the epitome of a grandmother to Bert. He couldn't help but be cheerful as he returned her infectious smile. He thought her to be very likeable.

"Hello, I'm Bert Lynnes. Thanks for meeting with me," he said.

She replied, "Hi, Bert, I'm Patricia, but most people call me Patty. I'm happy to do anything which might somehow bring peace to Robert. He's had a very hard time without Vicki." While her English was good, she had an underlying Spanish accent. An aroma of a flowery perfume accompanied her.

He thought her perfume to be a bit strong, to the point of being distracting. "I know we don't have much time before church starts. How do you know Robert's mother?"

"Vicki and I attended the same church for probably ten or fifteen years. We even worked together there for a couple of years before she started going to this church."

"So, she didn't always go to this church, then?" he asked.

"No," she said. "We were both going to the Catholic church out west of town."

"You said you both worked there for a while before leaving. What did you do?" Bert said.

"I became a part-time administrator the last three years I was there. Vicki was their bookkeeper for several years before that. She kept working there up until she died," Patty said.

"You're sure that she's dead, then?"

"Oh, for sure," Patty said emphatically. "There's no way she would have left Robert. He was the love of her life."

Bert then asked, "You said you both left that church to come to the Calvary Community Church. When was that and may I ask why?"

"It was about May of 2009, roughly a year before Vicki

disappeared," she said. "I changed churches a few months after Vicki did. She never did tell me why she wanted to change. I just decided to go with her to CCC. She was my best friend."

"You were her best friend, but she didn't tell you why she wanted to change churches," Bert said. "That seems a little strange. Was she upset about something?"

"Oh yeah," Patty said, "something made her very mad and she didn't want to talk about it. I respected that and didn't ask. I always figured it had something to do with the books. She was a meticulous bookkeeper and the church administration was quite loose in that regard. They probably blamed her for some of their oversights. She'd had enough and said she would keep working there but wasn't going to go to the services anymore."

"Hmm," he muttered. "I find it interesting that she would get mad about something to do with the work and change where she went to church yet continue working there."

Patty continued, "Well, if you knew Vicki it wouldn't be too surprising. She worked contractually with her various places, so maybe couldn't leave. In addition, she took a lot of pride in her work. She wouldn't want to turn it over to someone else if she didn't have to."

Bert asked one more question. "So, you and Vicki attended church at CCC with Robert for just over a year before she turned up missing. Did it go smoothly at this new church?"

"Yes," Patty said, "we had a good time here. A neat church with good people. We enjoyed it and we'd usually go to eat lunch together afterwards. Robert was almost always with us, too."

"So, you don't know what upset Vicki. How did she act during that last year?" Bert asked.

Patty seemed to be pulling up those memories before answering Bert. "As I recall, she seemed to be kinda like an earthquake. No visible signs of any underlying ruptures, but you knew it could crack at any time. I always knew she was deeply troubled about something, but she tried to hide it and didn't want to ever talk about it. She would get moody sometimes and clam up for a while. Then it seemed like she'd resolve it in her head and would act normally for a while."

Bert checked the time on his phone. "Patty, I can't thank you enough for meeting with me. I appreciate your insights. Would it be okay if I call you again sometime if more questions come up? I know church will be starting in a few minutes."

"Oh yes. By all means. Call anytime," she said. "If you'd like to sit with Robert and me, you're welcome to. He and I always sit together, and we usually go for lunch afterwards. I feel that's the least I can do for Vicki."

Bert thanked her for the invitation and left to get his car. Missy was waiting patiently in the cargo area and jumped around excitedly when he approached and opened the door. He smiled to Norah in the passenger seat as he escorted Missy outside and to a grassy area behind the station. Her walk would be short for now, as they needed to get to the church in the next ten minutes. Her disappointment was obvious as he commanded her back into the doghouse. Ears down and her tail tucked, she reluctantly jumped into the cargo area and flopped down, her back to Bert. He couldn't help but wonder if that was an intentional snub. What does it say about you when your coyote hybrid thinks you're a POS, he wondered?

Back in the car and driving to the CCC church, Bert asked Norah what kind of thoughts or visions she might be having today about the case. He knew she'd been reading Patty after the meeting. With the clear blue sky in the background through the passenger window, Norah's red flowing hair seemed to shimmer. In her spirit life, as when she was alive, she was so beautiful to him. He kept glancing at her as he drove the five minutes to the church.

"I have good feelings about her," Norah said. "I'm seeing a vision of her standing in front of a closed door. Then she reaches forward with a key and begins to unlock the door. I get the feeling that there is something she knows which is key to solving this case. I don't think she even knows what it is that she knows. You need to stay in touch with her and continue to talk with her, though, Honey. Somehow, you have to draw that knowledge out of her."

"That's tough, when you don't even know the questions to ask," he replied after some thought. "Maybe we should go to lunch with them after church and talk some more. I think you should go in the church with me, Sweetheart. You might pick up on something."

In the church, Bert made sure to keep a portion of the pew beside him open for Norah. Nobody else would know she was there. Or would they? He noticed a teenage girl, seeming to be about seventeen, looking at them occasionally. She appeared to be looking at Norah, too. Another medium in the room, he wondered. Or was she an empath and just sensed Norah without seeing her? He made eye contact with the girl during one of her glances, and he smiled and nodded. Norah also looked straight at her and gave her beautiful smile. The girl seemed to understand and resumed her involvement in the service. It was the first time he and Norah had encountered another medium. He wasn't quite sure how to handle it. Hopefully acknowledgement and nonchalance were the way.

The service went normally without any issues. As they were leaving the church, Bert noticed that a lot of people seemed to know Patty and Robert, and many asked him how he was doing. They gave Bert the impression that they knew Robert had been having problems. Robert answered them meekly and politely, without saying much. He seemed uncomfortable around people.

One fellow named Frederick patted Robert on the back and introduced himself to Bert. He invited Bert to come back and become a member of their church. Bert thanked him, said he was impressed with the church, and asked Frederick what brought him to this one.

Frederick answered, "If you've ever heard Marty Robbins' song, The Master's Call, you'd glimpse my journey which led me to this little congregation. I'd have to tell you that story over a beer sometime." Then he added with a gleam in his eye, "Also, Mr. Bert, if a Nebraskan is to have any meaningful conversation with his equal, he has no choice but to talk with God."

Bert tried very hard to contain his laughter. He just couldn't do it. For the next couple of minutes, he kept recalling this man's gleeful words and would start chuckling and then laughing. He knew this was close to a phrase from the movie, Braveheart, but it was still funny as hell. Sometimes, you just need a good laugh. Thanks, Frederick, he said to himself as he struggled to regain his composure and get back to the case at hand.

Bert accepted Patty's invitation to join her and Robert for lunch at a little diner. He had just entered the doghouse, where Norah already occupied the passenger seat, when the teenager from inside the church approached his door. He rolled down his window and greeted her.

She extended her hand and shook his. "Hi, I'm Dori," she said. "I'm really glad to meet someone else, finally, who has the same gift that I do."

"Yes, I knew you did when I saw you looking at us inside," he said. "I assume you see my wife?"

Dori said with a smile, "Yes, I see you, ma'am. I'm Dori and glad to meet you."

"Glad to meet you, Dori," Norah answered. "You're the first person besides my husband that I've been able to communicate with."

Dori answered, "I know the opposite side of that. I see a number of spirits around town, but they don't try to talk with me."

"Dori, I'd like to talk more with you later. We're going to lunch with the couple over there, so must go now. Can I exchange numbers and talk later?"

Dori was eager to trade phone numbers and asked him to call her when they could talk more. As she walked back to her parents, Bert pulled out of parking and followed Patty's vehicle.

He saw that Norah was smiling. She genuinely liked knowing that another medium could sense her and talk with her. Something about that seemed to make her feel a little more whole.

The lunch with Patty and Robert was friendly and enjoyable, but it provided no additional information of significant value. Both did confirm what Bert already knew from the police report, that Vicki had dated an avid golfer for a while. Patty felt that Vicki liked this guy, Daniel Simmons, better than the three or four others she'd dated during the previous ten years. She said that Vicki didn't go out very often with any of them, maybe a couple times a month, nothing too serious.

Patty had no explanation for why Vicki's car was at the golf course parking lot. Daniel was out of town, she said, and Vicki wasn't one to eat alone at the clubhouse. She couldn't think of anyone else who Vicki might have met there. There was no reason for her to park so far away from the church to work on the books.

When they all left the restaurant, they said their goodbyes. Patty agreed to meet with Bert again whenever he felt the need. The grandmotherly little woman hugged Robert tightly and kissed his cheek.

She told him, "I'll see you in a few days again, Bobbie, you please take care of yourself, Honey. You call me anytime if you want to talk. Your mom would want that."

A sweet little lady, Bert thought to himself. He told a teary-eyed Robert that he'd get back with him, probably the next day, and see where they were in the investigation. Turning to Norah as the others drove away, he suggested they go to the golf course unless she had another idea. She agreed with that. Both were realizing that her psychic world was probably the best chance they had of solving this case.

Bert pulled off the entrance drive to the Table Creek Golf Course so he could let Missy out for a relief break and a short run. Before he exited their vehicle, Bert laid Vicki's silver hairbrush on the dash. He hoped that it might help Norah to channel anything about Vicki. Then he walked with Missy down this empty drive. No golfers were out on this cold day in

January. As usual, Missy almost smiled as she gleefully trotted down the fence line, stopping several times to drain her bladder. Bert sauntered down the road, keeping her in sight as he inhaled the cold air and cleared his head. He would need all his brain cells functioning if he was to help figure out this cold case.

After he and Missy were back in the doghouse, they drove on up the snowy lane to the course parking lot. Upon entering, Bert stopped to check the police report and see where Vicki's car was found. After identifying the parking spot, they drove across the large lot and parked on the exact place where her car was discovered. He turned off the vehicle engine, leaned back, and told Norah this was it.

Norah looked at the hairbrush for a minute, and then stared straight ahead without seeing. She tried to clear her mind of everything and let it drift back to a time seven-and-a-half years earlier, when Vicki's car mysteriously arrived at this position. Norah closed her eyes and focused on the faint video playing inside her eyelids.

She finally opened her eyes and spoke. "It's so faint, Honey, so hard to tell much. But I'm seeing the fuzzy vision of a small car, a sedan, I'm assuming it's her car, pulling into and stopping on this spot. I see the door swing open. That's it, Honey. Someone is about to get out of the car, but I can't see them get out. My vision just stops there. I can't even be sure it's her car, though I think it is."

"That's okay, Sweetheart. That's more than we had before,"

Bert said. "Maybe more will come to you in time. For now, how about we swing by the church where Vicki worked. I think it's about a mile from here, to the north." He could sense her disappointment.

They got back on highway 75 and drove north about three-fourths of a mile to the entrance drive of the Holy Mother Catholic Church. This was possibly one of the last places Vicki visited before her disappearance. By now it was about 4 p.m. and the sun was getting noticeably lower in the southwestern sky. The driveway was clear and empty, denoting the heavy traffic from the earlier services. The church now appeared to be virtually vacant. Bert only saw one woman going toward a side entrance to the main church building. She disappeared from his view. He drove slowly into the main parking area and stopped where they could survey the front of the large stone church. As he was marveling at the beauty of the construction and surrounding grounds, he noticed that Norah seemed anxious.

He asked, "What's the matter, my Love? I get the feeling that something's bothering you."

"You're right," she replied. "I'm getting a much stronger sense of her here. It's nothing specific, I can just feel that she was present here. That's maybe nothing, since we know that she worked here and went to church here for a while. Maybe my feeling is just validating what we already think we know. Or maybe it's vice-versa."

He thought about that for a couple of minutes. "Well,

Sweetheart, that could be significant because it means that you're channeling her, even if faintly. I think it means that the doorway between you and her is at least opened a crack. You have a chance to open it further as time goes on. It's going to be dark soon, so let's go back to the room and relax a bit. We can try to make sense of it after that."

"Yes, I can see that it's getting colder out again," she said.

"Yeah, I know, I couldn't believe that woman was running around the side of the church with just a skirt and short-sleeve shirt on," he said. "Guess these are hardy people here. Or she wasn't going far. Or, maybe she was in a hurry to talk with her equal." He laughed. "I'm more than happy to have this fleece-lined coat on."

He turned around in the parking lot, slowing as he studied the figure of the Holy Mother on top of the central church building. He thought the artwork to be very beautiful as he drove down the entrance lane and on highway 75 back toward the motel. The lengthening shadows from the late afternoon sun gave a new look to Mother Nature's palette as they splayed across the low rolling hills and intertwined among the scattered trees. A handful of geese were winging their way across the southern sky, probably looking for a night resting place. Bert imagined he could hear their distant honking, despite the hum of the vehicle engine. As he glanced at Norah, he was mesmerized by the fiery glow of her hair as the sun shown in the passenger window. He wondered if he was seeing the natural intensity of her spirit or if the sun really could create such a patina around the head of a ghost. It didn't matter. Either way, her light shined brightly, silhouetted against the setting sun. He felt himself a blessed man that he had the gift of this second sight.

Tonight, Bert would relax and enjoy the companionship of this lovely spirit and their working companion animal. This seemed to be one of those insignificant, nickel-dime days when the nuggets received were small. Tomorrow would bring a new day in their hunt for the missing. Vicki was somewhere out there, perhaps around here, and he believed that her spirit was trying to be found. He, like Norah, could sense some faint vestige of the woman and mother, waiting to be brought back to her son. Waiting to be brought back into the light.

CHAPTER EIGHT: A NEW DAY

Monday morning was another typically cold day with high thin clouds hinting at the approaching front, which promised that another storm system was on the way. Becky Thompson checked her winter weather traveling gear before she left Cody at 5 a.m. The roads were clear for her six-hour drive to Laramie, but she knew to plan for the worst case. With a couple of stops, she planned to be there by noon. She'd be meeting with the Assistant Director for the Young Un's Daycare, a lady named Sonya. This lady should be able to shed more light on Jeremy's personality and traits in dealing with small children.

Becky entered the small town of Thermopolis around 6:30. Appropriately named from the Greek words for "Hot City," this would be one of those expected stops. She kept wishing she could spend some time in this seat of Hot Springs county, with its population of about 3000. The hot mineral water sounded great to her, especially in this cold weather, and she really wanted to bathe in the famous "Big Spring," purported to be the world's largest geothermal and mineral hot spring. Because of a treaty signed in 1896 with the Shoshone and Arapaho tribes, the springs were free to the public. Being a self-proclaimed naturalist, Becky also wanted to visit the nearby Dinosaur Center and browse over the many fossils recovered from the area. Unfortunately, such a visit would have to wait for another time.

This morning, she proceeded straight ahead to the east on Broadway where highway 20 turned south in downtown Thermopolis. Making the U-turn on Broadway Street, Becky returned and pulled in front of the Storyteller bookstore. It was a neat little book, gift, and coffee shop. Right now, she needed a cup as well as a brief break to stave off the sleep monster which was tormenting her the past twenty minutes. She dared to hope that they were open this early in the morning. To her delight, they were.

Ten minutes later, she removed her winter coat before hopping back into her warm truck. Travel cup in hand and filled with her favorite hot beverage, she resumed her journey to the south on highway 20. The remaining drive to Laramie would be bearable now.

Soon she was driving along the huge Boysen Reservoir and Boysen State Park. Formed by a large earth-filled dam on the rustic Wind River just south of the majestic and stunning Wind River Canyon, this water and camping playground was another of the favorite stops for Wyoming travelers. She knew she had better enjoy the scenery here, because the next two hours were mostly what she considered drudgery. It was mostly undulating hills, gullies, and arroyos, interrupted by the frequent antelope, before hitting Interstate 25 at Caspar. An hour before Caspar, though, Becky passed up another point of interest. She once again made note of the covered bridge over the old highway just north of highway 20. Every time she passed this relic of the past, she continually reminded herself that she needed to learn about its history.

The last four hours to Laramie passed as if in a trance, lulled into a semi-hypnotic state by the interstate highways. Becky rolled into Laramie just after noon. She found her way downtown to the Turtle Rock Café, where she was meeting Sonya. Another opportunity for coffee, and another opportunity to struggle for the willpower to resist the many dessert temptations. She looked over the menu while waiting for the woman to show and battled the hamburger and fries demon until deciding on a tossed salad. Around her was the increasing hustle and bustle of the noontime rush of college students from the University of Wyoming. She enjoyed watching and listening to the ideological gamesmanship of these young people, so confident in their beliefs despite their lack of meaningful experience in the real world. Her people-watching was interrupted by the arrival of a neatly dressed brunette, looking to be about forty years old. Becky knew instantly that she was Sonya.

Sonya Olivette was a stocky woman with a stern, unsmiling face. She came across as a stereotypical teacher: firm, direct, and authoritative. She had barely sat down at the table with Becky before she wanted to see Becky's driver's license and P.I. license. Then she demanded to know about the company that Becky worked for.

Becky smiled sweetly as she entertained a quick thought to herself. "Bossy bitch." She handed her licenses to Sonya and waited for the woman to study them as if evaluating an entrance exam.

After Becky described her company and answered several questions about herself and very general questions about the case she was investigating, Sonya seemed to kick one stirrup from atop her high horse. She had the demeanor of someone who was too busy to put up with such trivia and had more important things to do.

"Make that an egotistical bitch," Becky thought silently. She smiled again and explained that Jeremy was working at a daycare school in Red Lodge and she just needed to know how he performed and related while here at her Laramie school.

"Well, to be honest, I always wondered why a 20-something male college student would want to work at a daycare with little kids," Sonya said.

Becky realized that Sonya's bias would probably taint about anything she had to offer about Jeremy. "Did he ever do anything that caused you to question him?" she said.

Sonya replied, "Oh, just his demeanor with the kids was too rough. And he was such a big guy that his size intimidated some of the children, especially the girls."

"Oh really," Becky said, "I didn't realize he was a big guy."

"He was probably about 6 feet 5 I'd guess," Sonya answered. "He was so tall that he seemed rather slim, but he must have weighed over 200 pounds."

Becky then asked the central question. "Did Jeremy ever do anything with any of the kids, especially the girls, that you considered inappropriate."

Sonya weighed her words carefully. "Well, no, not really, but many of the little girls didn't like him. I think he was just too firm and unfeeling with them. I couldn't help but wonder if there was more that I didn't know about, but I never became aware of anything blatantly inappropriate."

"Okay, well thanks for sharing those observations. I do appreciate it. You can't be too careful when you're considering whether a man is going to be allowed to care for little kids." Becky was ready to get this interview over with. She did not like Sonya.

Sonya added, "You know, it might just be that Jeremy's size is intimidating, even to me. I think some of the kids were scared a little because of that. Maybe he's in the wrong profession."

"I think you may be right, Sonya. Again, thanks for your inputs about him. I need to be going, so I hope you have a great day." Becky was about to call for the check but realized she hadn't even had her salad.

Sonya said good-bye and left. Becky called the waitress to her table. "I'd like a small hamburger with the works, no fries." The diet and salad could wait. Her taste buds craved a burger.

A half hour later and with happy taste buds, Becky left the café and headed for the University of Wyoming. She was glad she'd made an appointment to talk with Jeremy's child development professor. Maybe he could shed some light on the lad's demeanor. She didn't feel that she got much from Sonya.

At UW, she located the student union, where the gentleman wanted to meet. At first she didn't see him, until she finally realized that Billie was a woman with a somewhat deep and raspy voice. It hadn't been hard to mistake her for a man. With that discovery, Becky introduced herself to the portly little grey-haired lady and sat down. She had an enjoyable talk with Billie, who was certainly a more reasonable woman to talk with. However, the only thing she took away from it was that Jeremy was perceived to be genuinely interested in the childcare profession, but as a business. Billie said he talked frequently about starting a system of childcare establishments. An ambitious guy, then, thought Becky, and maybe he realized his shortcomings in dealing directly with the kids.

Becky checked the time. It was just 3 p.m. and she was done in Laramie. A new storm system was supposed to reach the region by Wednesday. If she got on the road now, she could be in Cody tonight and back in Red Lodge tomorrow, before the storm hit. She hugged and thanked Billie for meeting with her and left the student union for her truck. She could feel the stares from several of the young guys she passed, and knew they'd be surprised when she got in her big Dodge Ram Hemi pickup. It was a source of pride for her that she was not your stereotypical blonde chick. Maybe she had the looks to draw glances, but she was happy to be a country girl who liked the outdoors and her truck. Oh yeah, don't forget the hamburgers. She sighed; nothing but fruit the rest of the day.

The six-hour drive back to Cody seemed to take forever. She listened to the radio at times, but often she liked to just think as she drove. It amazed her how many issues she could solve while driving. If she ever wrote a book, she'd probably write the bulk of it in her head while on the road.

It was 10 p.m. when Becky pulled up to her B & B in Cody and went inside. She was exhausted from the long day's drive. This night she didn't even feel the usual loneliness very much. She just wanted to get in bed. One looks out the window to check the temperature. It read a chilly 20 degrees. It would be going down again in another day, so she knew she'd better enjoy this relative heat wave.

She realized that she hadn't called Bert and Norah today. This had been one of those days with plenty of time but also plenty of distractions and she simply forgot. There really wasn't much to report about this day's efforts, anyway. She hadn't learned any great revelations about Jeremy. He was no more or less a suspect now than he'd been yesterday. Tomorrow, she'd call on her way to Red Lodge. Tonight, as she snuggled under the covers and felt the creeping warmth from the cotton sheets and thick comforter, she wondered how their investigation was going over there in Nebraska. She tugged the covers up to her chin and worked her head into the pillow. The question faded as she drifted into sleep.

* * *

In eastern Nebraska on this Monday morning, Bert sipped a coffee in the motel room as he chatted with Norah. He was taking his time before taking Missy out for her morning outing. They were discussing how best to proceed with Robert's case. Missy was starting to pace the floor, so Bert knew he couldn't delay very long. The glow in the eastern sky hinted at the coming sunrise.

"Well, my Darlin," Norah said, "it seems to me that we have the phone call question on the day that Vicki disappeared. There's also the matter of her car. Why was it where it was?"

Bert answered, "You're right, Sweetheart. Are you still having the vision about the phone call, and about Patty holding one of the keys to solving this crime?"

"Yes," she said. "I keep seeing a phone; just a phone. And I feel that Patty knows something of great importance, but she doesn't know it."

"The phone, Honey," he asked, "what kind is it? A cell phone?"

Norah was at first surprised by his question. "Why, it's like a wall phone, I think. Doesn't look like a cell phone. I've been seeing it as a generic phone of any kind. Maybe it really is a wall phone that I'm seeing."

"I'm not sure what we can learn from that at this point in time," he said. "Probably no records now. But, what if she did go to make a call, as Robert thinks, and her cell phone was out of charge. She might have used a wall phone. That would explain no cell phone record of such a call."

Norah replied, "Yes, you're right, Honey. It doesn't sound like the police considered that. Maybe that's why I keep seeing a phone."

"Well, what do you say to a visit back to the Buck Snort bar and see what we can find out?" Bert said.

"Good idea, Sweetheart," Norah replied. "Maybe the phone office would still have the record. We won't know unless we ask."

Bert and Norah took Missy to a different field a bit farther west on highway 20 toward Lincoln. It was just a couple miles before he saw an ideal spot on the north side of the highway. The small hillside field, about five acres in size, had a wind break of twenty-foot pine trees defining the west and north sides. A dirt road led into the place. Bert parked just off the road. There were no houses or people in sight, so he walked Missy along the line of trees, enjoying her sometimes hectic pace of investigating the sights and sounds. He wished he could perform his investigations as quickly as she did hers. After about ten minutes, he called her back to the doghouse. With ears lowered, she reluctantly got back in the cargo compartment and turned her back on him again.

"Geez," he said aloud, "I can't spend all day walking you out here. Look how wet you are."

They both laughed as he entered the vehicle and drove back to the motel. He needed to see when the bar opened as it was only about 9 a.m.

Back at the motel, Bert called the bar. They didn't open until 11. They needed to go with plan B. They'd go to the local phone company office and see what they could find out. Before going back to the doghouse, Norah suggested that they call Dori, the young medium they met at the church, and see if a local medium might know of spirits which she and Bert couldn't connect with. To Bert's surprise, she answered immediately. He half figured she would be in school. She was in school, but on a short break. She said she could talk for about five minutes.

"Do you connect with spirits in specific locations around the city?" he asked her.

Dori said, "Yes, absolutely. There are numerous old historic sites around town with considerable activity. Of course, the cemeteries and a couple of the churches."

"Do you ever connect with a woman who disappeared and died about seven or eight years ago," Bert asked.

Dori answered slowly, "Well, I don't know for sure. You know, they don't really talk with me much. There is one entity who thinks she was killed about ten or eleven years ago. She says she was never found. She just kinda wanders aimlessly. Could she be the one you're looking for?"

"I doubt it," Bert said. "The one we're looking for is more recent than that. Out of curiosity, though, where do you usually see her?"

"Oh, I always see her near one of the churches. She just seems to roam around. She only talks a little about being killed there. She's just a lost soul."

"Which church?" he asked her.

Dori responded quickly, "The catholic church out west of town. The Holy Mother, I think it's called."

Bert had a thought flash through his mind. "What does she wear when you see her, Dori?"

"She was killed and disappeared during the summer, so she's always wearing a skirt and a short-sleeve shirt."

Bert asked her, "Are her clothes light blue, by chance."

"Why yes they are," Dori replied, surprised. "Have you seen her?"

"Yeah, I think I did, yesterday, when we drove out to look at that church."

"Wow, that's pretty amazing," Dori said. "Hey, guys, class is about to start up, so I have to go. Please call me again sometime if you'd like."

After they hung up, Bert turned to Norah. "Hmm, Honey. So,

if the spirit we saw at the church is a woman who died maybe ten or more years ago, she can't be Vicki."

"No," said Norah, "but, why is she at Vicki's church and why is she missing like Vicki?"

"I know," he answered. "Is that just a coincidence? Or is there a connection between the two?"

Bert leaned back on the chair and looked at Norah, where she stood near Missy and the window. Did they just stumble onto a second cold case? If there's a connection, maybe her case could help them find Vicki. If only a coincidence, would that poor woman's demise pull them away from the case they're being paid to solve? Norah heard his thoughts and slowly nodded. They had to check it out further.

Twenty minutes later, they arrived at the Nebraska City News-Press. A sweet little lady looking to be in her sixties offered to assist Bert in going through some of the old paper archives. She got him onto a computer, gave some basic instructions for searches, and turned him loose. With Norah looking over his shoulder, Bert began scanning the articles beginning with the year 2009 and going back in time.

It wasn't too long before he found an August article which talked about the still-missing woman, a woman named Janice Campbell. The reporter discussed how Campbell's disappearance was still a mystery, two years after she vanished.

It went on to say how her devastated husband had taken their son, twelve years old at the time of the article, and moved to Utah. Reportedly the boy was having serious psychological problems and the father hoped that a complete change would help the lad cope.

Bert scrolled back in time to early September 2007. He found an article discussing a press conference by the Chief of Police at that time, asking for help from the public in finding Mrs. Campbell. Her car had been found at the Lake Ridge Golf Course, northwest of Nebraska City and near Beaver Lake. Her family were members of the Holy Mother Catholic Church. The church was hosting a fund-raising the next Saturday for the family.

He scrolled to the more recent past. It didn't take long to find an article in August 2012 about Nebraska City's second missing woman, Vicki Sturdevant. Two women in the past five years had gone missing in the west part of the city and the crimes remained unsolved and their bodies were never found. Despite intense searches and investigations, both cases had gone cold.

Bert closed the computer, scooted the chair back, and looked silently at Norah. They shared the same thought. This is not a coincidence.

Back in the doghouse, Bert drove the ten minutes to the Buck Snort tavern. It was now after 11:00. Leaving Missy in the vehicle, he and Norah went inside. Bert first went to the men's room. Then he ordered a small glass of a Nebraska beer and asked the bartender if he or anyone else there at the time had been working for a long time. The bartender said that one of the cooks had been with the establishment for nearly ten years. He called the cook, a woman named Betty, out to talk with Bert for a minute.

He had noticed that there was no sign of a phone in the establishment, certainly none in the hallway leading to the bathrooms. He asked Betty if there had ever been a public phone in the tavern. She told him there was a phone on a small desk near the bathrooms when she first started work there. However, she said it was removed during her first couple of years there, because everyone had a cell phone. She thought that occurred in about 2008 or 2009.

Bert finished sipping the small beer and sharing thoughts with Norah. She pointed out that if Vicki disappeared in 2010, then the phone would have been gone by then. He agreed and wondered if there was a way to exit the building to perhaps a phone on the street. He hadn't seen a door leading to the street when he was back there. Norah agreed with him that he should go back and look specifically for an exit.

He went back toward the bathrooms. At the end of the hallway, he paused to study the small storage closet at the end of the hall and after the door on the right to the men's room. While it matched the rest of the hallway, he could see that the paint and trim looked to maybe be newer than the hallway and ceiling adjacent to it. It might have been built into the hallways in recent years. Perhaps someone on the staff would know.

When he returned to his stool at the bar, he again asked the bartender if Betty might answer a question. The fellow walked to the kitchen and called for her.

Bert thanked her profusely for taking another bit of her time for his question. She was nice about it and didn't seem to mind. He asked if there had ever been a door at the end of the hallway leading to the street, before the closet was built. She nodded and said that there was a door there until about five years ago. The owner needed more storage space and was also concerned about undesired people coming in off the street out of view. Bert shook her hand and thanked her again for that information. He explained that he was a P.I. trying to solve a case, which seemed to have some connection with the bar. She was thrilled to have that bit of information and contribute, not to mention something to talk about back in the kitchen.

He paid the bartender and left the tavern with Norah by his side. She knew they were going to the phone company office.

Missy hopped around in the cargo area of the doghouse as they entered. Bert could see that she needed to get out again, but here on a main street was not the place. He put his cap and gloves aside and drove west on the street until they found a vacant lot. She had to stay next to him as they meandered around the lot, but she was still happy to be out of the car. When he put her back into the doghouse, she didn't turn her back on him.

They drove to the local office of the phone company. The clerk that morning was a plump little woman, probably in her thirties, named Genny. She was a pleasant sort, another redhead, with a helpful attitude. After Bert explained his reason for being there, she was more than willing to assist. She told him, though, that most of their records are discarded after seven years, so there might not be any that he sought. He said he understood and would just hope they got lucky.

He watched as she searched for any record of a street-side phone outside of the tavern. They got lucky. There did used to be a pay phone booth just across the street from the Buck Snort bar adjacent to the old bathroom door. It had been removed as being obsolete in the spring of 2011. So far, so good. Call records were a different story.

Genny tried to find the call registry records for that phone, but initially could not find them. Either they hadn't been properly entered or they had already been purged. She needed to take her lunch break but told Bert she would look in a couple of other files when she returned. She promised to call him in either case and let him know.

It was still a chilly day with a light wind blowing, although the temperature had climbed up to about 30 degrees. It was shortly after noon, at this time, and Missy hadn't had a good walk in a while. Bert suggested that they go back to the motel, have lunch from the cooler, and he would take Missy out to the usual morning field. Norah knew that Bert was a little hungry and Missy needed some exercise. She agreed.

Back at the motel, Norah chose to remain in the room while Bert took Missy out to the field where they'd been walking in the mornings. It was remote and expansive enough for her to have a good run, checking out all the sights, sounds, and smells. He strolled around in her general area, mostly thinking about the case and trying to figure out what they needed to do to solve it. He thought about calling Becky to see how she was doing on her case. Not wanting to give the impression that he didn't trust her, he decided to just wait for her to call. After about thirty minutes, he called Missy back to the doghouse and they returned to the motel and Norah.

Norah was happy to see them return. She caressed Missy's coat softly and was pleased to notice Missy cocking her head from side to side with ears flicking forward and back. She gently wagged her tail. Missy could sense her presence.

Then Norah turned her attention to Bert. "It felt like you were gone a long time, Honey," she said, "I'm really glad you're back."

He smiled that endearing smile that she loved. "I'm glad to be back with you, too. Have you got any ideas for proceeding from here?"

She nodded. "Yes, besides waiting to find out about the phone records and continued glimpses of my previous visions, I'm beginning to channel the first missing woman, Janice Campbell. I'm sensing a connection between her and Vicki. I don't know what that connection is."

"Do you think they knew each other?" he asked. "Maybe there's something they had in common which led to their disappearances."

"I'm not sure," Norah said. "But the feeling keeps getting stronger that something ties them together. I think if we can find Janice, we will find Vicki, Bert."

"So, this has become about solving two cold cases in order to solve the one we've been hired to solve. Nothing too complicated about that is there." He laughed. "Gotta love a challenge, huh."

"Yup, Darling," she said, "if we find either of them, I have the feeling that we'll find the other. Perhaps death is their connection."

"Then how do you think we should go about figuring this out, Sweetheart?" he asked.

Norah mulled that over for a few seconds before answering. "Maybe Patty knew Janice as well. I think we need to get together with Patty again."

Bert replied, "Yes, and with Robert, too. We owe him an update today, I think. I wonder if we went by the Holy Mother Church if we'd be able to communicate with Janice."

"Might be worth a try," said Norah. "I'm getting the impression, though, that she isn't a communicative spirit. Dori can't find out much from her, and she was getting away from us. Bert, it could be that she's confused because she doesn't know what happened to her. We may be her best hope of finding out."

"Why wouldn't she know what happened to her, Honey," Bert asked.

"I think that if she was unconscious before she died," Norah answered, "then she might not have any memory of how she died. She could just be one of those lost souls that we hear about."

"Oh, I see your point, Sweetheart," he said. "So, trying to pry much out of her might be a poor use of our time, then."

"Yes, my Darling, I think we are better served to go around Janice's spirit for now. I'm still seeing Patty holding the key, or at least a key, to figuring this out."

Bert knew there were now several tasks to be completed, if possible. Robert possibly held some knowledge that might be helpful, but he was such a troubled soul there was no telling if they could get it out of him or not. The lady at the phone company might have tracked down the records for that pay phone by now. There was no way to know if that would help. Did the teenage medium have any further information which might help? For now, he decided to first contact Robert, bring him up to date, and see if anything could be pried from his memories. After that, he'd set up another meeting with Patty.

How do you get the key from someone when neither you nor they know what it is?

It was now mid-afternoon and there wouldn't be much daylight left. Bert called Robert, who said he'd be able to meet in about 45 minutes. He loaded Missy back into the doghouse, Norah took her usual place in the passenger seat, and they proceeded to Robert's house. This would be their first look at where and how he lived.

Robert's house was a modest, one-level, three-bedroom, brick house in a nice neighborhood in northwest Nebraska City. It was well maintained outside. Knowing that Robert was left essentially wealthy by his mother, Bert and Norah were surprised by the simplicity inside. It could best be described as sterile. There were no dishes out and nothing seemed out of place. It almost looked as if nobody lived there. Except that Robert met them at the door and escorted Bert to the kitchen table. Norah remained near the wall opposite the main appliances.

Bert declined Robert's offer of a water and proceeded to brief him on the status of their investigation. After giving a brief rundown on what they'd learned so far, he asked Robert two central questions.

First, he asked if Robert or his mother knew Janice Campbell. Robert had to think about it for a bit, but finally said that he'd heard of her but didn't think he or his mother knew her. Janice had attended their church some years earlier, he remembered. He knew that she and her family had left a few years before his mother vanished.

"Do you know what happened to Mrs. Campbell," Bert asked.

"No," he said. "She left and a short time later her family left, from what I remember."

"So, you do remember something about them," Bert said. "Did you know her son, Terry?"

"Oh, yeah, I did kind of know Terry I guess. He was a few years older than me, so I didn't know him very well. He became weird."

Bert thought about that statement. "So, you knew Terry well enough to know he was a bit strange. Is that why you didn't get to know him very well?"

"Yeah, I guess so. I just don't remember much about the time before Mommy disappeared." Robert seemed to be clamming up.

"On a different note, you're an eligible bachelor with a good income. Do you date a lot of the ladies around here?" Bert asked.

He was quick to reply. "No, I don't date anyone. I don't feel comfortable around people very much. I have a hard time talking with girls."

"I don't mean to get too personal," Bert said, "but what kind of things do you like to do for enjoyment?"

"Not much," he answered. "I mostly stay at home. Sometimes, I do like to go to the Arbor Day farm and walk some of the hikes. I like that if there aren't many people there. I like to listen to the birds."

"Another question we have concerns your mother's car location, if you don't mind, Robert. Do you have any idea why her car was parked at the golf course?"

He answered, "No, I have no idea. The police must have asked me that a hundred times, but I just don't know. All I know is that she did date a guy who golfed there."

"Did you like the golfer she dated," Bert asked.

"I think so," Robert answered, "I just don't remember much about all that time. What I can remember, I think he was okay.

Robert seemed to be getting a little flustered with the questions, so Bert looked at Norah and noticed her nodding in agreement. He thanked Robert for his time, promised to continue keeping him informed of their progress, and said good-bye.

As they drove away in the direction of their motel, Bert wanted to know what Norah thought of the time with their client.

"You know, Bert, the thing I noticed is that he does seem to have some memories of the period that he originally told us he doesn't remember. He told us a couple days ago that he didn't remember much of anything prior to his mother's disappearance. He remembers some things. What else might he remember?"

"Yeah, Sweetheart, you're right. He knew of Janice and her son, and that family had left the area by the time his mother vanished. He remembered that the boy, Terry, acted weirdly. It makes you wonder if he's hiding something or selectively remembering."

Norah replied, "Robert was old enough to have had some influence on his mother's disappearance, but he was probably too young to have anything to do with Janice's. So, I don't think we can go down that rabbit trail."

"Yes, and from all indications, he and his mother had a loving relationship. While it's possible that he had something to do with his mother's demise, I think it's highly unlikely. We need to keep the possibility in the back of our minds, but not spend much time on it."

"What is strange, is Robert himself. Talk about acting a little weird," Norah had observed. "He lives a very mundane and sad life, I think, Honey. How many twenty-something young men do you know who don't date and are uncomfortable around girls their age?"

"I found all that to be sad, too," he said. "You know, Norah, it would be interesting to know what Robert was like before his mother vanished. I wonder who can shed light on that."

"I bet Patty might have some inputs to that question, Honey. Maybe we can locate one or two of his schoolteachers. They would know."

Bert contemplated everything. "Then I think we need to get on Patty's calendar and see what else she might tell us about Janice Campbell, Terry Campbell, and Robert."

They had arrived back at their motel room. Norah settled into a spot near the window and close to Missy. She wanted to just let her mind relax and see if she could channel anything more about the case. Bert called Patty. She was busy with a sewing group meeting soon but was very happy to meet the next day. They agreed to meet at Jonny's Café on Central Avenue at 9 the next day, Tuesday.

It was a good time for a nice walk with Missy. The sun was just dropping below the horizon and it would be dark soon. They drove to the nearby field, which had become their go-to place. Bert and Norah strolled side by side across the higher ground while Missy explored the low places and checked out the ravine and its tree line. Twilight had brought out a couple of mule deer from the farmland to the west, and it didn't take Missy long to discover them. She took off after them. All three had crossed the ravine before Bert noticed the chase. He whistled for Missy before she got out of his range. It was with great reluctance that she grudgingly obeyed and gave up her pursuit. As she returned, she paused several times to watch her prey as they slowed, stopped on a knoll, and turned to watch her retreat. Bert couldn't help but notice the irony of the prey taunting their tormentor. He and Norah both laughed.

They meandered back toward the doghouse. The sky had turned from twilight to darkness and the stars were just beginning their nighttime brilliance in the cold winter temperature. The moon was just above the eastern horizon. Missy had caught up to them and circled loosely around them as they walked in the growing darkness. It was a setting made for lovers, and tonight it was made for Bert and Norah. The cold of that Nebraska night was no match for the warmth and depth of their devotion to each other. Side by side they slowly returned to the motel and the reality of an unsolved mystery.

CHAPTER NINE: A DEEPENING MYSTERY

The brisk wind had a bone-chilling effect at 6 a.m. when Becky left Cody Tuesday morning. Combined with the falling temperatures and increasing cloud cover of the approaching storm system, there was a sense of urgency as she hustled to get on the road to Red Lodge. Survival gear and travel bags all securely loaded, she cranked up the heat in her Dodge truck and headed north. The private investigator was back on the job.

Her drive this morning was uneventful. Becky made it to Red Lodge ahead of her schedule and she popped into one of the local restaurants for breakfast and coffee. There were about two dozen patrons, several obviously skiers readying for the slopes, already sitting in the dining room. It didn't seem unusual that a bearded man wearing a black hoodie entered about a minute behind Becky and took a seat at a distant table, facing toward a side wall. She smiled at a couple of the guys who made eye contact, but otherwise paid little attention to any of them. She needed this boost before meeting back up with Lizzie to continue the quest to find the reason for Summer's torment.

With some ham and eggs and a couple cups of coffee under her belt, a revitalized Becky left the restaurant and drove to the Hayden's house. The heavy cloud cover, 20 MPH gusting wind, and plummeting temperature heralded the onset of the winter storm, now only a half-day away. She was definitely going to stay in their little cabin for the duration of this visit.

Lizzie threw open their front door before Becky could even knock and gave her a warm hug and a hearty welcome back. She reminded Becky to get her bags in the cabin before the storm hit. Then Becky heartily accepted the offer of another cup of coffee. She knew that the Hayden's coffee was hands-down better than that of the restaurants in town.

Guy was at work for the day, and Summer was at her school. This would be a time for the ladies, the client and the investigator, to have time to talk. Becky said she wanted to take advantage of this storm time to get to know Summer better. Lizzie liked that and was enthusiastic to talk about her daughter.

They talked for a couple of hours, mostly about Summer and how some of her behaviors seemed to be intensifying. Lizzie said the drawings were now pretty much a daily occurrence. It seemed like thc additional attention being given to her by Becky was focusing the child's attention onto her own feelings to a greater extent. Lizzie didn't know if that was a good thing or not, but she found it to be of concern.

As they talked and the minutes became hours, Becky began to feel an odd sense of emotions coming from Lizzie. She had felt the mother's concern and fears from the first meeting, but there was a strange feeling of guilt emanating from Lizzie's persona. While most parents would wonder if they'd done something to cause their child's behavior, this felt different to Becky.

"Lizzie," Becky said, "you're a great mother to your little girl. Whatever is going on with her, I don't see any reason to think it's your fault."

Lizzie looked away and it was obvious she was trying to hide the sudden onrush of tears. She tried to discreetly wipe them from her cheeks, but the slight quiver around her lips gave away her emotion.

"Lizzie," Becky said. "What's wrong? I have this new and overpowering feeling that something is really bothering you today."

Lizzie turned to face Becky, not making any effort to hide the tears flowing down her cheeks and falling upon her shirt. "You're very perceptive, Becky. Yes, something sits in the background of my consciousness most of the time, but for some reason it's taking center stage right now. I can't seem to put it away."

Becky inhaled deeply, allowing her mind to relax and her senses to focus on her client and friend. "Do you need to talk about it, Lizzie? It's my business if it has anything to do with Summer, so it's a matter of strict confidence for that reason, as well as friendship."

"Yes, I think I need to get this out and share it with someone. I've never told anyone before, and I don't think I can keep it to myself any longer, Becky. Are you sure you don't mind being my confidant?"

"Lizzie, I know you're my client, but I already feel a good friendship developing with you. Your secret is my secret, if you want to talk about it."

Through a renewed gush of tears and with an emotionally strained voice, Lizzie blurted out the secret that had tormented her for years. "I don't know if Guy is Lizzie's father."

Becky sat in stunned silence for a few seconds, trying not to say anything that would give away the shock she was feeling. Finally, she found the words. "Well, what makes you wonder about that, Lizzie. That's something you would know, isn't it?"

Lizzie composed herself and wiped away her tears. "When I first moved here after college, I became friends with the priest at the church I began to attend. We became close friends, very close. Shortly afterwards, I met Guy and began to fall in love with him. The priest and I started drifting apart."

"That's just a natural way that it works, Lizzie," Becky said. "There's no harm in that."

Lizzie continued. "The night before our wedding, when Guy was having his bachelor's party, I and my friends had a bachelorette party. I got a little drunk and decided foolishly to walk back to my apartment. My priest friend happened to drive by, saw me walking, and gave me a ride home." She drew a deep breath, and then resumed. "One thing led to another, Becky. I didn't know the depth of my feelings for him until he kissed me. We ended up in bed."

Becky shifted in her chair and adjusted her shirt. "So, you went ahead with the wedding to Guy the next day. That must have been a very emotional day for you."

"You don't know the half of it," Lizzie said. "I was a basket-case of emotion before and during the wedding. Afterwards, I became resigned to my decisions and began to make myself look only forward."

"Oh my God," Becky said, "I can only imagine how conflicted you must have felt, Lizzie. I had this growing feeling that something was bothering you. I could sense your feelings of guilt, but I just didn't know why. I am so sorry for you."

"To put it bluntly, the priest's sperm had a day head start on Guy's," Lizzie said. She hung her head and stared blankly at the floor.

Lizzie then sat upright and wiped her eyes and cheeks with a tissue from a nearby box. "Well, my friend, I made that bed and have to sleep in it. But most of the time I'm okay. I rarely even think about it until something starts to push it to the surface. Your investigation into Summer's strange behavior has been pushing it into my conscious mind."

"Lizzie, the fact is that you don't know for certain that Summer isn't Guy's child. She could be. You do know that he believes her to be his, and she sees him as her father. So, I think you should just go with that; believe it yourself, go forward, and try not to look back."

"Thanks for that; I needed to hear that, I think," Lizzie replied. "I just want to go forward and focus on what's bothering my daughter."

Becky felt the need to investigate a little bit more before they moved on. With Lizzie's permission, she asked, "Where is the priest now."

"He got a reassignment a month later and left. He didn't tell me where he was going, and I didn't try to find out. We both just realized it was the only way." Lizzie leaned back and let out a deep sigh.

"What did he look like, Lizzie?" Becky asked. "The priest, I mean."

Lizzie said quietly, "He was slender and tall, quite a bit taller than Guy. Dark hair. Good shape. He was a nice fella."

Becky asked, "Have you thought about a DNA test."

"Oh yeah," Becky said emphatically. "But that possibility is buried under a mountain of fear and hope that it will never happen. I don't want to know; I don't want to risk hurting Guy."

"But there really is a chance that Guy could be Summer's father," Becky reminded her.

"Did he, the priest, ever try to see Summer? Or does he know that he might be the father of a child?" Becky asked.

"No, we haven't been in contact since he left. We did speak

once during the second week after the wedding, when we agreed to not stay in contact for the sake of my marriage. The subject of a baby didn't come up."

Becky then asked, "How do you think he'd react if he thought he might have a child back here with you."

"At the time we were dating, he was very family oriented. He really was a good guy, we just had strong feelings for each other and made a mistake. He was a very passionate man; that's why he became a priest."

"Lizzie, if you don't mind telling me. What's his name?"

Lizzie's brow furrowed as she said, "His name is Marvin Finegan, with one N. Please don't contact him or anything, though, Becky. I don't want him brought back into this. Okay?"

"I promise to not contact him, Lizzie. I just think as your PI that it might be prudent for me, and only me, to keep tabs on him. Nothing more."

Lizzie was okay with that. The two women changed the subject back to something more light-hearted for a while. They talked about their mutual love of downhill skiing and some of their favorite slopes, before shifting back to Summer. They couldn't believe how fast the time had slipped by. The child would be home from school in just a few minutes.

Outside, the approaching storm had the trees and shrubs whipping around like spirits on Halloween. Through the kitchen window, Becky noticed that the thermometer now read eight degrees. Half a block away, a dark pickup was visible through the light swirling snow as it sat with the exhaust fumes billowing out from the idling engine. It caught her attention for just a second because nobody parked on the street around this neighborhood. Summer's school bus would be coming past it very soon. Becky turned away and gave it no more thought as she suppressed the chill that swept down her back. She shrugged her shoulders to spread the warmth within her flannel shirt, and asked Lizzie if she could have another cup of coffee.

As the two ladies were stirring their coffee, Lizzie noticed the school bus coming down the street. She pointed out to Becky that Summer was home. Leaving her coffee on the kitchen table, Lizzie went to the front door to greet her daughter. Becky followed her.

Becky watched as Summer made her way from the bus toward the door of the house. The strong wind gusts made it difficult for the little girl to walk, and she weaved somewhat as she moved in her heavy winter coveralls. The snow was already over her ankles in some places along the street. Glancing past the bus, Becky noticed that the pickup was still sitting on the street. She couldn't tell for sure, but the nearly obscured driver seemed to be doing something; maybe taking pictures with a camera. That struck her as strange, or maybe even suspicious. Maybe he's a reporter for the paper.

They ushered Summer into the house as wisps of wind-driven snow spun happily inside with her through the open door. With Lizzie tending to her daughter's clothing, Becky made one more look outside before closing the door. The school bus was making its way to the next stop, and the pickup had left. She could see taillights well down the street, and she assumed that was the vehicle. The snow made it difficult to identify it for sure, as it quickly faded from view. It was probably completely harmless, yet she was a paid investigator and she needed to be suspicious. She was suspicious. Something just didn't feel right.

Once Summer was out of her winter gear, Lizzie sat her down at the table for a hot chocolate and a talk about her school day. Outside, it was snowing more heavily by the minute. The storm had arrived. Winter storm watches had transitioned to warnings a couple hours earlier, and now a blizzard warning was repeatedly coming to their cell phones. Guy was due home in an hour, and Lizzie walked to the window and stared into the dancing whiteness. Darkness wasn't far off and the storm clouds were already hurrying day into night. Becky knew she was wondering if Guy would be able to get home from the airport.

Unable to do anything about the situation with the storm, Becky asked Summer if she would show her some of her schoolwork. The little girl's eyes lit up as she eagerly agreed and pulled out her school bag.

The first item out of the bag was Summer's beloved doll, her Be-be. She moved the doll toward the center of the table as she pulled out her file folder of papers. She began to rifle through the papers to find her several math assignments. Math was one of her favorite subjects.

While Summer was gathering her papers, Lizzie whispered to Becky, "Wow, I've never seen her take that Be-be doll out of her bag anywhere but in her room. That's like her sanctuary. She makes sure the doll is near her when she's in bed. You seem to have a magical influence upon her."

Becky just smiled and nodded. She rested her elbows on the table and watched Summer. The little dark-haired girl was a real cutie. Becky found herself looking for characteristics she could associate with Guy. The dark hair for sure, but then both Lizzie and her priest had dark hair, so that didn't prove anything. Lizzie had blue eyes, so did Summer. Nothing particularly stood out as telling her that Guy was her father. Similarities for sure, but nothing you could point to.

Summer had her math papers out and was ready to show her work, so Becky put her attention on the papers laid out neatly in front of the girl. It was obvious from the work, grades, and neatness that Summer was quite intelligent. Her artistic flair was evident in the care she took to make her numbers and letters almost pretty. The child moved on to her science work and was also very interested in the wildlife and plants around her. This was not unusual for a child of Montana.

Becky asked Summer what her favorite class was. She, of course, already knew it was art and wasn't surprised when the art papers were pulled out. Summer began showing her artwork and drawings to her friend and her mother. The crayon and pencil drawings were quite good for a 7-year-old child, and it wasn't difficult to tell her subjects. The little girl needed more room to display her papers, so Becky asked if she could sit the doll upright and back a little so he could see, also. Summer was a little hesitant but nodded in agreement.

Among the next ten pages of drawings suddenly appeared the familiar but mysterious circle drawing. Summer placed it in front of her and stared at it. Her demeanor seemed to change at that instant from a child actively engaged with her spectators to one totally focused on only one thing. The big red question mark at the top of the page indicated that her art teacher had no idea about this, either. For a while, the little girl just looked at the drawing. Then, her eyes shifted up to her doll, in a sitting position as if looking at it, too.

Becky and Lizzie sat silently and barely breathing, just watching. Waiting to see how Summer would react. Becky wondered if this was the first time that circle drawing was shown to the doll. If so, how would that change the girl's perceptions. It didn't take long to find out.

Reaching into her bag for a pencil, Summer remained fixated on her drawing as she began to trace the circle, slowly at first, then faster and more aggressively. She seemed to become angry. After a minute of threatening to tear her paper with the pencil, she began to mutter quietly at first, then rising in volume, "Be-be, Be-be, Be-be." Her actions became those of a frantic child as she forced the pencil to the paper, tearing through her drawing.

Her cries turned into screams. She went from sitting on the chair to her knees, bending over the paper as if attacking it. Her mother couldn't take it any longer.

Lizzie wrapped her arms around her daughter and picked her up, hugging her tightly. She softly told the girl that she was okay and was loved. After about a minute of continued crying and screams, Summer gradually began to relax and settle against her mother, arms wrapped tightly around her neck. Becky took the cue to remove the circle drawing and folded it up on her lap. She would put it in her investigation file at first opportunity. Out of Summer's view, Becky laid the doll on its back. It had seen enough.

While the two women talked softly and soothingly as they had an early supper with Summer, Guy arrived home. He reported that many of the streets were nearly impassable from the snow, but he knew enough of the side roads to get through. His biggest challenge was the visibility, since they were in full-blown blizzard conditions. At times he said he could barely see past the front of his truck. He noticed the still tear-stained face of his daughter and asked what happened. Lizzie pulled him aside and brought him up to date. When they returned, Guy picked up Summer and held her lovingly on his lap while they talked about the weather. Becky couldn't help but notice the love between the two of them.

After putting Summer to bed, along with her Be-be, Guy donned his coat, cap, and gloves and excused himself to go check on Becky's cabin accommodations and get her fireplace started. When he returned about fifteen minutes later, he said he'd walk Becky there when she was ready, because he almost couldn't find his way in the intense blowing snow.

It wasn't long before Becky was ready to get to the cabin and to bed. She held onto Guy's arm as he carefully led her to the cabin through the driving and whirling snow. The intense wind periodically whipped so much snow about that the one-yard light even disappeared momentarily. Only an eerie glow gave hint of its presence. Guy made sure she was settled okay with her bags, and they said their good night. He stepped back into the howling storm and closed her door.

By herself again, Becky chased off the demon of loneliness and replaced it with a recap of the earlier incident. She just couldn't figure out what that circle represented to the child and why it brought out such an intense reaction. It seemed to be one of the key pivotal questions, maybe the key one, to solving this case and understanding this tormented little girl.

Becky got ready for bed, stoked the fireplace again for the night, crawled under her covers, and sat back against the headboard. The raging storm outside was probably going to be good for sleeping, but it was too loud to consider calling Bert and Norah. As soon as the blizzard subsided, reportedly by late afternoon tomorrow, she'd update them on the case. She was interested in how they were doing in Nebraska City. She also wanted to ask if Norah could shed any light on the guy in that dark pickup. Was he just a reporter? Or was he something else, maybe sinister? She knew she needed to keep an eye open for him from now on.

As she scooted under the covers and turned out the light, Becky felt that twinge of aloneness hit her again. She was not a loner, never had been. She enjoyed the company of a mate, a companion, someone to share life with, a lover. Maybe someday the right guy would come along. She had to believe that. For now, though, her job would govern her life. Her eyes closed to the dim light of the flickering fireplace. The storm raged on.

* * *

Tuesday morning dawned cold and clear in eastern Nebraska. The brilliant red sunrise was giving way to the blue sky of another brisk winter day, as Bert and Missy finished their walk. The only sign of an impending winter storm was a gathering cloud cover far to the west on the horizon. He knew that Becky would be experiencing blizzard conditions by afternoon, and he wondered how she was doing in Red Lodge. He needed to talk with her soon. As he thought about her, Bert wondered what it was about her that was both attractive and intriguing. Sure, she was a beauty and easy on the eyes, but there was a lot more to Becky Thompson. There was an attraction of personality and character which was as magnetic as her looks. He felt fortunate to have her on their team. He knew it wasn't just because of her abilities as a P.I. Norah was a psychic; she knew that also.

He gathered Norah and Missy into the doghouse for the short drive into Nebraska City to Jonnie's Café. Missy settled into her usual bedding in the car, while Bert and Norah went inside to meet with Patty. Norah stood beside Bert where he sat across the table from Patty, who was already inside. Norah had repeated her insight that Patty somehow held the keys to solving this mystery. Bert just had to help her discover that bit of hidden knowledge. It would be tough, since none of them knew what it would be.

They exchanged the usual greetings and small talk for a few minutes. Patty still used a bit too much perfume, for Bert's liking, but she had such a sweet grandmotherly personality that he could overlook it. She was as interested in helping now as during the previous meeting.

"Patty, there's a couple of questions I'd like to ask you," Bert told her. "One is about Robert. As you know, he seems to be a very introverted guy and lacking in confidence. Has he always been like that?"

"Well, no," she replied. "He was a normal, outgoing little boy until several years before his mother disappeared. Vicki was getting concerned about him as time went by. We talked about his change of personality many times but couldn't understand it."

Bert asked, "Did his personality changes occur after they changed churches? Or before?"

"Oh, he was changing for a year or more before they transferred. It was probably closer to two years, maybe even three."

"Could you and Vicki tie it to anything about the churches?" he asked.

"No," she said. "Robert's doctor thought it might be a growing social or mental disorder. He referred Vicki to a psych, but she was offended by that and never took him. Vicki really clammed up the last year. She didn't want to discuss it and seemed to be lost in her own world a lot. I was her best friend and she wouldn't even talk with me about it."

"That seems unusual that she wouldn't even talk with her best friend. Any idea why?"

"I had the impression that she was very conflicted about the situation. It felt kind of like when a close person is diagnosed with a terminal illness, but you hide from the reality of it. I guess that's being in denial, huh?"

"Yes, in denial," he answered. "Maybe the question is whether she was in denial of the condition her son had, or in denial of the cause? Perhaps she felt that she was a part of the cause?"

Patty answered, "Yes, that could be some of it, I suppose. I did have the feeling that she felt a lot of guilt about Robert's poor social skills. As if she was somehow to blame."

"Another question I have concerns Janice Campbell and her son, Terry. Did you know them?"

"I knew of them," Patty said. "But I don't know that I ever really met them. I learned about them mostly from the disappearance. There was a big manhunt for months, trying to find Mrs. Campbell. Nothing turned up. Two or three years later, Vicki disappeared. Everyone tried to connect them to each other, but only their disappearances joined them."

He asked, "Did you know anything about Campbell's son, Terry."

"Just that he was apparently a strange kid, always kind of distant from what I heard," she said. "He and his father left the area a few months after the mother disappeared. That caused some speculation that maybe the father had something to do with it."

"Did Mr. Campbell return to the area at any time, that you know of? Bert said.

Patty seemed to stare out the window, searching for an answer. Finally, she said, "Yes, I believe he came back at least a couple of times, for sure on the yearly anniversaries of his wife's disappearance for the first three or four years."

"Would he have been back here around the time that Vicki disappeared," Bert asked.

"Well, yes and no," Patty replied. "His wife disappeared during the early summer as I recall. To avoid our winters, I think he came back primarily during the summers for a few years. I do remember either seeing him or hearing comments about him. Even though the police could not connect him to her disappearance, many in the congregation still felt like he had something to do with it."

Bert's phone rang and he noticed it was from the phone company, so he placed them on hold and said good-byes with Patty. She told him again to just call if he needed to talk again. As Patty left the café, Bert answered the call from Gennie, the phone company representative he'd spoken with earlier.

It was not good news. After several minutes on the phone with Gennie, he hung up and briefed Norah once they'd returned to the vehicle. Gennie could not locate any records from the pay phone in question and concluded they had been purged. There was no way to draw any conclusions about whether Vicki used that phone on the day she disappeared. Apparently a dead end. Apparently Norah's vision was wrong.

"Norah," Bert said, "I can't see any real connection between Vicki and Janice other than the church they attended. But what could that mean? Do you suppose they were both stalked by a member of that church?"

She pondered that, then replied. "Honey, I have a weird feeling about that church, but I'm not getting anything specific to hang a hat on. I have the growing sense that the church is somehow a part of this mysterious disappearance, but I just don't sense how. I wonder if Janice's spirit would open up more to the teenager?"

"That's a good idea," he said. "I'll ask Dori if she'd keep trying to build a relationship with Janice's spirit and try to find out what happened to her. Since we have no other real leads now, let's go to the Holy Mother Church and see what we can find out about any of this."

Bert drove back out to Highway 2 so they could give Missy a brief walk at their favorite hillside field. It was becoming obvious that she needed to get out of the car for a bit. She covered the entire field in just a few minutes, giving extra attention to the game trails and smells down along the wooded ravine. The clear sky of sunrise was giving way to thin, wispy clouds as the winter storm approached from the west. He thought he could perceive a slight drop in the temperature.

It was close to noon when Bert piloted the doghouse up the driveway to the Holy Mother Church. Rays of late morning sunshine through the thin clouds illuminated it with a surreal quality. He pulled to the edge of the driveway near the parking lot to the front of the structure. Zooming in with his phone's camera, he took a couple pictures from several angles. The next time he talked with Becky, he'd show her a few pictures from Nebraska City and their case. Perhaps something would occur to her that he and Norah hadn't yet considered.

He rolled down the windows enough that Missy could stick her head out, and he and Norah entered the church and headed for the business office.

When Bert entered the office, a perky and friendly little woman introduced herself as Deloris and asked how she could help. Returning the introduction, Bert explained that he was looking into the missing mother of Robert Sturdevant. Norah remained behind her husband and to the side of the door, where she could watch and listen.

Deloris was apologetic as she said she'd only been at the church for about five years and had no direct knowledge about Vicki or Robert. As Bert was starting to shift his mental gears into plan B, Deloris added that another lady, Phyllis Overland, was doing some errands inside the church and she'd been here a lot longer. Deloris was sure that Phyllis could shed some light on the issues.

"Could I give you a tour of our church," Deloris asked. "It is one of the most beautiful churches I've seen, anywhere. Phyllis should be back by the time we finish."

Bert nodded in agreement. "Sure, I'd love to see your church. It's quite beautiful and unusual on the exterior. I even took some pictures this morning."

With that, Deloris led Bert down the hall to the entrance door to the main congregation chamber. Norah followed just behind Bert. As they entered the large, and very exquisite, worship chamber, Bert noticed a woman leaving the altar area and quickly walking to and out the side door, disappearing from view. She wore a light blue skirt and matching short sleeve blouse. She appeared to be exiting the church. A glance at Deloris told him that she did not see the woman. Bert knew this apparently was the side door that Janice Campbell was going toward from outside, the first time he saw her.

The church was indeed both large and beautiful. As they toured the altar and returned to the main door, he made note of the placard which stated that the seating capacity was 600. Back at the office, Phyllis Overland extended her hand in greeting. Following introductions and his explanation for the visit, Phyllis invited him to sit near her desk and she would do her best to answer his questions. Perhaps they could continue over lunch soon, if they weren't completed, she stated.

At first Bert wanted to know more about the church. She told him it was now about seventeen years old and she had started working there about nine years ago. Her first major issue was the disappearance of Janice Campbell and the subsequent attention that brought to the church. Although Janice had disappeared several months before Phyllis started work there, the ongoing search for her continually involved the church for the next year or two as the police attempted to connect the church with the disappearance. The questions gradually tapered off as the case turned cold.

"Why were the police so interested in the church," Bert asked her.

"Mr. Campbell kept alleging that his wife was involved with a church member. He couldn't be more specific, but his claim brought the investigation back to us, time and again," she said.

"I take it that his claims could not be substantiated," Bert asked.

Phyllis answered, "That's right. It seemed to be more of an assumption on his part than founded on anything concrete. He was apparently suspicious but had nothing to base it on."

"I guess when Vicki Sturdevant disappeared under somewhat similar circumstances, it probably brought the church back into the limelight again."

"Oh, yes, you bet it did." She said emphatically. "This time, though, there were no allegations of wrongdoing by anyone in the church. A few people, including her son, reported that Vicki was very angry about something, but nobody could explain about what. It was part of the mystery. No connection was ever made to anyone associated with the church."

"Just to cover all the bases," Bert said, "do you suppose I could meet with your priest and get his thoughts about these cases?"

"I'm sure that Father Romero would be happy to talk with you. He'd love to see these cases solved. I'll see if he's available right now." She pulled out her cell phone and called. After a brief discussion, she told Bert that the Father could meet with him right now. She motioned for him to follow her.

Bert was introduced to Father Romero, a short, portly fellow, about fifty, with a booming voice and a laugh to match. The man was instantly likable.

"How may I help you," the Father asked. "I understand

that you're looking into the unsolved disappearances of Janice Campbell and Vicki Sturdevant. We've spent a lot of time with the investigators in past years."

"Thank you for talking with me, Father," Bert said. "I have reason to believe that Janice's disappearance is somehow associated with this church. I was hoping you might be able to shed some light on that."

"All I can tell you is that we answered probably hundreds of questions related to the same issues, following the second woman's abduction. None of us have been able to make any connections to members of this church. Although both were before my assignment here, I feel that I know the women personally."

"You weren't here then," Bert asked. "When did you get here then, Father?"

"I was assigned here in the summer of 2012, about five years ago. Interest really peaked during the two-year anniversary of Vicki's disappearance. For about six-months or so, there was a renewed interest in solving the two cases."

"There was another priest here before you then. Did you know him very well and where is he now?" Bert inquired.

"Father Riccardo DelFranco was the shepherd of this flock before me," Father Romero answered. "He'd been here for quite some time and was up for reassignment. I worked with him during my two-months transition. He was a good man, very distressed about the missing ladies. I think it was heartbreaking to him that these cases remained unsolved. The heartache probably followed him to his grave."

Bert took instant note of the Father's words. "Are you saying that the Father isn't with us anymore?"

"Yes, Mr. Lynnes, Father DelFranco passed away a couple of years after leaving here and going to his new assignment."

"I'm very sorry to hear of his passing. Where was he assigned after here, Father?"

"He went to the church in Boise, Idaho. The beauty of the mountains and the people called him there, he told me. He went there to eventually retire; it's a shame that he died so soon."

"Can you tell me what Father DelFranco was like, Father," Bert asked. "It sounds like he was very concerned about his congregation."

"Oh yes, he took his role very seriously. He was always mentoring our youth and giving his time to those in need. The congregation loved him."

"What was he like as a man, beyond the robe? Did he have interests outside the church?"

"He was a rather tall and athletic man, with an interest in physical fitness. He ran almost every day and participated in numerous marathons throughout the region. He loved to go on organized hikes, and several times a year he would travel to regional events, often taking other parishioners with him for fellowship."

"What happened to such a man," Bert asked. "Did he die in an accident?"

Father Romero was subdued. "No, well, it was kind of an accident, I guess. My understanding is that he had a reaction between sleeping medication and a prescription he was taking for a bronchial infection. It was very sudden and unexpected."

They continued talking for another half hour. Father Romero could not shed any more light on the mysterious disappearances of the two women. All leads were dead ends. Bert thanked the Father for his time and departed the church.

Bert knew that Norah was deep in her thoughts, thinking about the visit. They decided to give Missy a walk around the church, despite the snow-covered grounds. In the greying light of an increasingly overcast sky, it was still obvious that the well-manicured lawn and shrubbery was a beautiful place to walk and meditate. Numerous evergreen and deciduous trees lined the property and created patches of summertime shade with benches and picnic tables for taking advantage of the serenity. In the southwest corner, a groundskeeper shed was nestled among medium-sized shrubbery and a few small trees.

They returned to the doghouse and loaded Missy. Once inside and driving away from the church, Bert broke the silence, asking Norah for her perceptions.

"Bert, when the Father was talking about his predecessor, I was getting a flurry of uneasy feelings. It's like when you first meet someone, and you just don't feel good about them; you don't know if you can trust them."

"Do you think Father Romero is hiding something?" he asked.

Norah said, "I don't know, Sweetheart, maybe. It feels like there's more to the story than we know now. It feels like we should know more. When Father Romero told us about DelFranco's death, I had this wave of doubt hit me. It felt deceptive."

"Do you think the Father was killed, Norah?" he asked. "If so, why would someone kill him?"

"Honey, I don't know. But something just doesn't feel right about it," she said.

"I think we need to take advantage of this coming storm to see what we can find out about Father DelFranco," Bert said. "Did he leave here because he was due a new assignment, or might he have been forced to leave? How did he die in Boise? Was it an accident? Or could he have been killed? If he was killed, why? Could all that be related to our missing women?"

"You're right, Bert, we need to look into him more. I'm feeling like my visions from the altar are probably from his eyes. Why am I receiving his view of his church? What am I supposed to be seeing?

They drove in silence back to the motel. Each lost in thought. Darkness was creeping in quickly along with the deepening cloud cover and increasing cold. The wind was now gusting up to twenty miles per hour. The storm was gathering. They would give Missy another quick run and then break out the cooler for an evening meal. Tomorrow would be a day to hunker down and ride out the tempest. A day to contemplate the next moves.

CHAPTER TEN: BAFFLING

Inside the Hayden's guest cabin, the last embers glowed brightly in the fireplace as Becky peered out from the comfort of her bed. She knew she needed to get up and stoke the fire, but the whistling wind outside convinced her to lie in her warm cocoon for just a few more minutes. The storm was forecast to begin subsiding around noon on this Wednesday in Red Lodge.

The pull of a freshly brewed cup of coffee gradually drew Becky from her nest among the pillows and blankets. She rolled out of bed, slipped on her fleece-lined slippers waiting neatly at the side of the bed, and made her way to the fireplace. The addition of a few pieces of kindling and a couple of larger pieces of split logs, accompanied by a good stoking with the poker, soon had the fire blazing. Next she moved to the kitchen and the stoking of the coffee pot. Outside, the snow whirled around the base of the trees and sprayed across the windows.

Coffee in hand, she propped herself in the rocker near the fire. This was a good time to plan out her day and how best to pursue the ongoing investigation into Summer's torment.

The first thing, she decided, was to contact Bert and Norah and compare notes on both investigations. Perhaps they could give her some ideas. She was also very interested in the case they were working in Nebraska City. She'd never been there but knew about the Arbor Day connection and hoped to visit it sometime. After that, Becky felt she needed to spend more time with Summer, this time trying to understand the second drawing. It was a mystery, but it didn't seem to elicit the strong visceral reaction that the circle did. She decided to spend any additional time learning more about Priest Finegan. She needed to know if he was behind the suspicious surveillance which seemed to be occurring. Did he suspect that he had a child here with Lizzie?

She called Lizzie and arranged to come over to their house in an hour to visit with her and Summer. Guy was going to work despite the ongoing storm, but Summer's school was still closed. Then she called Bert.

Bert answered on the second ring. He was genuinely happy to hear from her and they talked about the storm and how she was doing. He was very interested in the issues with Summer and he said Norah found it all intriguing, also. Becky was curious why she didn't hear Norah in the background. She was sensing that something unusual was at play. When she closed her eyes, she felt that she could almost see Norah.

Bert said they both agreed with her plan of attack for Summer. The drawings seemed to be pivotal in solving the case. Bert expressed concern about the mysterious guy who seemed to be surveilling them. If he was another private investigator he'd not be a physical threat. However, if he was a rogue or freelancer, he could pose a danger.

Becky asked him about the case of the missing woman. She was amazed to find out that it had morphed into a search for a second cold-case missing woman and might include the suspicious death of a priest.

"It makes one wonder, doesn't it, why there seem to be so

many priest related questions in both our cases," she said.

Bert replied, "Yes, it sure does. We're going to try to find out more about the circumstances of Father DelFranco's death. Right now, it feels like we aren't getting the whole story. Maybe that's intentional; maybe not."

"Bert, I'd like to ask you a question if you don't mind?" Becky said.

"Sure," he said.

"I think you mentioned that a teenaged medium has seen the first murdered woman. I'm assuming she was murdered, though you don't really know that for certain. Bert, you haven't said, but I'm getting the feeling that you're able to see the dead, also. Are you a medium, also?"

He knew this was going to eventually be a discussion. "Yes, Becky, I began to acquire this gift, if you want to call it that, a few years ago. It was either dormant until then or just something that I pushed down and ignored. I've also seen the spirit of the first woman who disappeared, hanging around the Catholic church. She seems to be something of a lost soul. The teenager said she, Janice, seems to not know what happened to her."

A suspicion was beginning to take shape in Becky's mind, but it was one she could not yet voice. "So, what does the church there look like? I suppose it's as awesome as most Catholic churches that I've seen?"

"Yes, it is a beautiful church, about twenty years old it sounds like. It's rather unusual looking and sits on a pretty piece of property, which is well maintained. I'll text you a couple pictures while we're talking. We are suspicious about the church role in these cases, and the original investigators were also. However, neither they nor we have been able to pin down anything specific."

"I can't wait to see it," Becky said. "I've always wanted to visit the Arbor Day Foundation sometime. Maybe when this case in Red Lodge is over, I can get out there and see everything in person. Maybe I can even help you, if you need any help." She didn't know how Bert would react to her offer.

His answer was reassuring. "That would be great. Right now, it seems that we could use your help. How would you feel about making a drive to Boise one day soon? You're a ten-hour drive from there and we may need to personally inquire about the circumstances of Father DelFranco's death. Of course, we wouldn't want to interfere with your case in Red Lodge."

"That'd be fine with me. If the January roads and weather let me go, I'd be happy to work that in. There's the other priest issue from here I need to stay on top of. Maybe I could do both at the same time."

With that, she and Bert said good-bye and clicked off their phone call. Becky went to her text messages and opened the two pictures Bert had sent her. She could see what he meant by the unusual architecture of that church. The explanation that he received from the current Father there, did make sense, though. For now, she needed to get dressed and brave the slowly deteriorating storm to the Hayden's house.

The walk next door to Lizzie's was as invigorating as Becky expected. The wind was still whipping the snow around her and the drifts ranged up to about three feet deep. The freezing cold air had her cheeks nearly bright red even after the two-minute walk required to get to their house. The storm hadn't been a big problem, but she'd be glad when it passed.

Lizzie was her typical warm and welcoming self as she invited Becky inside. They made small talk about the weather until, coffee in hand, Becky reviewed her plan for the day. They discussed how best to bring out the post drawings and get Summer to talk about them. Lizzie felt that Summer should be encouraged to do some of her normal drawings of animals until the opportunity seemed right to ask her to draw the posts and figure.

Summer soon came into the kitchen for breakfast and when she'd finished eating, Becky asked Summer if she'd draw pictures for her. The child was happy and eager to comply. Aided by a favorite animal book, the little girl was soon carefully drawing her favorite animals and birds. Her creations were surprisingly good, for a seven-year-old, and Becky could identify nearly all the animals being portrayed.

For nearly an hour, Summer seemed to be having a great time drawing for her adult friend. When she began to run out of ideas, Becky saw her opening. She asked Summer if she would be okay drawing the figure and posts for her and Lizzie.

Summer's demeanor changed. She went from a happy and bubbly little girl to one with a look of not wanting to do as asked. She didn't seem too upset, so Becky persisted in saying she'd really love to know what Summer was thinking when she drew that set of figures.

There was no answer. Summer just stared at the paper, pencil in hand, for several seconds. Finally, she began to draw the strange figure. Becky noticed that the girl seemed to draw this automatically with little forethought. She scribbled out the two strange looking posts and the figure between them.

Becky studied the drawing, trying to make sense of it. She couldn't. It was a human figure seeming to stand between two large posts. That was it. She began to encourage Summer to expand upon her drawing.

At first, Summer was reluctant, but with enough prompting she began to slowly add a little more detail. It seemed like she was having to reach into her mind to find it. She scribbled on the two posts so that they took a squarer shape, rather than round. Becky asked if she could add anything to the human figure.

Summer sat sullenly, lost in her thoughts. Eventually, she drew a line from the location of the hands to the posts, one on each side. She put her pencil down and turned away. She was done and she was getting upset.

Becky knew not to push any further. She could sense a mixture of emotions in the little girl. There was an element of anger and fear, but also confusion. Summer was angered by whatever it was that she was drawing, but she didn't know what it was. Becky thanked Summer and changed the subject to birds. Opening the colorful bird book which they'd brought with the other books, she began to draw the child back into the more acceptable and interesting topic.

After Summer tired of the books and drawing, Lizzie let her go to her room to play and rest. The two women sat down with another cup of coffee and looked over Summer's drawing.

"You're amazing with her, Becky," Lizzie observed. "She has never attempted to develop either of her strange drawings for us."

"I think I'm more baffled now than I was before by this one," Becky said. "Why are these posts appearing to be squarer than round? And what are those lines?"

"Exactly," Lizzie replied. "Is my daughter seeing a premonition of a woman being tied between two posts or pillars? Do you think she's psychic, Becky?"

"I'm wondering that, too. Psychic ability can come on at an early age and is probably going to be very confusing to a child. If she's seeing some future event, then who is the woman? Where does this occur?"

Lizzie sat with her elbows on the table and hands under her chin, contemplating the questions. Was all of this explained by her daughter having psychic ability? How would that explain her child's occasional bouts of terror, though? It just didn't add up.

It was about lunchtime, so the ladies worked together to fix up a good garden salad. Lizzie called Summer to join them and they had a good chat over the meal. After eating, Becky said she needed to get to a couple other things on her agenda, excused herself, and walked back to the cabin. The storm was lessening now, and patches of blue sky showed briefly between the rapidly moving clouds.

Getting out her laptop, Becky proceeded to the third item on her list for the day. It didn't take her long to locate Marvin Finegan in Bozeman, Montana. He was married and preaching at the Evangelical Free Church. Becky realized that she had to confront him directly if she was to know if he was having Lizzie or Summer surveilled. Fortunately, Bozeman was on the road to Boise. She could continue and check on Father DelFranco for Bert and Norah.

She called Bert and discussed the situation. They all agreed this looked like a good time for her to make the trip through

Bozeman to Boise. They did some strategizing about how best to deal with the respective issues at both locations. Pastor Finegan could be difficult if he either refuses to talk or denies involvement. They will need to develop connections in Boise for Becky to meet with. Bert said that he and Norah will work on making contacts there this afternoon. Becky told them that she would get on the road right away and drive to Bozeman, only a couple hours away. She'd spend the night there so she could get a jump on meeting up with Finegan. The drive on to Boise, probably the following day, would be shortened to about eight hours. Before getting off the phone, Becky wanted to ask Bert something, for Norah.

She asked if Norah had any insights into Summer's possible psychic abilities.

Norah had been listening to the conversation and was reading the tea leaves.

Bert passed her thoughts on to Becky. "Norah says she isn't getting a clear vision about Summer. There's something unusual going on with the child, but she's not sensing a psychic ability. She continues to have the unknown church and portal visions. No idea what they may mean. Maybe they don't really mean anything."

"Hmmm, that's good to know. Lizzie and I are wondering if these behaviors might be explained by clairvoyance. In such a young child, perhaps the ability has not fully developed and might explain some of the strange things we're seeing. If not, then we still have no real idea about the underlying cause."

Bert then added, "Well, don't let the Pastor Finegan issue divert too much of your attention. My guess is that even if he is involved, his interest is personal about the little girl. If he's genuine, he won't want to do anything to harm the child. Once he knows, he'll probably back away. However, that begs the question if he should know about the child. Lizzie doesn't want that, you said. So, you have to approach him in a way that doesn't violate your trust with her."

"Good points," Lizzie answered. "I'll try to figure out how to do this before I get there. I guess I'd better get on the road so I'm not driving after dark. Thanks for all the advice and insights. I'll let you know how it goes."

They said their good-byes and Becky leaned back in front of the fireplace, thinking about the suggestions. Then she pulled up the number for Finegan's church and called. To her surprise, she reached Finegan himself. He was receptive to talking with her the next day and didn't ask too many questions. They arranged to meet at the Coldsmoke Coffee House. It was situated close to Interstate 90, so she could get back on the road to Boise easily.

She called Lizzie to tell her of the temporary diversion and her plans regarding Finegan. Lizzie was at first concerned and reiterated her desire to keep him out of her life and especially out of Summer's life. Becky assured her she would not jeopardize Summer or Lizzie's trust. As she packed a quick bag and headed out of town, she couldn't help but wonder exactly how she was going to do that.

The clearing and increasingly blue sky gave her a good view of Red Lodge Mountain ski resort to the west of town as she headed north on Highway 212. The wide ski runs were bluish-white in the afternoon sun. She knew there were likely hundreds of people sliding down the mountain and having a great time. Red Lodge was truly one of the best-kept secrets of the ski world. She missed the exhilaration of the cold air on her cheeks, the challenge of making perfect turns on a dime, of catching the line, and the mild adrenaline rush of sliding down a half mile of steep slope at sixty miles per hour. A beer with friends at the lodge after a day's skiing was icing on the cake.

Before she knew it, Becky arrived at the town of Joliet, where she turned northwest on the Joliet Road to the city of Columbus. There, she skipped over to Interstate 90. Proceeding west on 90, she soon passed Greycliff, with its Prairie Dog Town State Park, dedicated to the little barking vermin, prey to about every predator that moved on the prairie.

Another of her favorite Montana towns, Livingston, was soon in her rearview mirror. Situated at the north end of the long and stunning mountain valley leading south to the north entrance of Yellowstone Park, this little community was known for its wind, wind farms, large number of artists, and proximity to the Yellowstone River. Sandwiched between the Crazy and Absoraka mountains, the stunning views of Livingston Peak gave balance to the brutality of the winters. If you were rugged enough, or rich enough, Livingston was another great place to live.

Traversing the high mountain pass which separated Livingston and Bozeman, Becky soon dropped down the descending western side to the college town of Bozeman, home to Montana State University. If she had more time, she'd love to browse through the Museum of the Rockies and look at the T. Rex exhibitions in the Siebel Dinosaur Complex. She wouldn't have the time, though, if she had any hope of making it to Boise tomorrow after her meeting with Finegan. Tonight, she would find a motel with a gym and try for a long overdue workout. After that, she might brave the cold temperature and get a beer somewhere.

* * *

Bert gave Missy her usual walk on this Wednesday morning. They were getting used to the cold mornings there, but this morning was much more intense. The storm had hit with its full fury during the early morning and the wind driven, heavy snow made it nearly impossible to keep Missy in view as she scoured the drifts. The temperature had fallen into the single digits. With the wind chill, it felt like somewhere around minus fifteen to twenty. Bert cut the walk short to about fifteen minutes this morning. Missy didn't seem to mind as she faced into the wind on the way back to the doghouse, her thick winter coat plastered in sweeping patterns against her body. Bert pulled his parka tight around his face to keep the wind from blowing it off his head. The snow stung his eyes and he had to go in the general direction of the vehicle, taking brief glances to find his way. The wind direction was his chief navigation aid, and he knew if he kept the wind from his left front, he'd get back to the road. Eventually the ghostly shape of the parked vehicle began to take shape.

Back in the motel room, he discussed the weather conditions with Norah. They were beginning to strategize about their day's plan when Becky called from Red Lodge.

Bert happily took her call. She was always so upbeat and enthusiastic that she was like breathing fresh air. She really was a lot like Norah, who was always a light in his life.

After the initial discussion of the weather at both locations and a review of her case, he shared Norah's sense that Summer was probably not psychic. Norah did stress that she couldn't be certain of that, though, since there seemed to be no other explanation for the unusual things going on with the child. Bert told Becky about the catholic church which seemed to somehow be at the center of the mystery in Nebraska City. He texted her a couple more pictures as they talked.

Bert was concerned about the apparent investigator who seemed to be doing a surveillance on Summer. He knew they couldn't now be sure of who the guy was watching, or why. Norah had an uneasy feeling about him. That concerned Bert, because she was usually right.

Becky threw him a curve ball, when she asked if he was a medium. He glanced at Norah, who nodded. They both knew the question was going to come up and they would have to eventually tell her about the situation. Bert was putting it off in the fear that it might drive Becky away at the very time when they needed her. Something like this had to come to light at the right time.

They discussed Becky's concerns about Pastor Finegan and compared ideas. They all concluded that she had to be very careful so as not to compromise Lizzie's trust. If he didn't already know about Summer, she couldn't let him find out, at least not from her.

Regarding Father DelFranco, Bert told Becky, "If you think you can make it to Boise safely and soon, it would sure help us. There's reason to think that someone in the congregation might have been involved in the disappearance of the two women here. If the Father had suspicions, he might have been killed to silence him. His death feels suspicious."

"I think I can head out later this afternoon, possibly," Becky said. "The weather is already starting to break here. Bozeman is on the way and I can check on Finegan as I go. Might be to Boise by tomorrow night."

"That would be great, Becky. We think that DelFranco may be one of the keys to solving our case here. The circumstances of his death could possibly shed some light on what he may have known or suspected. We'll do some calling around and see if we can find any people who might know details about his passing."

"I'm thrilled to be able to assist you, Bert and Norah," Becky said. "I can actually use the break to collect my thoughts on how to proceed with this Red Lodge case. I think my brain is about to mutiny. I'm feeling like I've run out of rabbits to chase."

Bert offered her some words of wisdom. "Sometimes, if looking at a problem from the top isn't working, try looking at it from the bottom."

He could almost hear her replaying his words before she answered. "You know," she said, "that is so wise. I'll give that some thought and see if I can look at this through different eyes. I see why you're the boss." She laughed. "Goodbye for now. I'll let you know what I can find out."

After closing his phone, Bert looked at Norah. He didn't have to say anything. She knew he saw the similarities between Becky's wit and her own. She didn't mind that Bert liked this new woman; Norah liked her, too.

He glanced out the partly frosted motel window at the swirling snow. The cars in the parking area were barely visible at the far side of the lot. It would be a day to figure out how to pursue this case.

"Norah, my Love," he said, "where do you think we need to go next?"

She also gazed out the window at the stormy scene, which faded into a ghostly white. "Well, that wind might even blow me away today," she laughed. "Not a good day to go back to that church, but I'm sensing that our answers are there, somehow, somewhere."

"I believe you're right, Love, all roads seem to converge at the Holy Mother Church. Both were parishioners there, at least at one time. Janice's spirit seems to be stuck there. Her husband evidently believed she was mixed up with an unknown someone there. You have recurring visions as if looking from the altar across the congregation. There's the strange death of Father DelFranco after leaving here. Did he know or suspect something and was he killed to silence him? Hopefully, Becky can shed some light on that."

"The one thing that still bothers me most is that vision of a portal. I just don't know what it could represent and whether it pertains to our case or Red Lodge," she said. "Whatever it is, it feels very sinister."

"Babe, I sure agree. The way you describe it, it can't represent anything good. For this stormy day, I'm thinking we should focus our efforts on the church. See what all we can find out about it. Any better idea, Sweetheart?"

"No," she replied. "The church is somehow a player in these disappearances. I'm getting the strong sense of that."

"I think you're right, Norah. I'm going to call the church office and see if I can dig deeper into the workings. Somewhere there is something that will validate our suspicions." Bert dialed the church.

He didn't know if anyone would be there during this storm, but Phyllis Overland answered quickly. The woman must live there, Bert thought. He explained his reason for calling and asked if she had time to review the church with him. She seemed happy to have someone to talk with.

Bert questioned Phyllis about the history of the church. Among other things, there had been a facelift about five or six years earlier. Much of the current landscaping was put in during that time. He asked about any physical renovations to the church. She said the same facelift resulted in upgrading the altar and church entrance. Bert asked about any exterior additions.

Phyllis said that, besides the shrubbery and landscape improvements, some maintenance buildings were added for storing the groundskeeping equipment. Bert asked her if, after the storm passed, it would be okay for him to look around the grounds. She said that would be no problem.

Almost as an afterthought, Bert asked her what the main push was behind the upgrades, since the church was beautiful and not very old. She said that the church board, chaired by Father DelFranco, felt the upgrades were necessary to keep up with their standards of excellence. The grounds especially seemed somewhat plain compared to the elegance of the church, itself.

He told Phyllis thanks for her information and said he would be back to look around soon after the storm passed. Then he thought of one more thing to ask her. He wondered if she could tell him how many phone lines there were in the church. After a minute of going over the phones in her head, she finally told him there were a total of five lines. Bert thanked her again for that bit of information and said good-bye.

He turned to Norah. "You know," he said, "I wonder if there's a way to confirm if a call was made to the church on the day that Vicki disappeared."

"Perhaps," Norah answered, "if the church maintains call records dating back more than seven years."

Bert called Phyllis back and asked her that question. After a short discussion, he hung up and reported to Norah that the church only maintains the past year's records.

"So, another blank," Norah said. "But what about the phone company, Bert? Maybe they would have the records on a church."

"It's worth a call to ask," he said. With that, he dialed the phone company and eventually got to Gennie. He asked her about getting such records. To his surprise, she said there was a possibility, but it would take her some time to get to it. Bert thanked her profusely and said he would check back later.

Next, Bert began the search for someone in Boise for Becky to talk with about DelFranco. It took about an hour of phone tag, but he finally found the current minister, Father Stewart, as well as the most senior nun, Sister Frances. Both understood his explanation for their interest and agreed to talk with Becky when she got there. He obtained their phone numbers to pass to Becky.

He then asked Norah what else she thought was important. He knew she had been in deep thought, looking inside for answers. After a long pause, she told him that she felt a strong connection between Vicki and Janice Campbell. She could feel there was a key something in common with the two women. However, she didn't sense a friendship between them. Whatever it was, she said, it was like a chain which bound them together in death.

"So, if we solve one case, we also solve the other, in all likelihood," he again stated. "Since we're struggling to find clues right now for Vicki, then maybe we should shift gears and focus more on Janice."

Norah nodded in agreement. Her mind was awash in flashes of the mystery portal, visions from the pulpit, phones, and two women, walking side by side with heads forward and hands clasped in prayer. A shadowy figure, or was it two figures, followed behind them. Who were they, she wondered?

Bert was already online, searching for information on Don Campbell. It only took him five minutes to locate a man by that name with a son, Terry, now twenty years old, in Salt Lake City. He keyed in the cell phone number.

When Don Campbell answered, Bert introduced himself and

explained his reason for calling. Don was at first skeptical and seemed on the verge of hanging up on him, but Bert noticed a relaxation and a sense of trust as he fully explained the situation he was investigating.

"I understand, Mr. Campbell, that you suspected that your wife was somehow involved with another member of the church here," Bert said. "Did you ever confirm this?"

"No, sir," Campbell answered. "She always denied it. Yet, she seemed to become more withdrawn and distant during the months leading up to her disappearance."

"Her car was found at a golf course, several miles away. Could she have been involved with a golfer who was a member of the church?"

Campbell replied quickly. "It's possible, but I couldn't get a sense of any of them. The same question pertained to the Sturdevant case. She actually dated a golfer, but he was not a real suspect. Small wonder, since he was a cousin of the police chief's wife."

"What?" Bert said. "I've never heard that before. So, he was related by marriage to the chief of the investigators."

"That's right, Sir," Don replied. "However, he seemed to have a solid alibi, being at a tournament in KC at the time Sturdevant vanished. Of course, you don't know from any of the investigation reports that Simmons' main alibi at KC was also a golfing buddy of the police chief."

"No kidding," Bert answered in amazement. "Was this golfer fellow, Daniel Simmons, a church member at the time your wife disappeared?"

"Yes, he sure was," Campbell said. "But I don't have any reason to think he and Janice were more than acquaintances. I thought about him but couldn't connect any dots."

"Did you know anything about Simmons, personally," Bert asked. "What kind of man was he?"

Don again answered without hesitation. He'd done his homework. "He was pretty much a prick. Had a reputation for a quick and bad temper; driven to always be in the limelight where golfing was concerned. I didn't trust him any further than I could throw him. At church he was a model parishioner; they all loved him. But if you were around him at the course, you got a different picture."

"Uh huh," Bert said. "Didn't see any of that in the report on Vicki. How is your son doing? I've heard he was having some problems."

"He's finally better the last few years," Don said. "For the longest time, he was very introverted and quiet. Bringing him here and getting him into a new culture with new friends finally started to bring him out of his shell."

"Do you think your son would be willing to talk with me some time," Bert asked.

"I don't know. You'd just have to ask him," Don said. "I'll give you his cell number before you go. I'll have to tell him to expect you because he doesn't answer unknown calls. He works during the day, too."

Bert couldn't think of any other questions now, so he said thanks and good-bye to Janice's widower. He could tell that their conversation had rekindled some old memories and opened old partially healed wounds in the man. Bert felt bad about that.

He leaned back in the motel desk chair and gazed longingly at his wife. She sat on the bed with her back to the headboard, her red hair shining with a beautiful luster. She smiled the beautiful smile which first captured his heart years earlier. Not even the blowing snow outside the motel room window could put a chill on her spirit. "What do you think about that call?" he asked her.

"It sure makes you wonder about the golfer boy, Simmons. He might not be the saint we first thought. Could he be behind both murders, Bert?"

"What if he's behind three murders? Maybe Father DelFranco was suspecting him and Simmons killed him out in Boise to silence him. But then again, we don't know that DelFranco was killed. We're being told unusual cause."

"Bert, I'm not sensing Simmons when I focus on the two women. What you say is a possibility, but I'm just not getting that vibe. Not yet, anyway. These things have a way of developing over time so I can't say this with certainty."

"Okay, Love," he said. "Then let's focus on the Father and see what Becky can find out for us. Before we leave Simmons, though, let's review what we know. First, he was a member of the church during the time both women were members. We know that he even dated Vicki and he was well liked by church members. We've been told that he had a bad temper and was very competitive. His alibi is suspect, according to Janice's husband. This because he had connections to the police chief by marriage. The fact is that Kansas City is less than a three-hour drive from Nebraska City. He could easily have made that round trip the day Vicki disappeared. She disappeared sometime that afternoon and her car was at a golf course. This seems to indicate she was meeting up with someone who golfed. Janice's car was found at a different golf course. These prove nothing, but they sure make him seem like a logical suspect."

"Logically I agree, but I still don't have the feeling that he's the killer, Sweetheart," she reiterated.

"Then we won't rule him out, but we won't spend much time on him unless something else comes up."

They decided to spend the rest of the day going back over the police report and getting hold of Dori, the teen medium. Perhaps she'd be able to get more information from Janice's spirit. By later this afternoon, the storm should be largely past and the roads well on the way to being opened. Tomorrow, they figured on visiting the church again, getting back with the phone company, and perhaps talking with Patty. Somehow, they had to figure out who killed Vicki and Janice, where their bodies were hidden, or both.

Bert first took Missy back out into the storm, which was subsiding in its fury a little bit. It still cut their walk short, but she relieved herself, which was the main objective. After that, he made his calls, opened the report, and began the tedious work of going over it again with Norah. Perhaps they missed something the first time. The day wore on and the storm slowly wore itself out as it continued east.

CHAPTER ELEVEN: SEEKING CLUES

Becky entered the Coldsmoke Coffee House a few minutes before 8:00 on Thursday morning. Pastor Marvin Finegan was already at a table and he motioned for her to join him. He was a somewhat tall and good-looking man, just as Lizzie had said. They had their introductions and ordered coffee.

"Well, what's up, Miss Thompson?" he asked.

"Just call me Becky," she said. "You used to be a minister over in Red Lodge. Right?"

"Yes. Why?"

"You must have been a good one; and popular," she said. "A guy, who wants to remain behind the scenes right now, knew I was coming through here and was wondering if you'd consider returning there. I think he's on a board trying to find candidates."

He shifted in his seat and sipped his coffee before answering. "No, I don't think so. I'm flattered that anyone would want me back there, though."

"Are you married?" Becky asked. "Is that because of family?"

"Yes, kind of. We have a four-year-old child and would not want to uproot from Bozeman. We've settled into this community, my wife is from here, and our daughter is in a wonderful daycare facility."

"I understand," she said. "So, you're settled and happy in Bozeman and there's really nothing to pull you back to Red Lodge."

He smiled at her. "Yes, Becky. When I left Red Lodge, I had personal reasons and do not intend to go back there, even to visit."

"Bad blood there. I understand that."

He became serious. "Not bad blood just made some errors in judgment and want to keep them behind me. I want to stay focused on my ministry here and on my wife and daughter. Please don't tell them that. Just say that I'm very happy here and don't want to leave. I do appreciate being considered, though."

Becky had her answers. He apparently didn't know about Summer and had no interest in finding out. "Well, sir, I sure appreciate all that and will relay your desires. Thanks for meeting with me and for the coffee. I do have to be going. I'm trying to be in Boise before dark. Better say good-bye."

As she guided her Dodge truck on the road to Boise, with the sun to her back in the southeastern sky and blue sky and mountains ahead of her, she thought about the meeting. On the one hand, she felt she could rule out Finegan as wanting to know about Lizzie or any child she had. On the other hand, though, she had a growing unease. If Finegan wasn't behind the strange surveillance, then who was?

During the remaining seven hours drive to Boise, Becky continued to ponder that troubling question. Was she misreading the apparent surveillance and was there another, innocent, explanation for it? If it was a surveillance, she'd assumed it was on Lizzie's family, Summer in particular. What if there was another purpose? Could they be gathering information on herself, and not on Summer. If so, who would be interested in me, she thought to herself.

By the time she was closing in on Boise, she was arriving at another disturbing possibility. When she divorced her abusive husband, he had tried to act all apologetic and remorseful. She knew it was an act, and knew he was mad as hell. That was one of the reasons she left the area and pursued a career as a private investigator. She was afraid of him and wanted to get as far from him as possible. Was he jealous and vindictive enough to have her followed? To try to get even. As she drove the last few miles into Boise and looked for a motel, she knew the answer was yes. She knew that she had better be extra vigilant from now on.

That evening, Becky had her daily call with Bert and Norah. Besides getting the Boise contact numbers for Father Stewart and Sister Frances, she brought up her concerns about the mysterious P.I. who might be surveilling her. They became instantly serious and Norah relayed that she was getting a bad feeling about that. Nothing specific, Bert said, but when Norah received an impression about something, it was worth considering. Bert reviewed his questions about Father DelFranco. Then they ended the call. Becky called the phone numbers for the Boise contacts, but it was after hours and she could only leave a message. She'd have to call first thing in the morning.

In keeping with Bert and Norah's tradition, Becky began to research Boise and glean some facts about her host city. The popular mountain city was close to all things natural and was a tourist destination known for its many attractions, including skiing. Its population of about 220,000, included a large Basque community, and the town square was often the center of their very colorful and fun dances. At an elevation of almost 3000 feet, it had a moderate climate. She knew she could expect the average winter nighttime temperature to be in the mid-twenties and daytime highs in the forties. A man named Spalding had introduced Idaho to the potato, for which the state had become famous. The mountain bluebird, appaloosa horse, and cutthroat trout were all state symbols. Boise State University was known as a research university and the Broncos were a football powerhouse. Founded in 1932 by the Episcopal Church, it now had a student population of over 25,000.

Satisfied with her new knowledge of her surroundings, Becky turned off the light near her motel bed and closed out the day. The next day would bring new challenges in helping gather information for her boss.

* * *

Bert and Norah looked out their Nebraska City motel room window at the first rays of sun peeking through the departing clouds stretching toward the eastern horizon. Through the partly cloudy sky overhead, small patches of blue sky were becoming visible. It would still be a few hours for the road crews to finish plowing out the streets and roads, but this Thursday morning gave promise to a fairly nice day.

Bert took Missy out for her beloved morning walk to their favorite field south of town. The snow had stopped during the night and there was only a light wind now, although it was still a chilly fourteen degrees. She barely noticed the cold, it seemed, with her thick winter coat. Bert thought she practically smiled as she ran around the field, bounding in and out of the drifts.

After returning to the motel and having coffee while talking with Norah, they decided to call Gennie and see if she'd had any luck with church phone records. Gennie said she might have some good news. At the request of area churches, their phone records were maintained for ten years. She would pull up the five lines for the Holy Mother church and see if she could correlate any calls with the pay phone on the day Vicki disappeared. Bert thanked her profusely and gave the good news to Norah. Maybe they were finally going to get somewhere with the phone issue.

Next he called teenager Dori and chatted with her a few minutes. Her school was cancelled for the morning, so she had a little time. He told her about his concerns with Janice Campbell's spirit and asked if she'd continue trying to communicate with her some more and try to find out any additional information. Dori agreed and said she'd drive over to the church as soon as the roads were cleared this morning.

He then called Robert and gave him an update on the case, even though they didn't have much more concrete information to go on. He asked if his mother had much interaction with Father DelFranco. Robert was quiet for a while and finally said that she didn't as far as he knew. He said he really couldn't remember much about any of that. It made him uncomfortable and Bert could tell he was anxious to get off the phone.

With this all done, he asked Norah if she was ready to stroll around the church grounds. She was, so they loaded Missy and drove the few miles to the Holy Mother Church. There were two to four-foot drifts along the sides of the road and streets, but they were mostly well cleared. Nebraskans knew how to deal with snow.

As for snow, the church grounds were covered with an average of nearly a foot of snow from the storm, and drifts made it more or less deep. They knew Missy wouldn't mind the snow and drifts since they were like a playground for her. They began a slow but methodical walk through the snow around the grounds, looking for anything that might be a clue.

Many of the shrubs and trees were evergreens, probably obtained from the Arbor Day Foundation, which was just a few miles up the road. Bert and Norah could tell that much of the landscaping and greenery were around five or six years old, in keeping with when the updates were made. Nothing stood out at all.

Bert Paused to look at the groundskeeper building. It was a

nicely painted, wood-frame, building about ten by twelve feet dimension. It was nearly hidden by the shrubbery planted neatly around it, as if to make it less conspicuous. Above the double doors was a brightly colored sign, stained wood with dark green letters. It read "Saint Brigit." They found it interesting that a groundskeeper shed would be named for a saint. This was the Catholic Church, though. They continued walking around the church itself, admiring both the architecture and the shrubbery.

Before they left, Bert stopped by the church office to say hello. A different lady was the volunteer secretary at that time. The middle-aged woman, named Tamara, was a very cheerful sort, and she greeted Bert warmly. She had been volunteering there for many years, she told him.

"May I ask you about the renovation that took place a few years ago?" he asked her.

She nodded in agreement.

"I find it unusual for a groundskeeper shed to be named after a saint. Do you know any of the history behind that?"

"All I know is that Father DelFranco wanted that name fixed to the shed. I think he found it amusing or something. For some reason he thought that was appropriate."

Bert pondered her words for a minute. "Okay, that's very interesting. Thanks for your time, Ma'am."

As they departed the church and were returning to the doghouse, they saw Dori as she was getting out of her car. They walked over to her and greeted her. She said she was just getting there to see if she could contact Janice's spirit.

"I see you've been over to the caretaker shed, judging by the tracks. You're the only one on the grounds today." Dori laughed.

Bert replied, "Yeah, we just wandered around there."

"Did you happen to see Janice around there?" Dori asked. "I sometimes see her hanging around there as well as by the side door or inside the church around the altar."

"No, sure haven't seen her at all today," Bert said as he contemplated Dori's words. "So, you often see her by that shed?"

"Yes, occasionally she's just hanging around the shed, kinda looking lost. Of course, she kinda looks lost all the time," Dori sighed.

Bert's mind was processing the growing list of questions. He needed to go back inside the church and ask a favor of the secretary, Tamara. He wished Dori luck on her attempt to reach out to Janice and said he'd check with her later to see if she had any success.

He and Norah went back into the church and located the

secretary, who had stepped out into the events room. Bert asked her if she happened to have a key to the shed and if she'd be okay with taking him out to look inside.

Tamara retrieved the key from a lockbox in the office and escorted Bert to the shed. He apologized to her for making her go out into the cold and snow. She laughed it off and said she didn't mind at all. She unlocked the door and stepped aside.

Inside it was well organized with rakes, hoes, shovels, loppers, and so forth hanging neatly from hooks on the walls. A riding lawn mower took up the lion's share of the floor space. The floor was made of poured cement, which looked professionally done. It was just a well arranged shed, nothing else stood out to him.

After they got back to the doghouse and were driving away, Norah finally spoke. "Honey, I didn't see anything there of note. However, I had this strange sense of dread come over me. I feel the shed has a connection to at least Janice. Maybe she was killed there, and her body taken someplace to be hidden."

"At this point, anything seems possible, Norah," he said. "That could explain why her spirit is hanging around here occasionally. But it doesn't get us much closer to finding either or both."

"Bert, I'm seeing that portal thing again. It's both strange and sinister. I have no idea what to make of it, Sweetheart, but it kinda scares me."

He could feel her fear. "The way you describe it, it does seem very sinister and threatening, Honey. Perhaps it's ..." He was interrupted by the ringing of his phone.

After a brief call with Gennie, the phone company clerk, he looked at Norah and brought her up to speed. Gennie had found a record of a call made by someone from the pay phone by the Buck Snort Bar at 12:42 p.m. on the day Vicki disappeared. The call went to the office at the Holy Mother Catholic Church.

"We can't prove that Vicki made that call, Honey, but it sure makes it more plausible that she called someone at the church during her lunch with her son. Where there's smoke, there may be fire, and this seems to establish a link between her disappearance and the church. The question is, who did she call there?" He stopped the car in front of their motel and turned off the ignition.

"Bert, my understanding is that someone is available at the office during normal business hours. When a volunteer or secretary isn't available, then one of the nuns, the Mother Superior, or even the Father may have to sit in at times."

"That's how I understood it as well, Sweetheart. I doubt there is any way to know who was at that phone on the day Vicki vanished."

Norah answered with her usual wisdom. "You're probably right about that, Honey. However, I think we can assume that the person she talked with had some connection with her apparent death."

"Good assumption, babe, however, the connection doesn't necessarily have to be direct involvement. Perhaps the call just confirmed that someone else, even a volunteer, was there at that time. The person answering the call may not have had any idea of the significance."

"You're right, Bert, but my theory is more likely." She smiled that big smile which always made him give in.

"Something else keeps nagging at me, Honey," he said. "Maybe it's nothing, but why name a maintenance shed after a saint?"

They were back in the motel room and Norah had taken her usual place near the head of the bed. She pulled up her legs and placed her arms around her knees, a favorite position for thinking. "Bert, I don't know anything about Saint Bridgit. Maybe you can find something online."

He agreed and began to search for information about the Celtic Deity, who was also known by several names, including Brigit, Brigid, Brigitta, and Brigantia. Her former Pagan tie is evidenced by her feast day of February 1st, the date of the Pagan festival of Imbolc, when the ewes begin to give their milk. She was considered in Scottish lore as the midwife of the Virgin Mary. Numerous holy wells were dedicated to her. She was known in Roman times as the Nymph Goddess, and several rivers in Britain and Ireland are named after her.

"So, what does any of that have to do with a maintenance shed?" Norah asked.

"That's the question, isn't it," he said. "I wonder who knows more of the history about that shed? Tamara said she'd been volunteering at the church for many years. Maybe there's more to that than meets the eye. Perhaps she knows something. Patty might know some of the history, also. Maybe we should have lunch with her."

Norah's red hair shimmered as she nodded in agreement and gave him that big smile which always melted his heart. Thank God, he thought to himself, that her spirit possessed the best of the living person's personality and characteristics. It was easy to stay in love with her, in both dimensions. He called Patty and arranged to meet her for lunch at Johnny's Corner Café.

Following another brief walk for Missy around the motel and the short drive downtown to the café, Bert, with Norah beside him, walked up to the table where Patty was already waiting. Greeting her with a hug, he sat, ordered, and began talking with her.

Patty said she'd never been to the site of the shed before but was aware of some kind of wooden structure there before the current shed was built. It was kind of like a platform of some kind, she told him. She'd just had glimpses of it from a distance, during the few times she walked on the grounds. It was somewhat overgrown with bushes at that time and was hard to see much. She hadn't found it very interesting. The new shed with its accompanying new shrubbery was much prettier and more enchanting, she thought.

They finished the nice lunch, with some discussion about the town and area. Bert was always interested in the places he traveled through. She told him she had to go see Bobby Boy that afternoon. It was something she felt she had to keep doing for Vicki.

"Bobby Boy," Bert repeated. "Was that a pet name that Vicki had for him? I heard you use it the other day, too."

"Oh, yes," she said, "Vicki used that nickname a lot when it was just the two of them, and sometimes when I was around. He kind of liked it, I think."

"Okay, interesting how pet names come about. You could probably write a book about that subject if so inclined. However, we, I mean I, need to go. I have some other things to check into. I also need to talk with our other investigator out in Idaho. By the way, we've confirmed that a call, most likely from Vicki, was made to the church during lunch with Robert on the day Vicki vanished. Any idea who she might have spoken with?"

"Oh, really! That's an interesting development, isn't it?" she replied. "No, but it would most likely be one of only a handful of people who would be at those phones. Sometimes, volunteers would man the office phone, but the church staff mostly answered the other lines."

"Who were the volunteers, usually?" he asked. "Did any of the men volunteer to help in the office?"

"Oh, Bert, you know men. Not many offered to help there. They'd rather help with lawn work. A couple did help inside a few times, including the guy Vicki dated, Simmons. In fact, I think that's how they met. She stopped in the office on a rare day when he was answering the phone."

"Okay, well that adds another element to the puzzle. So, it's possible that Vicki might have called to talk with Simmons if she knew he was at the office. Her cell phone was apparently dead that day during lunch, according to Robert."

"That would be possible," Patty returned, "but wasn't he at a golf tournament in KC?"

"Oh, that's right. I forgot that for a minute. So, unless he drove back to the church from KC for some reason, he would not have been volunteering there. Maybe he just stopped in and just happened to answer that call, since he was used to helping out sometimes."

Bert looked at Norah, and knew they were both thinking the same thing. There were a lot of maybe's in there and not many certainties. He thanked Patty for her time and information, and they all left the diner.

As they drove back toward the church, Bert called the office there. Another volunteer was working now instead of Tamara. This woman was about forty, her name was Susan, and she was very talkative. She seemed to be a ball of fire and said she'd been a member of the church since it was first opened. She was very happy to talk with him when he got there.

After they drove up and parked the doghouse, Bert was again taken by the stunning architecture of the church as he walked inside to the office. He introduced himself to Susan. She leaned forward on the desk, seemingly anxious to answer any questions. He told her he only had one question at the present time. What was the history of the groundskeeper shed?

"When I first came to the church," Susan told him, "there was only a wooden platform about the size of your average bed. It was weathered as if it'd been there for a number of years. I never saw under it, but I've been told that it was a cover over an old hand-dug well, what's often called an artesian well. Apparently it was covered to keep anyone, especially children, from falling in."

"So, if I'm getting this correct, then, Susan, the old well and cover were embedded in the cement floor of the maintenance shed."

"Yes, Bert, you're correct. When the renovation took place

and a decision made to have a maintenance or groundskeeper shed, it seemed logical to just eliminate the issue of the old well by cementing it into the floor."

He recalled his visit to the shed. "That explains why the foundation and floor sit about a foot or more high and there's a concrete ramp leading up to the double doors. The well covering necessitated that thickness of concrete to fully encapsulate it."

"You're right about that, Bert," she said. Father DelFranco insisted upon that design to ensure that no accident ever occurred with the old well. Nobody knew for sure how deep it was. They only knew that it contained water of an unknown depth."

Bert's thoughts were racing as he thanked Susan for her time and returned to Norah and Missy in the doghouse.

It was getting late and the sun was dropping below the western horizon. As he drove toward the motel, he looked longingly and lovingly at Norah, her spirit silhouetted against the darkening landscape. "We have some answers, my Love."

She'd been waiting for him to speak. "I knew you had something to tell me, once you were ready."

"Brigit is associated with water, my Love, and she is supposed to have blessed holy wells. There is an old well under the floor of that building, covered over by inches of concrete flooring,

probably reinforced with steel rebar.
The name now makes sense."

"Bert, every time I get around the church now, I'm seeing the portal vision. What if I'm seeing that well, as if looking down into it from above? If that's it, what is it telling me, Honey?"

"Honey, what if we're not looking at a murder here. What if one of these women fell through the old, rotting, cover. To an untrained observer, it might have just looked like the cover collapsed, which led to the eventual decision to bury it in concrete. It seems very unlikely, but what if the same fate befell both women."

She considered that for a while. Eventually she said, "I suppose anything is possible, Bert. However, my sense is that their disappearance was not by accident. How do you explain the angry moodiness exhibited by both victims for months before they died? No, I feel they were killed.

He added one more thought. "We've only seen the spirit of Janice Campbell around here. Same with Dori. So, if anyone was killed at the well or is somehow in the well, it is probably her."

"That makes perfect sense, Honey, except I keep having visions which seem to link them together. Not necessarily as friends, but as victims."

They arrived back at their motel. There was much on their minds. If the old well held clues or a body, how would they convince the authorities or the church to tear down the shed and destroy the floor. Bert took Missy out for a bedtime walk. As he turned up his coat collar against the January chill of a moonlit night's breeze, he pondered that question. It was the same challenge they always had, not only with psychic evidence, but evidence from the spirit of the psychic. As with the other cases they'd worked, they just had to find the way.

Back at the motel, he and Norah talked for a while, watching Missy's usual bedtime antics. She moved from the bathroom floor, to in front of the door, and eventually settled down in her favorite place in front of the window. She only settled down to curl into a ball after doing her spin move a dozen times. It always made her human companions chuckle. They smiled at each other as Bert climbed under the bed covers.

"Good night, my Love," he said. "I'll see you in the morning and someday on the other side. I love you, Norah. I'd be lost without you."

She smiled her devilish smile. "Honey, you are lost without me. But I'm here to keep you on the path, Sweetheart. I love you, my captain."

Bert turned out the light as a tear trickled down his cheek. His life was like a mirror. He could see the image of what he wanted; but he could never reach through and touch her.

CHAPTER TWELVE: FRIDAY

Friday morning was crisp, clear, and cold as the sun rose with a crimson brilliance over the eastern mountains of the Sawtooth National Forest and on toward Yellowstone Park. It promised to be a beautiful January day in southern Idaho. Becky was up and having coffee and breakfast in the motel dining area as she began to call the church to make her appointments. She would be meeting first with Sister Frances at ten, and eleven with Father Stewart. After that, it all depended upon how those meetings went.

While waiting for the first appointment, she went first to the newspaper office and asked for help in finding articles about DelFranco's death. She found three articles which referenced his unusual death. One in particular caught her attention, because it talked about how his body had been found by the church staff and moved to a bed in the house he was provided. She closed the article and left for her first appointment, wondering as she drove why it was necessary to move him.

Becky arrived at the Catholic church and introduced herself to the current church secretary, an elderly woman named Mrs. Talbert. She visited with the lady while waiting for Sister Frances to return to the office. There was an almost instant connection with Mrs. Talbert and Becky liked her from the first hello. They were having a lively discussion about all manner of things related to Boise when Sister Frances returned. Excusing herself to Mrs. Talbert, Becky turned her attention to the Sister and exchanged introductions.

Sister Frances was a middle-aged, friendly, yet stern woman.

She was short and a little on the chubby side but seemed like a ball of fire when it came to managing her business at the church. Becky liked her, yet she felt a sense of caution or maybe a little distrust. She explained her purpose in being there and asked if the Sister could shed any light on Father DelFranco's death.

"Oh, it was very unfortunate," the Sister said. "The poor Father got his medication mixed up it seems and had an adverse reaction. At least his death seemed to have been peaceful."

"Why do you say that?" Becky asked. Was he found lying on the bed or couch?"

"Yes, he seemed to die peacefully," Sister Frances replied. "He was a good man and a fine example of a Godly man. We've missed him terribly."

"May I ask who found him, Sister," said Becky.

Sister Frances quickly answered, "One of our volunteers, a young man who was helping take care of the Father's residence, was concerned about him and went to check. He said he found the Father and didn't know if he was unconscious or dead. He came to the office and told me, so I hurried down to the residence to make sure the Father was presentable and called 911 for the ambulance."

"Was he not presentable, Sister?" asked Becky.

The nun was slow to respond. Finally, she said, "Miss Thompson, the Father had just returned from a shower and was nearly nude at the edge of his bed. He had slumped down on the bed. So, I felt the Lord telling me to make him presentable before the responders arrived. We didn't want his death to be embarrassing to him or his position in the Church."

"Oh, I see," said Becky. "What condition was he being treated for, Sister?"

"He wasn't actually being treated for anything, but the poor man suffered from joint pain from his years of running, I think. He took herbal supplements and aspirin daily to help ease the pain."

Becky knew that many people handled their pain the same way, to avoid prescription pain meds. "I guess the autopsy showed that, then?"

The Sister responded in a firm voice. "We asked them not to do an autopsy. There was no reason to defame the body of such a man of God. The coroner agreed."

"Then I suppose that Father Stewart was called in on rather short notice to replace Father DelFranco?" Becky surmised.

"Yes," the Sister said. "He came as a temporary priest but decided to stay here. He fell in love with the area. Speaking of Father Stewart, I believe he's here and ready to talk with you also."

Becky was introduced to Father Stewart, and Sister Frances left the office to make her rounds of the church. The Father seemed like a very personable yet strong man. It didn't take long for her to see that he was a man driven for greater things. He didn't have anything to add to what Sister Frances had said. It was obvious that his information largely came from what she told him. What he did mention, though, was his ambition to move up in the ranks of the Catholic Church. It wasn't lost on Becky when he said that Sister Frances also was moving on to the diocese as soon as it could be arranged.

The Father said that he needed to go as one of the parishioners was having problems and needed his counsel. Becky told him good-bye and thanks for taking the time to meet with her. She paused after he left to resume the discussion with Mrs. Talbert, who had been in the office the entire time.

They continued to discuss some of the history and people of Boise. Becky asked her how long she'd been acting as a church secretary.

"I think about six years, now," Mrs. Talbert answered. "I was here during the last year or so of Father DelFranco's tenure."

"So, you knew Father DelFranco, then, reasonably well. Was he a good match for the church here?"

Mrs. Talbert looked around and, seeing nobody else within earshot, leaned toward Becky and said, "I don't think he really liked being here. He never seemed very happy to me."

"Oh really," said Becky. "That seems to run counter to what others are saying.

"Yes, well other people have their own reasons for reading things into other people that really aren't there." She gave a wink of understanding toward Becky.

"You're saying that the Church tends to protect its own interests," she said.

"You're right about that, Becky." Mrs. Talbert again looked through the window in the door to the office. Nobody was outside or in sight. "Becky, they aren't completely leveling with you about what happened to DelFranco."

"You know, ma'am, I kinda felt that. It felt like they might be leaving something out. Could you talk with me now? Or would you be able to meet for lunch in a few minutes and discuss it?"

Mrs. Talbert straightened up and said that she'd be taking a lunch break in about fifteen minutes and she'd love to share it with Becky. She said with a big smile that the Cheesecake Factory was a good, and tasty, place for lunch.

Becky thanked her for the offer and left the church quickly.

She did not want to cause any problems for this lady. She used her phone's mapping application to locate the Cheesecake Factory and drove there. She waited outside in her truck for Mrs. Talbert. Her instincts were apparently correct about the woman.

She greeted Mrs. Talbert again when she arrived a few minutes later, and they went to a table in a back corner and ordered a light lunch, which, of course, would be topped off with cheesecake.

As they ate, Mrs. Talbert leaned toward Becky and said as quietly as she could that there were some things Becky should know. "For one," she said, "Sister Frances did make the Father presentable and did get him laid on his bed. I overheard enough of the discussion with the male volunteer to know that."

"Why did she feel compelled to do that, Mrs. Talbert?" asked Becky. "She could have gotten in trouble with the law for moving his body."

"Do you know the Catholic Church's position on suicide?" asked Mrs. Talbert.

"Oh yes, I've heard it clearly defined. It's strictly forbidden and a reason to lose one's grace," said Becky. Are you saying that he killed himself?"

The older lady didn't answer that. "Do you also know that

the Church tends to not air its dirty laundry in public. It keeps its secrets."

"Yes, I'm aware of that."

"Becky, the Church has always rewarded those who are team players for the Church."

"So personal ambition could play a part behind the protection of the Church's reputation?"

"Yes," Mrs. Talbert said. "Becky, Sister Frances brought back a handwritten note from Father DelFranco's residence that day. She meant to file it away, but a phone call interrupted her, and I happened to be working and to see it for just a few seconds. It was in the Father's handwriting."

"I'm listening, Mrs. Talbert," Becky answered. "What did it say?"

Talbert said in a hushed voice, "I'm very sorry. I can't live with this any longer. May God forgive me."

Becky leaned back in her chair and ate a couple more bites of her salad, thinking about what she'd been told. What exactly did the note mean, she wondered. What could he not live with? Painful joints, or something much worse? What did he want forgiven? His apparent suicide in the face of Church doctrine? Or had he done something terrible? The note raised more questions than it answered.

"What do you think he was referring to, Mrs. Talbert?" asked Becky.

"I don't know, Becky," she said. "From the time he arrived here two years earlier, he was often quiet and seemed distant. It was as if he carried a weight around his neck. When I asked him about it once, he just looked at me for a while and said that he would be coming for him. I assumed he meant that God would be coming for him."

"Could he have meant someone else, besides God, might be coming for him, Mrs. Talbert?"

The secretary mulled over that with a spoonful of cheesecake. "Well, I suppose so. I never thought about it, really. Why would anyone else be coming for a pastor?"

"I guess that's the $24,000 question, isn't it," Becky said. "Why do you think Sister Frances hid the note he left?"

"You hinted at it before," Mrs. Talbert said. "Primarily to protect the reputation of the Church and limit involvement with the authorities. Also, to eliminate serious speculation about a suicide motive. Perhaps most importantly, the Catholic Church rewards loyal servants, and Sister Frances has ambitions beyond just being at a lone church in Boise, Idaho."

"Hmm. Well, ma'am, you've given me a lot to think about and I appreciate all your time and answers to my questions. I'd better be going, but I can't thank you enough, Mrs. Talbert. I envy you for being able to live and work in such a beautiful part of the country. Boise seems like a marvelous little city."

Mrs. Talbert continued sitting for a few seconds. Finally, she told Becky she wanted to tell her something. "It has it's darker side, Becky. There was a terrible crime here just a few weeks ago. I was hesitant to tell you, but you should know that we also have crime. So far, it's unsolved. I get this feeling that you should know about it."

Becky settled back in her chair. "Okay, I'm listening. What happened?"

"A poor woman was found murdered several weeks ago and they have no suspect, yet. That's bad enough, Becky, but what's more disturbing is what we know about the manner of her torment and death. She was found tied between two pillars by her wrists at a residence in rural Boise."

Becky sat in shock. Finally, she asked, "You're saying she was tied with a rope by the wrists between two pillars at a residence and eventually died that way?"

"Yes, ma'am," said Mrs. Talbert. "She was apparently tormented and eventually killed and left in that position. The killers are still unknown."

Becky held back the tears as she thanked Mrs. Talbert for the information and told her she had to get going. Her head was filled with visions of Summer's drawing. Was the child seeing this crime before it even happened?

Becky bought the sweet little lady her lunch, and then they went their respective ways. She was feeling the burn to get back to her Red Lodge case, so decided to drive part of the way the rest of the afternoon. She could be back on the case by early afternoon the next day. She set her sights on Whitehall, Montana, for the night. This small community of just over a thousand people sat along Interstate 90, roughly halfway back to Red Lodge. It would be as good a place as any to spend a quiet night and reflect upon the information she'd gathered.

While she was driving, she would call Bert and Norah and discuss the puzzling mix of information she'd obtained.

* * *

Friday morning in Nebraska City was clear and very cold. As he walked Missy in the five-degree temperature, Bert's mind was occupied by the previous day's revelations and questions. Were they closing in on at least one of the murders? Was the well just an irrelevant coincidence? Perhaps one or both women were killed in the relative seclusion of that spot but transported somewhere else. Someplace where they'd maybe never be found. Perhaps one or both bodies were in that well. How do we find out, he wondered?

Back at the motel, he discussed the questions and options with

Norah. They agreed on a plan to get to the answers. It would start with their client, Robert.

Upon reaching Robert, Bert arranged to meet him back at the Buck Snort café, perhaps a fitting place to discuss his help. Robert seemed anxious to find out where the investigation was taking them. They would meet there as soon as it opened at 11 a.m.

While waiting, Bert tracked down and called the main investigator for Vicki's case. Detective Bryan Louden was still on the force in Nebraska City, a little to Bert's surprise. He was skeptical at first when Bert explained his role in looking into the cold case for the victim's son. However, as they talked, the detective seemed to warm up to Bert and began to open to the idea of meeting. Bert told him he'd like to meet soon, possibly Saturday, and bring him up to date with their investigation findings. Bert knew he would eventually need the man's help if they were to prove or disprove the growing suspicions. They tentatively arranged to meet Saturday morning for breakfast.

Next, he called the church and made an appointment to meet with Father Romero at four in the afternoon. For the plan to work, he would need the Father's support.

With the wheels set in motion, he and Norah discussed Missy. Could her nose become a key factor in solving the case?

"Norah, we both know that Missy can sense your presence,"

he said. Do you think she can pick up your scent even now, or is it a sixth sense?"

It was a bit of an awkward topic, but Norah replied, "I'm not sure which, Darling, but it's one of those."

"We know that people report all manner of manifestations from spirits, Honey," he said. "Many feel a chill in the presence of a spirit, some report smelling things such as cigar smoke, others hear sounds or feel the presence."

She knew where he was going with that. "So, Bert, you're wondering if Missy might be able to somehow track either of those women, despite the many years since they were killed."

"Yes, Sweetheart, I wonder if it's possible. There's only one way to find out, I guess, and that's to just see. I wonder if Dori might be available this afternoon at four to meet with Father Romero, also. Her gift, along with being a local girl, might give us a convincing edge." Norah's nod of understanding was all he needed. He called and spoke to Dori.

"She's good with meeting then," he told Norah. "Fact is, she's totally excited about helping with this."

Bert leaned back against the motel desk, facing Norah, and checked the time. If they left now, they could be a few minutes early for the meeting with Robert, but early was good. They were both anxious to get moving. He gathered Missy and got her excitement contained enough to get her in the back of the doghouse. She seemed to sense a growing excitement. It made her excited, too.

After the ten-minute drive, they arrived at the café to find that Robert was already there, waiting outside. He waved for Bert to get in his car and they sat there rather than going into the bar. It was as good a place as any. Bert briefed his client on the status of the case and the questions they now needed to find answers to. The young man was guardedly less timid as he agreed to meet at the church at 4 p.m.

Bert realized he hadn't even eaten yet, so invited Robert to have a burger with him inside the tavern. They just sat and talked about unrelated things while they each ate the hamburger plate special. Bert felt that he should just help Robert relax rather than continue to fill him with information. Norah remained in the vehicle with Missy, keeping her company. It was true, Missy did sense her presence.

After the lunch, Bert and team returned to the motel. He made one more call, this time to Terry Campbell. Mr. Campbell had evidently alerted his son to the possibility of a call, because Terry answered quickly. After the usual introductions and explanation for his call, Bert proceeded to discuss the case with the son of the first victim.

"Terry, it sounds like you had it pretty rough for a long time, but you're doing well now. I'm glad to hear that," Bert said.

"Yes, sir," the young man said. "I had some very bad years before and after mom vanished."

Bert acted upon a feeling. "Terry, you said you had some bad years before she disappeared. Do you remember about when those bad times began?"

"I think I was probably about eight, so that would be around twelve years ago," he said.

Bert asked, "What was going on in your life at that time? Was there anything significant which caused or added to the troubles for you?"

Terry was silent on the phone for an uncomfortably long time. Bert was beginning to wish he hadn't asked the question. Finally, Terry replied. "Mr. Lynnes, I don't remember a lot about that time. Maybe I just want to forget it. I can't really say what bothered me, it was just a bad time of my life. I've tried hard to just put it all behind me since we moved here to Salt Lake City."

Bert sensed the lad's reluctance and knew he couldn't press. "Oh, no problem, Terry. I'm just trying to understand the situation. The more I know, maybe the closer I'll be to figuring out what happened to Vicki, and maybe your mother, too."

"That's okay, Mr. Lynnes, Bert, I understand you're just doing your job. You know, it's taken me about ten years to get to the point that I can put all of that behind me. I'll always miss mom, but I want to forget everything else."

"Terry, I'm sure she was a good mother and would be with you if she could. Whatever happened was beyond her ability to control."

"Yeah, once she knew, she tried to control it. But she couldn't. I know she loved me and wanted the best for me."

"So, there was something that she found out?" he asked.

Terry seemed to be nervously moving around with his phone. Bert began to wonder if he was coming back. At last, the young man responded. "Yes, Mr. Lynnes, I was one of the altar boys for the two years before she disappeared."

Bert digested the words carefully. "Okay, son, that's very admirable of you. Why is that important to her disappearance, though?"

Once again, a long pause. When he finally spoke, Terry sounded very emotional, "Mr. Lynnes, I've never told anyone that, not even my dad. I don't think anyone would understand."

A growing realization was forming in Bert's mind. He was beginning to understand. "Terry, some might not try to understand you, but I'm paid to understand. It's my job and duty to try to feel what you're feeling."

Terry's voice was breaking and interrupted by effort to contain his emotion and sobs. "Sir, I was raped at the church, many times. I didn't know what to do about it. I didn't think I could even say anything to mom or dad, because nobody would believe me."

Bert was shocked by what he'd just heard, but it did not surprise him. That thought had been slowly taking shape for some time. He suspected that it could explain Robert's weird behavior, too.

"Your mother must have found out or at least suspected that," he said to Terry.

"I think so," Terry answered, "she even asked me if anything unusual was going on. But I just couldn't tell her, Sir. I didn't think even she could understand and believe me."

"Why wouldn't anyone believe you, Terry? Why not your mother?"

"Because of who it was," he replied.

"It was someone who was well known and respected in the church, wasn't it, Terry," Bert said.

"Yes."

"Was it Father DelFranco, Terry?"

"Yes."

Bert bit his lip to hold back the tears that were welling in his eyes. His heart went out to this boy, and to the years of isolated torment he had endured. Drawing a deep breath, he got in control of his emotion and asked another question. "Terry, if your mother suspected something, do you think she confronted the Father about her suspicions?"

Terry seemed to be pulling his own emotions back. "I don't know, sir. I know she was becoming quiet and almost angry for several weeks before she left us. I don't think she knew what to do, either. I couldn't tell her, and she wasn't sure."

Bert drew another long breath, again to maintain control of his feelings. "Terry, I admire the courage it took just now to tell me this. I won't violate your trust with this knowledge. Just know that it might help us solve one or both cases. It might help us find your mother, so you've done the right thing. I would encourage you to talk to your dad about this, son. I get the feeling that he's able to understand you. I need to go now but take care of yourself. I think you'll find that a big weight has been lifted by talking about this."

They ended the call, and Bert looked at Norah. The tears in her eyes told him that she had heard it all.

"I just realized in my vision from the church altar, that in the front row are seated two boys, wearing the robes of altar boys. They were in my vision all along, but I didn't know what I was

239

seeing, Bert."

"Two boys?" he asked.

"Yes, Honey, two boys. I feel like the second boy is Robert. I'm sensing they were both victimized."

* * *

Becky called about 3:00 that afternoon, as Bert, Norah, and Missy were getting ready for their meeting at the church with Father Romero. Both Bert and Norah listened with great interest as Becky brought them up to speed on her meetings with Pastor Finegan, Sister Frances, Father Stewart, and Mrs. Talbert.

When Bert told her the new revelation about Father DelFranco, she decided to pull off the road. She wanted to focus on the discussion and she didn't want to risk outrunning her cell phone reception.

"Oh my," she said. "His apparent suicide makes more sense now if he was raping altar boys and feeling guilty about it. But what about the mothers, Bert, what happened to them?" Do you think he might have hired someone, like that Simmons guy, to silence them?"

"That's a possibility that I hadn't really considered," he told her. We just don't know at this time. There's some reason to suspect that well on the church property, but we have nothing solid to go on."

Becky then asked, "Any suggestions about the apparent surveillance going on here? I'm convinced that Mr. Finegan doesn't care to know and isn't behind it. So, if it isn't being conducted on Summer or Lizzie, then I'm the only other option, I think. In that case, it would likely be my ex who's behind it."

"I suppose you could just confront him and ask," Bert suggested. "But if you don't want to do that, then see if you can get the license plate number and I'll run it. If we find out who has the truck, we can probably figure out the rest."

"I'll try to get the plate, boss, because I have no desire to talk with my ex. I don't want him to know anything about me, either. Does Norah still not think that Summer could be psychic? It just seems uncanny that her one drawing so closely depicts the murder in Boise."

Bert looked to Norah for her answer. She slowly shook her head but also mouthed, "I don't really know, but I don't sense that." He relayed that to Becky.

"The child is just too purposeful about her drawings, Bert, they have to mean something. If Summer isn't psychic and the Boise killing is purely coincidental, then what else can it be?"

"I don't know, Becky, but we think you're doing the right approach, just slowly drawing it out of Summer. Asking for more details. Since we have so many church connections to our cases, maybe you could go online and start going over church pictures with her. Perhaps something in the architecture or scene will relate to her and help her be more explicit."

Becky agreed. "That's a great idea, guys. Soon as I'm back tomorrow, I'll start searching for churches to review with her. If she is psychic, maybe she's channeling another church or parishioner, somewhere. It's worth a shot."

"Sounds great, Becky. I guess we'd better be getting off to our meeting with the Father here. Drive safely to Whitehall tonight and on to Red Lodge tomorrow."

They ended the call as Becky got back on the road and Bert loaded Missy in the doghouse and they pulled away from the motel. They reviewed their notes again as they drove the ten-minute drive to the Holy Mother Church.

Upon arriving at the church, they saw that Dori was already there. She got out of her car and came over to talk with them. Bert explained the situation and that it would probably be hard to convince Father Romero of the evidence which pointed to the well. He told her that her credibility as a member of a nearby church and a witness to Janice's spirit might make all the difference. She was very anxious to do anything she could to help.

As Bert, with Norah and Dori at his side, walked toward the church, Robert drove up, parked, and joined them as they waited for him near the entrance. They all entered and went to Father Romero's office.

Father Romero was surprised to see three people. He had only expected Bert. Norah stood to the side, unseen by the Father, while her husband explained his reason for bringing Dori and Robert. Father Romero seemed to accept the explanation and offered them a seat as he learned forward on his desk.

"So, Mr. Lynnes, what's this all about?" he asked.

"Father Romero, I'll get right to the point. There is a growing body of evidence, some of it what you would call supernatural evidence, that one or both of your missing women were killed at the old well, which is embedded under the floor of the caretaker building, the Saint Brigit building. There is also reason to suspect that one or both bodies may be in the well."

Romero sat back in his chair with an air of shock and disbelief. "Okay, Bert, if I may call you by your first name, what evidence indicates this?"

Bert went on. "Sir, my other investigator went to Boise, Idaho, and discovered strong evidence that Father DelFranco committed suicide there. A note was discovered but quickly hidden, which said he was remorseful and sorry for what he'd done. His death was made to look like an accidental overdose of medication, to hide the embarrassment of his apparent suicide."

"I take it there is no evidence of this, which would stand up in court," he said.

"No sir, Father, however, the circumstantial evidence is very strong. Especially with what I'll tell you next." Bert let that sink in for a minute.

"Okay, Bert, I'm listening," Romero said.

Bert continued. "Father, I have spoken at length with the son of Janice Campbell, his name is Terry. He's now twenty years old and lives in Salt Lake City. Terry told me that, as an altar boy at this church, he was repeatedly molested and raped by Father DelFranco."

Father Romero sat silent and expressionless. Bert could tell that a combination of disbelief, denial, and anger was passing through his mind. Was the anger at DelFranco, or was it at Bert for raising the question of church integrity?

Bert glanced at Robert, who was listening intently but also sat silently and without visible reaction. Bert had not told him about Terry's admission. He wanted to know if the shock might awaken any of Robert's sublimated memories. Robert simply sat, looking down at his clasped hands.

Father Romero broke the silence. "Mr. Lynnes, for you to make such an accusation, I hope you're prepared to defend that position if challenged."

Bert expected that reaction. "Yes, sir, I'm quite certain that both Terry and his father would corroborate that in court, if needed." He glanced at Robert, who continued to sit without obvious emotion. "There's more, Father Romero."

"And what's that?"

"Father Romero, in all likelihood, the suicide note still exists in the files of Father DelFranco's church in Boise. At least one witness can testify to its existence and what it said. Janice Campbell suspected that something was going on with her son. It's logical that she suspected DelFranco and eventually confronted him. She disappeared as a result of that confrontation. Her spirit seems to be trapped at this church and around the old well."

Father Romero was now getting angry. "Mr. Lynnes, do you know what you're alleging, against not just this man but against his church?"

"Yes sir," Bert replied. "However, there's a big difference between simply claiming something and suggesting something which the evidence supports. The evidence supports this claim, Father Romero. Part of that evidence is what you'd call paranormal. I'd like to introduce you to this young lady, Dori, who is a member of the Calvary Community Church, where the other missing woman, Vicki, attended after choosing to leave your church. Dori has a gift of second sight; she's able to see and communicate with dead people. I'll let her tell you why she's here. Dori."

"Hello, Father Romero," Dori said nervously. "I'm here

because I've often seen the spirit of Janice Campbell here at this church. She's stuck here between the walls of this church and the grounds outside. She's often around the groundskeeper shed."

"Dori," Romero said, "I appreciate that you think you're seeing something. However, I don't believe in such things. I can't buy that such a spirit is either here or that you're seeing her."

Bert interjected. "Father, you're a Christian, right?"

"Of course, I am. How do you even ask that?"

"You believe in the Father, the Son, and the Holy Spirit or the Holy Ghost. Right?"

"Yes, of course. It's scripture," Romero retorted.

Bert went on. "So, Father, how can you believe in the concept of a Holy Spirit, the concept of life after death, and then not believe it when presented with the evidence of individual spirit and life after death? Isn't that a bit two-faced?" Bert chose to put this man on the spot.

Romero wasn't sure how to answer that. "Well, convince me then, Mr. Lynnes."

"Listen to what this young lady has to say, Father Romero.

Take off your blinders and actually hear her," Bert said. "Dori, please go on."

"Father, I've been a psychic medium for most of my life, all that I can remember, anyway. I've always seen things on the other side. It was terrible at first before I began to understand it. Eventually, though, I realized that I could do good with my gift. Many spirits just need help. If they could cross into the light, they would. They just can't break whatever is binding them here. That's where Mrs. Campbell, Janice, is. She's stuck here and she doesn't know what happened to her, so she wanders aimlessly from inside your church to the grounds and that shed, outside."

"How do you know it's her," Romero asked.

"She's told me her first name, Janice, and that she died a long time ago, in 2007. She wears a skirt and short-sleeve blouse, because she died in August."

"Well, Dori, that's impressive and I appreciate your sharing, however, that's nothing that you couldn't have gotten from newspaper articles," the Father said.

"I've read many of those same articles, Father Romero," Dori replied. "None of them tell you that she was strangled, do they?"

Romero was slow to answer her. "Uh, well, no, they don't because her body was never found so nobody knows that, Dori."

"I know that, Father, because she's told me. The last thing she can remember is losing consciousness as she was being strangled." Dori looked him straight in the eyes. He looked away. It was too much for him to digest at one time.

Bert took the pause as an opportunity to speak. "Father Romero, I know this is a lot for you to consider. It goes against some of what you believe. However, I'm also a medium, Father, and I have seen Mrs. Campbell's spirit twice now when visiting the church. She doesn't talk with me but keeps moving away, but she's here, Father."

Two people who see ghosts, thought Father Romero. What's next, he wondered. It didn't take long to find out.

"Sir, we have reason to believe that Janice's body very well may be in the old well which is encased in the floor of your shed," Bert told him. "We need your permission to move the shed and have the authorities access the well. Then we very well may solve the case of her disappearance."

Bert could see that the man, as expected, would need more convincing. He would not want to create a stir among the congregation without very good reason. He told Father Romero that he would be meeting with the police detective who worked the case, the next day, to discuss these same things. He said that if the detective was convinced, he would probably order the well to be entered. Bert wanted the Father to think about that, overnight.

With thanks and good-byes all said, Bert, Norah, and Missy drove back to their motel. They reflected on the meeting. Norah nodded at him and smiled in approval.

A package was waiting for them at the motel. Upon opening it in the room, they found a pink "Race for the Cure" baseball cap. The note from Don Campbell said that this was the only thing he could find which was likely to still have Janice's scent. He said she wore it all the time. Bert had asked during their phone call if there was anything he could send.

With the pieces seemingly in place and night fast approaching, Bert took Missy for a quick outing as the sun disappeared over the western horizon. He wondered what his client, Robert, was thinking tonight. Would the knowledge that Terry admitted to being molested awaken anything in Bobby Boy?

Back in the motel room, he chatted with Norah for a while before going to bed. She looked at him in the loving way that always touched his heart, and she told him how proud she was of his handling of the meeting. He told her how thankful he was to have her in his life and what a blessing it was to still be able to connect with her. When the light went out, tears flowed on both sides of the great divide which separated them. Both wanted what they could not have.

CHAPTER THIRTEEN: REVEALING

Shortly after noon on Saturday, Becky arrived back at the Hayden's cabin in Red Lodge. She had already called Lizzie and arranged to have tea at their house after she returned. A quick unpack of her bag in the cabin, and Becky donned her coat for the short walk to the house. It was still cold, but there was a slight warming trend on the way. The temperature was just above freezing on this sunny day and patches of melting snow replaced the previous icy spots.

Inside the Hayden's house, Lizzie gave Becky a warm hug and welcomed her back. They sat at the kitchen table, discussing Becky's trip to Boise and reviewing the plan for Summer. On this Saturday, Guy was working at the airport and Summer was visiting one of her classmates. She would be home within the hour. Becky described in some detail the grisly murder in Boise and how much Summer's drawing seemed to foretell the scene.

"Lizzie, my bosses don't perceive that Summer is psychic, so I just don't know if that similarity means anything or is just a coincidence."

Lizzie responded, "Well, Becky, you're the one who is here and dealing with Summer. I trust your judgment over theirs in that matter."

"Ordinarily, I'd agree with you," said Becky. "But Norah is also psychic so has some authority in that arena. She thinks there is some other explanation. They suggested going over pictures, especially religious pictures, with Summer. Just to see if anything seems to trigger a connection to the one drawing."

"That seems to make sense, Becky. Her one drawing is becoming more explicit since you had her expand upon it the other day."

"The good news, Lizzie, is that I don't think the priest, Finegan, has any interest back here at all. He's married, has a child, and said he's not returning here. I believe him."

"That's a big load off my mind," said Lizzie, "but then who is that other guy watching, then?"

"I don't know, Lizzie. Maybe nobody and just coincidence; maybe me."

"You," she said. "Why would anybody be watching you, Becky?"

"My ex was a very jealous guy, that's partly why we divorced, Lizzie. He's the only one I can think of who might be crazy enough. Probably just a coincidence, though. We'll see if it continues and go from there."

"Okay, sounds good. Oh, I see that Summer is home. I'll have her sit down with you in a minute."

They both welcomed Summer back and chatted about her time at her friend's house. The little girl was very engaged and bubbly. She'd had a good time, obviously. Becky took her cue from Lizzie and asked if Summer would look at some pictures with her. She told the girl that she'd like to know what she thought of them.

Becky had brought along her laptop and she began to find various church websites, starting with those in Red Lodge. They scrolled through pictures of the outside, inside, and various events, paying attention to the people. Summer became interested as a kind of game, telling Becky what she thought of them. Other than that, she had no unusual emotions about any of them. The one exception was that she did become a little subdued when looking at the priests in their full vestments.

They continued this exercise for almost two hours, without any discernable result. Summer was getting tired of it and wanted to go to her room and play. Becky and Lizzie moved to the living room and watched the fire burning softly in the fireplace. They collaborated on how best to proceed.

Becky was reiterating how she, as well as Bert and Norah, felt like a key to figuring out what was tormenting Summer was to understand the two drawings. Just then she received a text from Bert, asking if she'd made it back to Red Lodge okay. She answered him back and they exchanged a couple of quick messages about the cases. After his last reply, Becky had a sudden flashback to an earlier message from Bert. The one he sent with several pictures of the Nebraska City church. She hadn't taken the time to really look thoroughly at them, but a couple were jogging her memory. She thumbed her way up to the pictures.

After saving the pictures to her laptop in order to make them larger, she asked Lizzie if Summer could come back down and look at the ones which Bert had sent. Lizzie was a little puzzled, but she went upstairs to get her daughter.

Upon return, Lizzie sat on one side of Becky and Summer sat on the other. Becky explained to them both that her boss had sent some interesting pictures of a church and she wanted to see what they thought of it. She pulled up a couple of pictures of the inside, showing the rows of pews and some of the ornate interior architecture. Lizzie commented on how beautiful the inside was, while Summer sat silently. She was just focused intently upon them. That changed when she brought up a picture taken of the exterior.

Bert had taken one of several pictures from the parking area, showing the entire front of the church. When Becky opened this one for Summer, the child pushed back into the couch as if to get away from it. Her eyes were open wide and her mouth quivered. Tears welled up in her eyes, but she made no sound. She jumped up and went around Becky to her mother and sat tightly against her, burying her face against her mother's side as Lizzie hugged her tightly. Lizzie was shocked by the reaction and looked closely at the image.

Her eyes followed the flow of the granite blocks up the front, past the large wooden, double doors, along the two guard towers which formed the left and right corners, to their top fortification, which both rose above the peak of the main church. On the peak, standing between the two towers, was a statue of the Holy Mother, her arms outstretched to both sides. She was holding onto a large chain in each hand, which was connected to the tower on each side. Bert's explanation said that it represented the Holy Mother's connection of the past to the future, the old church to the new. Lizzie realized that she was looking at the refined reality of her daughter's one drawing.

Summer was casting quick glances at the picture and then burying her face back against her mother. She began to sob, at first subdued, but soon uncontrollably. Lizzie asked her what was wrong, but Summer just continued to cry. Finally, she just uttered, "Be-be, Be-be, Be-be."

Lizzie and Becky's eyes met. Both were wet with tears. Both knew the other was thinking the same thing.

Becky spoke first. "This is it, Lizzie. This is her second drawing. I have no idea how she's connected to it or even knows about it, but that's part of what haunts Summer. I can feel her connection and her sense of fear. She's afraid of that church for some reason. We have to find out why."

Lizzie nodded in agreement, but emotion prevented her from saying more than, "Yes, I know. We have to take her there."

* * *

Darkness had settled upon Red Lodge. The winter stars twinkled brightly in the night sky. The temperature was a balmy 25 degrees, reflecting the warming trend that was expected for a few days. Becky had stoked the fireplace in the cabin, settled into her pajamas, made herself a hot cocoa, and called Bert. Time to bring them up to date on the new development.

"Hey, boss-man," she said when Bert answered. "We have new news for you guys. We're going to be joining you there. Soon."

"Oh, really! To what do we owe that pleasure?" he asked.

"We just miss you guys and want to see you," she replied with a laugh. "I haven't gotten to know Missy yet, either. Need to get in her good graces."

He laughed back. "Well, I know you two will hit it off, swimmingly."

She became serious. "Actually, Bert and Norah, we have had a development here that concerns the Catholic Church there. Summer had a serious reaction to the outside pictures you sent. Her one drawing has obviously been a fledgling attempt to show the statue on the top. The minute she saw the real picture, she became very emotional. Both her mother and I saw the connection. We just don't understand it."

Bert was quiet on the other end of the call. Finally, he spoke. "That's absolutely amazing, Becky. Now it makes us wonder if she really is psychic and is somehow channeling into the case here."

"We're asking the same questions here, guys," Becky answered. "Is it possible that she could somehow help solve your case there?"

They discussed Summer's potential clairvoyance and how to tap into it. After that, Bert ended the call. Becky's question followed everyone to bed that Saturday night.

* * *

Earlier that Saturday, in Nebraska City, Bert and Missy, accompanied by Norah, had taken their morning sunrise stroll around the field. It was also warming up a bit there, too, and the wind chill in the light breeze was barely noticeable with the 26-degree temperature. Missy had a blast when she found a rabbit to chase. It barely managed to escape her teeth as it dove under a brush pile in the ravine.

Back at the motel, Bert had his usual breakfast of fruit and sausage in the motel dining room. Then he called police detective, Bryan Louden. They arranged to meet at Jonnie's Café at 10:00.

On the way to the café, Bert asked Norah if she still had the perception that Summer wasn't psychic. She was slow to answer but shook her head and said she just didn't have that feeling. She still felt there was some other explanation.

He nodded in understanding. This was one time, though, that he wasn't sure if his wife was correct. How else do you explain the goings-on with that child? He parked the doghouse in the lot of the café and went inside with Norah.

Detective Bryan Louden entered a short time later and came over to their table. Despite his civilian clothes, the handgun and badge attached to his belt gave away his occupation. He introduced himself and shook Bert's hand. He and Bert had a short but lively talk about college football. Louden, of course, was a Husker fan and was enthused about the prospects next fall with a new coaching staff. Bert had equally high hopes for the Wyoming Cowboys. They soon tabled the discussion to talk about the Campbell and Sturdevant cases.

Bert got right to the point. "Detective Louden, I'm asking you to order the opening and inspection of the old well which is encased in the floor of the shed at the Holy Mother Church."

"Why do that, Mr. Lynnes?" he asked. "We saw nothing around that well during my investigation to justify an inspection. We had no evidence of any foul play taking place at the church, so nothing to base any warrants upon."

"My team consists of a psychic who provides inputs and perceptions, some of which lead us to believe the dead women are somehow tied to the church and possibly to that old well."

"Dead women?" he asked. "How do you know that?"

"Not only am I a psychic medium, often able to see and

converse with the dead, but a local teenager has the same gift. We've both seen the spirit of Janice Campbell at both locations."

"Bert, if I may call you by your first name, psychic evidence is almost never admissible in court. You undoubtedly know that, sir."

Yes, Detective, I do know that," Bert said. "However, many law enforcement agencies are learning that legitimate psychic inputs can be used as a tool, which can often lead to hard evidence, which is admissible. If you think about it, a detective's hunches are often followed to unravel clues leading to the solving of crime. Psychic inputs are really just refined variations of your hunch."

Louden thought about that for a minute. He finally said, "Well, you do have a point there. So, what else do you have which changes the equation from seven years ago?"

Bert answered, "The priest, Father DelFranco, who was here during the disappearance of both women, very likely committed suicide in Boise a year or so after leaving here. There is evidence there, which could be subpoenaed, to support that presumption."

"Okay, interesting," said Louden.

Bert continued. "Most telling, though, is the admission by Terry Campbell, son of Janice Campbell, that DelFranco was molesting him sexually for some time before the mother vanished. If she confronted the Father about that, you have a motive for murder, sir."

Detective Louden took a couple more sips of his coffee and another bite of sausage, collecting his thoughts. At last, he told Bert, "We'll need some solid evidence to go with if we're going to go up against the hierarchy of the Catholic Church by accusing one of their own of rape and murder."

"I realized that, Detective," Bert said. "If you can indulge us and meet at the church with my team on Monday morning, about 10:00, there are some things I want to do which might persuade you and the Church."

Detective Louden agreed to the Monday meeting. They soon wrapped up their breakfast with a little more football chat, and Louden headed back to the station, since he was on duty today. Bert and Norah went back to the doghouse and an excited Missy. She was obviously needing another walk. They drove back to their favorite field.

The 36-degree temperature and light wind had the snow melting, and Missy was wet when they returned to the motel. She didn't care for the rubdown with a towel. Once that chore was completed, Bert began to make the calls and arrange for the meeting on Monday. Norah laid near Missy, listening to her soft breathing as she dozed in front of the window.

The afternoon passed quickly. After darkness had descended upon eastern Nebraska, Becky called. Bert was happy to hear her upbeat voice on the phone. He was a little shocked, though, when she called him boss-man and announced that she had new news for him and Norah. "We're going to be joining you there. Soon."

They discussed her development that Summer had an obvious reaction to the pictures he'd sent of the Holy Mother Church. She said that Lizzie strongly agreed that they needed to bring Summer to that church and try to understand the connection. Lizzie had discussed it with Guy when he returned from work. While he didn't think he could leave his work on such short notice, he was supportive of the trip.

Becky said that she, Lizzie, and Summer were leaving Red Lodge early in the morning, Sunday. They should arrive in Nebraska City sometime Monday afternoon. Bert told her he'd arrange rooms for them at their motel.

Becky's final statement followed him and Norah to bed: "Is it possible that she could somehow help solve your case there?"

As he turned out the light and stared into the darkness, he asked Norah, "Honey, is it possible that the child is somehow channeling this case in Nebraska City, hundreds of miles from her home?"

He heard her answer, "Sweetheart, I guess I just don't know. I'm not sensing it but how else do we explain it?"

CHAPTER FOURTEEN: THE WELL

It was about 7:00 on Sunday morning when Becky, Lizzie, and Summer left Red Lodge in Becky's truck. The nearly eleven-hour drive to Nebraska City would take a little bit longer than usual because Summer would need a stop now and then. Becky figured they'd get to someplace in central Nebraska along Interstate 80, before stopping for the night. That would leave an easy drive of around four hours Monday morning to their destination. They would miss the meeting that morning but could catch up on everything once they got there.

Becky initially had her sights set on the coffee shop in Thermopolis. She knew Summer would need a bathroom stop by then, and a coffee would be welcomed by herself and Lizzie. After passing her new home of Cody, they started a game of antelope with Summer, seeing who could spot most of the speedy creatures. They were easier to see than usual because of the patches of snow.

The sharp-eyed little girl was a formidable competitor, and she held a commanding lead by the time they reached the first stop.

As the miles faded behind them, Becky's mind kept drifting to the strange circle drawing. It was still an unknown entity. Did it also have some connection to the Nebraska City church? Or was it something entirely different and unrelated?

Watching Lizzie and Summer both dozing in their respective seats, Becky felt a calmness and confidence that she hadn't felt before about her case. She felt like the answers they sought were a day ahead, somewhere around the Holy Mother Catholic Church.

She turned on the radio and tied it to her ear buds so as not to awaken the other girls. An old-time singer, whom she liked, was just coming on. She listened to the catchy lyrics and tunes of The Masters Call, Faleena, and then El Paso City, all made familiar and popular by the late, great, Marty Robbins. When the songs ended, she sighed a deep breath, and felt a sadness come over her. She knew that this country girl would forever be linked to the past, more-so than the present, at least where music was concerned. Her remorseful reflection was interrupted by another good one. The Highwayman with Waylon, Willie, Johnny, and Kris was starting. Life was good.

Being a Sunday, there was almost no traffic on the road. The only vehicle she had seen in the last hour was a lone vehicle which was apparently going the same direction as they were. She just had occasional glimpses of the vehicle, a truck she thought, well behind them.

* * *

Sunday in Nebraska City was a down day for Bert, Norah, and Missy. He had decided that they needed a break from the mental pressures of digging for the bones of these unsolved cases. The only work they did was to review the plan for Monday's meeting and ensure that all the pieces were lined up. Satisfied that they were as ready as they could get, it seemed like a beautiful sunny day to take a hike in the Wilson Creek State Wildlife Management Area, which was about ten miles west of Nebraska City. It was in the middle of winter, so there was little chance of running into many other people. Missy was guaranteed to have a blast with a free run.

Hours later, they returned as the sun was sinking onto the western hills. Missy was happy as a clam, literally grinning as she hopped with muddy, wet feet onto the old army blanket in the cargo area. She flopped down and was asleep before Bert got the vehicle into gear. He and Norah both laughed. They could hardly stop smiling as they drove the fifteen minutes back to the motel.

That evening was mostly about relaxing. They did some talking about their business and the cases but didn't want to stress their minds with too much thinking. "You can overthink these things, I think. Are you thinkin' what I'm thinkin', Honey?" he asked with a big grin.

She laughed and her eyes flashed. "Yeah, I agree, we wouldn't want to do too much thinking, or we could overthink it, I think."

They laughed so much that Missy raised her head from the floor where she was napping by the window. She gave them a look as if to say, "quiet, please. Some of us are sleeping."

They discussed Becky for a few minutes. Both agreed that she was a great choice and a good fit with their business. They liked how she had taken the challenge at Red Lodge and was running with it yet making good decisions.

"Let's keep her, Bert," Norah said. "I'll learn to live with her looks." She laughed.

It was a good day, a fitting respite before the challenges that tomorrow would bring.

"Good night, Norah," he said as he turned out the light. "You're really something, Honey."

She laughed in the darkness. "I have to be something, because you'd be nothing without me, Sweetheart."

He chuckled and smiled broadly in the darkness, even as tears welled up in his closed eyes and trickled down his cheeks. So close, and yet so far away.

Norah leaned back on the bed. She didn't know if she could cry real tears, but she knew she could feel the ache of real longing.

* * *

Becky lowered her sun visor as she entered Interstate 80 from their overnight stay in North Platte, Nebraska. She and Lizzie had taken Summer to dinner last night at the Bill Cody restaurant. The little girl was totally enthralled with the western folklore and she must have asked a million questions, thought Becky, with a smile.

For now, they all donned sunglasses as they drove east into

the low, but rising, sun on this Monday morning, January 15th, 2018. In about four more hours, right around noon, they would be in Nebraska City.

As she piloted her Dodge Ram Hemi truck toward the east, Becky was oblivious to the stares from passing truckers. She was lost in thought about how to figure out how this church was somehow drawn into Summer's life. As before, the only conclusion she could reach was that the child was psychic. Somehow, Summer had connected to the church and maybe to the missing mother of the other client. Somehow, she seemed to be developing the vestiges of clairvoyance. Becky wondered, however, if the child was picking up on what happened in the past? Or, was she seeing where they were now headed into the future?

It was hard for her to believe that she just started working for Bert and Norah only two weeks earlier. It was even harder to grasp the fact that she'd been on the Hayden's case for most of that time. Her first case for B and N Investigations was well into its second week, and it was taking her two states away from where she'd started. Talk about your whirlwind beginning, she thought to herself.

They were driving this distance for a reason, Becky thought. It was as if an invisible force had taken over her investigation and now, she, Becky Thompson, Private Investigator, was just along for the ride. She was no longer driving this case; she had become a passenger.

* * *

On the same Monday morning, Bert, Norah, and Missy had completed their morning ritual. They took their deep, relaxing breaths as they entered the parking lot at the Holy Mother Church. It was twenty minutes until 10:00. Bert wanted to be well early. This was a critical day to his case. It had to go right.

Bert and Norah were thrilled when Robert arrived just a few minutes later, followed closely by Dori. He got out of the doghouse, leaving Norah with Missy. Missy sensed the excitement and needed Norah's calming presence to keep her from getting too wound up. Bert greeted both Robert and Dori. They had just started to discuss the meeting when Detective Louden drove up.

After introducing Louden to Robert and Dori, Bert led him to the left rear door of the doghouse, ordering Missy to stay as he opened it so she could sniff and meet the Detective. Bert said his usual intro to the coywolf and quickly explained Missy's history and role. With that formality completed, he led the group to the church and inside to Father Romero's office. Since Missy had calmed down, Norah left the vehicle and also entered the church and office, standing in the front right corner. Bert nodded at her.

Taking the lead, Bert introduced all parties to each other. He said that he was going to present a theory, which was based upon the facts and evidence they had acquired to date. He explained that Dori might interrupt him at any time if she saw the spirit of Janice Campbell, because he wanted to try an experiment, one whose outcome was unpredictable. With that quick explanation, he began.

"Father Romero and Detective Louden, the premise of my theory is that Father DelFranco, formerly of this Church during the time the two women disappeared, was involved in both disappearances. It is a fact, as stated by Terry Campbell, now twenty, that DelFranco had abused him sexually while he was an altar boy. The abuse lasted at least two years, until Janice, his mother, disappeared. It's highly likely that Janice confronted DelFranco. I believe he lured her to the old well, due to its seclusion, and killed her to silence her. I believe you will find her remains in that old well." Bert glanced at Robert, who continued to sit, stoically.

Father Romero interrupted him. "How do you explain that the cars were found miles away at separate golf courses? That strongly suggests that someone else was involved."

"Father Romero, that's a good question and easily answered. Father DelFranco was an athlete and especially a runner. He ran numerous marathons throughout the year, often taking others with him. Even the ten miles from the Lake Ridge Golf Course would've been an easy jog for Father DelFranco. He could have dropped the vehicles off, unnoticed, and ran back to the church without anyone suspecting anything. On the weekdays when the ladies disappeared, the church would have been mostly empty. Anyone seeing him would have known that he ran nearly every day, so that would not have been suspicious."

"Father DelFranco has passed away, so how can you get his side of this?" asked Father Romero.

"Our other investigator, Becky Thompson, will be here later today. She interviewed several people in Boise, where DelFranco last served and died. One lady can testify that she saw a note left by the Father, expressing his remorse for something he did. It's an obvious suicide note, which can be subpoenaed from the church files. It doesn't take a big imagination to see that he very possibly was remorseful for things he did here."

Detective Louden began to speak. "So, Mr. Lynnes, what leads you to believe that the . . .."

Bert interrupted him when Dori motioned to him. He knew that she saw Janice's spirit. He quickly gathered the group up as he asked Dori to see where she went. Dori indicated that she was going toward the side door from the altar.

Asking everyone to exit the front of the church and focus on Dori and the site of the well, Bert ran to the doghouse to get Missy. He put her on her leash and ran with her toward the outside door on the side of the church, ball cap in hand. He knelt beside Missy, offered her Janice's pink ball cap, and ordered her to find. He removed the leash. It was now up to her to prove or disprove his experiment.

Bert moved next to Detective Louden. He quietly explained what he was doing with Missy. He told him he'd never tried this before and didn't know if she could pick up the scent of a spirit.

Dori came beside him, as well, and told both men that she had seen Janice's spirit go to the shed and seemed to disappear inside. Father Romero and Detective Louden looked skeptical yet were engaged in the process. Their skepticism seemed to be wavering.

Missy moved very slowly around the side doorway, sniffing diligently. She moved her head from side to side, as if straining to pick up the slightest sound or molecule of scent. After about twenty seconds, she began the same methodical search movements as she began to make her way across the untracked snow, toward the maintenance shed. She would move a few feet, then stop and sniff from side to side, rotating her head. Every movement seemed intended to gather as much residual scent as possible. She wasn't getting much, however, she was getting just enough to keep her slowly moving toward the shed.

Bert's heart was pounding out of his chest, by the time his prized animal slowly reached the shed and finally sat down beside it. She looked back at him; her cue that she'd found what her nose was looking for. They all walked briskly with him to the shed and stood back in amazement as he petted and praised her and rewarded her with a piece of jerky.

He turned to the group. "Folks, you've just witnessed two bits of evidence to support our belief that Janice's body is in this well. For one, Dori, a psychic medium in her own right, saw and sensed the spirit of Mrs. Campbell as she went to and entered this locked shed. Secondly, Don Campbell, Janice's husband, sent me her pink ball cap which she wore all the time. Using her scent from the cap, our tracking animal, Missy, was surprisingly able to glean just enough residual scent from the spirit to track her to the same shed. I didn't know if she could do that, but she did it. Her nose believes that Janice Campbell is inside that shed. The old well is embedded in the floor."

The group was silent. Even Father Romero had nothing to say. He didn't want to believe what he was hearing and seeing, yet he couldn't make himself deny it. Robert watched everything with keen interest, but he continued to remain stoic.

Finally, Detective Louden spoke up. "Lady, and gentlemen, I'm convinced that sufficient reason exists to open that well. I'm going back to the office and draw up the order to move the shed and open the well, hopefully tomorrow. After ten years, it's time we know what happened to those two mothers." He turned, marched quickly to his police car, and departed. He had a lot of coordination to do if he was going to make his deadline.

Father Romero was silent and only said good-bye when they reached the doorway of the church. He was obviously both dismayed and overwhelmed by the firestorm he knew was sure to come from the upper levels of the church.

After thanking and saying good-bye to Dori, who had even gotten an excuse to miss the half day of school, Bert pulled his client, Robert, aside. He endeavored to answer any question that Robert may have had and asked him how he felt about everything. The young man was even quieter than usual, and very withdrawn. He was obviously grappling with his demons from the past. Bert felt for him, yet he knew that this was something which Robert had to do if he was to move on with his life. Since he had little to say, Bert said good-bye and promised to keep him updated on the next events.

They had just gotten to the motel when Becky called to say they were about ten minutes away. She reconfirmed the motel address. Bert felt an awkward mix of excitement and subdued restraint at the thought of Becky being with them. He liked her and was impressed with her, yet he had the conflicted feeling that he shouldn't like her as much as he did. It seemed like months since she'd been with them in person. He took a deep breath and exhaled slowly. His eyes met Norah's. She held his gaze for a second, then smiled her sweet smile, and turned away toward Missy. He knew she knew; she was psychic, after all. Damn it, why did he feel so guilty about liking an employee.

When Becky's truck pulled into the parking lot of the motel, the first order of business was introductions all around. Becky started to take Bert's handshake, but gave him a warm hug, instead.

"We're huggers, remember?" She laughed.

He laughed at that, as he knelt to one knee to meet Summer. "Wow," he thought to himself, "this is one to tug at your heart. What a little cutie."

He met Lizzie next, and took a liking to her, instantly, just as Becky had said he would.

When Missy was introduced, just as Bert half expected, she was instantly mesmerized by both Summer and Becky. She had Summer hugging her around the neck and burying her face in her soft coat within minutes, while she could barely refrain from wiggling out of the child's arms. A couple licks on the girl's cheeks had her laughing gleefully before they even headed for the motel room.

With Becky, Missy was at first slow and a little shy to approach her, but from the first smell of her hand and stroke on her head, she was attached. She rubbed circles around Becky's legs, whining joyously. She followed her as she hauled her suitcase toward her room, although Bert quickly took the bag for her.

With Lizzie and Summer in their room, to freshen up, as the ladies like to say, Bert saw Becky to her room, which was next door to Lizzie's. He was starting to explain the day's events, when she asked, "How's Norah doing? I take it she's staying out of sight and behind the scenes."

"Yes, you're right. She's doing very well, thanks. Just staying low key." He glanced at Norah as she stood beside Becky's window, smiling at his awkwardness.

Becky could almost sense Norah's presence. She felt that Norah was listening to her. "Well, you be sure to tell her that I'm glad to have this chance to work directly with you two and I hope I can be a help in some way."

Bert started to return to his own room, but as he stopped at the door, Missy just stood in Becky's room, looking at him and then at her. "Oh my gosh," he laughed, "are you wanting to stay here with Becky for a while?"

She did a couple of excited spins with her tongue hanging out. It was obvious that she wanted to continue getting acquainted with Becky, so Bert bade her good-bye and went back to his room. Norah was already there, giggling and giggling from Missy's betrayal.

"So, another girl dumped you, huh?" Norah laughed.

He nodded and smiled. "Yeah, but she'll be back. Nobody can leave me for long."

The remainder of the afternoon was taken up with a couple of hours for napping, more chats about the cases, and eventual order for pizza delivery. Bert took Missy for her evening outing. Becky asked to go along so she could see how he handled Missy. They walked her for about fifteen minutes in the chilly air of the darkening night. Bert knew that Norah was with them, also. He realized that he was lucky to be in the presence of two beautiful women; beautiful both inside and out.

When they returned to the motel, Becky made an unusual request. "Would you mind if Missy stayed with me tonight? I feel a real bond forming with her and would love to continue it. Besides, it would be the first time that I haven't slept alone in a long time."

He cast a glance at Norah, who nodded approval. "Sure, Becky, she can stay with you tonight. I told you that you two would hit it off. I'll bring her leash over in case you need it. She'll need to go out to the edge of the parking area right before you go to bed."

With everyone else settled for the night, Bert could finally relax with Norah in their room. They both realized how awkward the afternoon had been. How much easier it would be if they could just explain the situation to people. Some would understand and be okay with it, but most would not. Bert pointed out to her that those who they needed most to understand, probably would.

"Yes, like Becky," Norah answered. "She will understand in time."

As Bert was about to brush his teeth, his phone rang. It was Detective Louden. After a brief call, Bert hung up and walked over to Norah.

"We're on, babe. Louden has a crew lined up for tomorrow to move the maintenance shed, the Brigit shed, and break into the well. Also, a crew to first drop a camera and dive, if necessary, into the well. That's if it's safe. They will start the move about 8:30 or 9:00 in the morning. He said we can come out anytime to watch the proceedings. It will probably take most of the day."

Norah was ecstatic! She repeated herself several times that

it was such a great feeling to know they might bring closure to those poor women. Bert called Becky to give her the news.

When he was off the phone and back with Norah, he had a worried look. When she asked about it, he said, "Becky reminded me that we still have no idea how any of this connects to Summer."

"We'll just have to see her reaction at the church and go from there, Honey," Norah said. "It sounds like that's a starting point."

Bert nodded as he leaned back in the desk chair, with his feet on the bed, and closed his eyes. A wave of fatigue just came over him. The pressure of the past few days was weighing on him, apparently. He got ready for bed, crawled under the covers, and turned out the light.

"Good night, Sweetheart," he whispered.

"Good night, my Love," she whispered back.

* * *

Three doors down the hallway, Becky and Missy were seated in front of the TV. Becky was running her fingers through Missy's coat as she caught up on the news. She realized that she hadn't yet closed the picture window curtains, and Missy was probably ready for that bedtime outing. So, she closed the curtains, donned her winter coat and boots, and led Missy from the room to the door at the end of the hallway. She instinctively felt for her .38 special, semi-auto handgun, in her coat pocket holster.

Missy evidently was more than ready to do her business, because she ducked out the door quickly to the right side of the building and to the edge of the parking lot. Becky strolled out into the parking area and turned to wait for her furry friend. She had noticed that a vehicle was getting ready to leave the motel and hadn't thought too much about it. It started down the drive lane from behind her at a normal speed and started to pass her.

She was taken by surprise when the dirty brown, extended cab, pickup suddenly stopped just in front of her and the driver and the passenger behind him threw open the doors and jumped out. When the driver demanded to see her identification, it made her pause for just a second. Just long enough for the passenger guy to bolt toward her. She tried to react, but he was just too close. She couldn't pull her weapon in time, before his left hand closed on her right wrist. His right arm was reaching for her neck.

The impact spun her partly down to her left knee on the pavement. The hand on her wrist let go of her and a startled yell replaced it. Forty-five pounds of furry fury bumped against her as Missy's attack carried her past Becky, the assailant's wrist clamped tightly in her teeth. She didn't let go, and the momentum pulled him to his knees, still yelling in pain. By the time the startled driver could react, Becky had pulled her gun, clicked off the safety, and had it trained on his chest. Missy held the man's wrist in a death grip, and her low growl was all the more menacing as she backed up, pulling him and keeping him off balance on one hand and knees.

Sensing that he was no longer a threat, Missy released her attacker and moved beside Becky in a guardian posture. Both men backed toward the open doors of their truck. Despite Becky's warning to stop, they entered the truck. They were going to drive away and she knew she wasn't going to shoot. So, she shouted at them, "Tell the sonofabitch that hired you to expect the law at his door. That's if he's lucky and it isn't me, putting a bullet between his eyes. Tell him, and don't come back. You won't get off this lucky a second time. Next time, I'll have her go after you in earnest."

She tried to get the truck license, but they pulled away too fast, and all she could tell is that it was a Montana plate. She had little doubt who was behind it. She felt like there was a good chance that he would not do anything again. If his boys gave him the message, he'd know she wasn't fooling.

As they disappeared, the fight-or-flight adrenaline was kicking in hard. Her hands were shaking, and she was slightly unsteady on her feet, feeling mildly dizzy. However, by the time she reached the door back into the hall and unlocked it, she was regaining her composure. As she let Missy in ahead of her, she dropped to her knees and hugged her close. The bonding was completed, she and Missy were now a team. Now she could cry, and she buried her face in Missy's coat and sobbed for over a minute. The shock of the incident was so sudden and dramatic that it hit her harder than she ever would have expected.

It was over, so no need to wake up her bosses. She'd tell them about it in the morning. Tonight, she knew she'd sleep well after a while, because tonight she had a champion guarding her room. Tonight, she vowed to never again be unaware of the vehicles behind her.

* * *

By 10:00 on Tuesday morning, The B and N team was fully assembled, fed, watered, and walked, and they were ready to see the Holy Mother Church. It was time to find out what was binding the little girl to this place.

Becky had told Bert and Norah about the attempted kidnapping last night, and they were both shocked and outraged. Bert promised her that he would see that it didn't happen again. He said nothing else. He didn't have to.

As they drove up to the church and parked in the middle of the vacant parking lot, with a good view of the structure, Bert asked if he could sit in the back seat with Summer. Once he was there, Norah also, Becky moved her truck so Summer could see out her window. She pointed to the church.

Norah was beside the child, watching her expressions and reactions. At first, Summer just stared at the front of the church. However, as her gaze went up the front to the peak and the guard towers, she began to show emotions ranging from anger to fear. She ducked back inside the truck, and began to cry and yell "No, no, no."

"No what, sweetie," said her mother. "What do you want to go away?"

"The man. Make him go away. Make him stop hurting me. Make him stop hurting us."

"Who is us, Summer?" Lizzie asked softly. "Who else is he hurting, baby?"

"My baby, he's hurting my baby," Summer began to cry.

They all sat, silently, not sure what to say as the little girl sat near Norah, sobbing. From the way she sat, she seemed to sense Norah, Bert thought.

His gaze shifted onto the grounds and down to the Brigit shed. The work supervisor had already moved the shed from its foundation, exposing the concrete floor. They were discussing how to safely remove the floor without damaging or caving in the old well.

Becky then suggested that they go into the church and look around. Possibly something inside would provide additional clues or stimulate more reaction.

When they were inside the church, Summer was more subdued for a while. However, when they approached the front altar and surrounding area, she became increasingly angry and didn't want to go any closer.

"Why won't you go any closer?" Becky asked her. "What's wrong, Summer?"

"He's bad," the child answered. "He's a bad man."

Becky had another idea. "There are pictures of all the priests during the history of the church. They're lining the one hallway. Let's take her to look at them."

When they began to look at the pictures of all the men who had served as the Holy Father at the church, Summer turned toward her mother and hugged her tightly around the neck. She held so tightly that Lizzie had to stop at each picture and turn around so Summer could see over her shoulder. At first, the girl just held tightly, without a word. She suddenly began to cry loudly, which quickly transitioned into a scream. They had stopped in front of Father DelFranco's picture.

Becky stepped next to Bert and whispered, "Bert, she's psychic. How else do we explain this? Somehow, she has tapped into this case. She's picking up on the evil that this man did."

Bert nodded in agreement. "I don't know how else to explain it. Let's take her into the office and see if she will draw the circle drawing you've talked about."

Back in the main office, volunteer secretary, Susan, was on duty again. Bert greeted her warmly and then asked if he could borrow a pencil and some plain paper. He handed them to

Becky. She sat Summer down at the nearby table and asked if she would draw her pictures.

At first, Summer just scribbled, drawing nothing that was coherent. After a couple minutes of that, though, she seemed to become stoic and rigid, almost angry. She began to draw the large circle with the pencil, tracing it over and over in an increasingly angry demeanor. Then she drew the smaller picture inside the other. She didn't go over it so many times.

Becky had an idea. She brought the box of crayons from the play area and asked Summer what color she would use for the walls of the big circle. She chose a black crayon and began again to angrily trace it in black. Then she asked about the smaller circle. Summer chose yellow. She asked her to color it. The child colored the inside disk a yellow color. When asked about the area between the large and smaller circles, she found a dark blue crayon and began to fill in the area with blue.

Bert was watching this with growing interest. Do you realize that we might be looking at a tunnel with a light at the end? Or," he said slowly and with emphasis, "this could be a view of the sun from inside some kind of portal."

"From the bottom of a well around mid-day," Becky suggested.

About that time, Patty entered the office. Bert greeted and introduced her to everyone. Then he asked her what brought her there today.

"I heard about the moving of the Brigit building," she said. "I wanted to see some of this with my own eyes."

"I'm sorry," Bert told her, "I should have invited you to the meeting yesterday and to this today. I couldn't think of any questions for you but should have known you'd be interested."

Patty answered unemotionally. "That's okay, Bert, I know you're busy. Besides, I've been talking with BB almost every day. So, I've been keeping up with most of the happenings."

Lizzie beat Becky to the question. "Ma'am, did you say BB? Who is that?"

"Oh, I'm sorry for using personal nicknames. My bad. BB was the most pet name that Vicki had for her son, Robert. She often called him Bobby Boy when it was just the few of us close friends around. Sometimes, she'd shorten that to just BB. He rode over here with me. He's outside, somewhere."

Both Becky and Lizzie sat in stunned silence for a minute, digesting what they'd just heard. Did they just get another piece of the puzzle?

Bert got up and said he wanted to see how the dismantling of the shed floor was coming. He hadn't yet perceived the significance of the nickname. He walked outside and stood near the doghouse, watching as the main section of flooring, which had been jackhammered loose all around the foundation, was being lifted off the old well. Whatever condition it was in, it would soon be exposed for inspection. The same crane that lifted off the floor was moving back into place over the old well. It was evidently going to lower an electrical cable, with light and camera, into the well.

Detective Louden was now at the scene, providing guidance about any evidence. From the increased pace of activity, Bert could tell that they'd found something. He continued to watch as the crane set up and lowered a lighted camera, along with something that looked like a grappling hook.

It took almost ten minutes, but finally the crane began to withdraw the hook from the well. As it passed the old broken rim of the well, Bert could see the shreds of blue material still clinging in places to the skeleton of Janice Campbell. He called Becky as the crane began lowering its grappling hook back into the well.

Becky, Lizzie, Norah, Patty, Susan, and Summer all came out of the church and walked toward Bert. The adults gathered around him as he explained what he'd observed so far. None of them noticed Summer as she drifted toward the well operation. During the twenty or so seconds that she wasn't being observed, the child began running across the grounds, dodging the patches of remaining snow as she ran full speed toward the operation.

"Summer!" screamed Lizzie. "Stop, stop, come back."

Bert and Becky began simultaneously to run full out down

the lawn toward the well. Lizzie was behind them. The little girl was running as fast as she could, and she was oblivious to the shouts. Bert could see that she was running straight at the gaping hole of the old well. Despite his desperation, he knew he couldn't catch up to her in time. All he could do was try.

Summer was only a few feet from the hole and running out of control. She couldn't stop even if she saw it in time. The gaping hole was waiting to swallow her, when a tall, thin figure leaped over the hole from the opposite side and grabbed her. He carried her the fifteen feet to the one bench which the crew didn't have to move.

Becky and Bert, with Norah beside them, and Lizzie almost caught up, stopped about ten feet from the man and little girl. They watched and listened in growing amazement.

Summer was clinging to Robert with her arms wrapped around his neck. Both were crying and sobbing. Summer was saying through her sobs, "BB, BB, my BB, I've come back to you, BB."

Robert was crying, but something was different, Bert realized. Robert was saying, "It's you. You've come back to me? I'm so sorry that I didn't say anything before now. I knew I should have but I just couldn't do it. I will tell them now, mommy. Everything."

Summer held him tightly around his neck and kissed him on the cheek. She continued to repeat, "BB, BB, my BB. I missed you. It's okay, BB, it wasn't your fault."

Becky turned to Bert, knowing that Norah and Lizzie were also listening. "Guys, do you believe in reincarnation?"

Bert turned to watch the crane slowly drawing the grappling hook from the well. He knew that Vicki, or at least what was left of Vicki's body, was in its grasp. Had this woman, this mother, found a way back to her son? Had Vicki's spirit found a conduit in the tiny child in Lizzie's womb, ready to be born within hours of her death?

As the shock of hitting the cold water brought her back to consciousness from near strangulation by the sash; as she stared up at the midday sun framed by the impossible walls of the well; as darkness replaced the light when the lid was back on the well; and as she slowly lost her grip on the wet rock wall, and on her life; had she found in this little girl, a way to come back to the son that she loved?

She appears to have found a pathway to come back into the light.

ABOUT THE AUTHOR

I grew up on a west Nebraska cattle ranch, the oldest of four children. Hills and valleys were my playground; cats, dogs, and a raccoon were my playmates until younger brothers took their places; windmills, BB-guns, and haystacks were among my playthings; horses and cattle were my workmates. Like the hardy people I grew up among, I have many hours working cattle on horses, using heavy machinery, and learning about the flora, fauna, and geography of the region. My early education came by way of one-room country schools. I often rode horses the three-plus miles each way to school or drove myself in a little Jeep. Two-hole outdoor toilets, coal stoves, and kerosene lanterns are among my childhood memories. Because of Nebraska weather, no phones, and no drivers' license, I boarded out most of my first two years of high school. I was athletic, loved sports, and participated in all available sports throughout high school.

Growing up without a neighbor in sight or other kids of my age to play with, I learned to live in my head and developed a vivid imagination. That imagination serves me well in creating fictional mysteries. Work ethic came from being the oldest son and starting to work full-time, outside of school, at the age of eight.

I have a degree in Animal Science from the University of Nebraska, and I've loved nature and animals all my life. Coyotes were part of the ecosystem, though largely unseen. Their howls welcomed most sunsets. The coyote-wolf hybrid was a natural character for this story, and I wanted to introduce it to the reader.

I first learned of the coywolf hybrid from an Animal Planet

documentary, "Meet the Coywolf." I felt I knew coyotes well and had almost no fear of them, only respect. Then, I happened to see another documentary named "Killed by Coyotes." This caught my interest immediately, because I knew of no adult human deaths by coyotes. However, an aspiring folksinger, Canadian, Taylor Mitchell, aged nineteen, was killed in 2009 in Novia Scotia by coyotes while hiking in a national park.

I feel that wolf DNA may have played a role in this tragic attack. Such behavior is not typical of the coyotes that I know. For this reason, I decided to introduce the coywolf to readers. While my female hybrid is a well-trained and domesticated fictional animal, the real hybrids are a blend of wolf and coyote and reflect the characteristics of both. The real animals are not necessarily pure coyote-wolf but may have varying degrees of DNA, to include dog.

Readers should understand that this hybrid is spreading across the United States as well as Canada, because of its resilient coyote blood. The wolf DNA makes it a larger, more aggressive, pack hunter, and therefore more dangerous than a coyote. The coywolf, like the coyote, can live and thrive in urban environments. It may be living and thriving in your city. With a typical weight of around forty-five pounds, it's large enough to be considered an apex predator.

I'm a retired Air Force officer and pilot, and I have traveled extensively across the United States, lived in three foreign countries, and have flown in about 40 different nations. I owned and operated a bed and breakfast in Cody, Wyoming for five years, during which time I was a freelance writer for the Wyoming Livestock Roundup newspaper. That experience developed my interest and love for writing.

I worked as a private investigator for two years, in Arkansas, conducting surveillance investigations in a variety of locales and situations. That experience is part of the background for the Bert and Norah stories. I've also had a lifelong fascination with psychic phenomenon.

Read on for a Sneak Peeks of the Books in the Bert and Norah Series.

Sneak Peeks Backwards

This third book in the "Bert and Norah" series follows the first, "The Nickel Dime Murders," and the second, "The Missing."

"The Nickel Dime Murders" introduces the team of B & N Investigations and highlights their unusual methods. It establishes the background and basis for the following books. Initially drawn into the search for missing couples, the private investigation team gets sucked into the hunt for what appears to be a serial murderer.

In "The Missing," the team calls upon all their unusual skills and abilities in order to find a kidnapped child of a high-level figure. The list of possible suspects is extensive and baffling and includes even some of the investigators.

"The Nickel Dime Murders"
Chapter One

"The few remaining deciduous leaves and evergreen needles flittered in the strong breeze. It was still too early in the spring for most of the dormant vegetation to return fully to life in receding winter's grip in rural, upstate Wisconsin. The grey overcast sky and 30-degree temperature made the wind chill and wet ground feel even colder to exposed skin. Marshland and meadow had given way to a shallow hillside, dotted with a mix of spruce, cedar, ash, and tamarack trees. One could hear the wind whispering through the trees and taste the odor of the damp pine needles, wafting in the background of the senses. This gloomy day was in stark contrast to a rescue mission, which was underway. Oblivious to the rescuers, the life they would save was destined to profoundly affect their lives and the lives of others yet unknown."

"The Missing"
Chapter One

". . . Samuel Patterson, sat in stunned silence for a few seconds, then slowly pushed his chair back and stood up. He quietly said, "Well, Mr. Lynnes, I think I'm beginning to see why you're the man I need for this job. The man I'll trust to get my little girl back safely." With tears struggling to roll down his cheeks, he turned abruptly and walked toward the men's room.

Bert and Jim turned to small talk, continuing to get to know each other.

Out on the sidewalk, a middle-aged man with dark but greying hair, wearing a brown leather jacket and matching hiking boots, seemed to look in Bert's direction through the window, then resumed his walk and motioned to his Husky. They disappeared from Bert's view as they passed the large picture window. Bert thought to himself, "I wonder who that guy is? Never seen him around here.""

Sneak Peek Forward

The fourth book in the "Bert and Norah" series will tentatively be called "Murder in the Ozarks."

Everyone in this small mountain town knew that Izack had killed his wife. He even joked about it and made lewd insinuations, literally taunting the local law. Yet, he walked freely among the community, causing a sense of both fear and disgust among his neighbors. The problem was that there was no proof, because there was no body.

Two years had passed since his aunt had vanished. Billy Joe couldn't take the anger and frustration any longer. He knew his hated uncle had killed his favorite aunt, and the murderer was getting away with it. The case was going cold. He contemplated bringing the uncle to justice himself. Being a crack shot, he knew he could do it. However, he didn't want to spend his remaining life in prison.

So, he searched online for someone who might have the resources to uncover the truth and see that an eye was given for an eye that was taken. He found a private investigation company in Cody, Wyoming, that might be unique enough. He called B & N Investigations.

www.ingramcontent.com/pod-product-compliance
Lightning Source LLC
Chambersburg PA
CBHW020238180626
46810CB00006B/2249